Also by O. N. Stefan

The Deadly Caress

SLEEP THEN MY PRINCESS

O. N. Stefan

NO ONE LOVES YOU MORE THAN ME.

NO ONE!

ACKNOWLEDGMENTS

Editing by Catherine Lenderi

Manuscript assessment by Victoria Chie and Kyle Sharpe

Cover design by Samantha Fury

Payella Pty. Ltd.

First published on Kindle October 30 2015

ASIN: B016G5T7AG

ISBN: 0-9942932-1-6

Dedications:

This book is dedicated to my family for

supporting my writing efforts.

Victoria Chie for helping me make this story better than it was and allowing me to pick her brains when I couldn't find a solution.

"There is an ultimate weakness in violence. It multiplies evil and violence in the universe. It doesn't solve any problems."

-Martin Luther King.

PROLOGUE

This was his night. He wouldn't allow anything to mar what he was about to set in motion.

He killed the engine and waited inside his van as darkness fell. He saw a light come on in an upstairs window of the contemporary clapboard house across the road.

Reaching for the bottle on the seat beside him, he gulped a mouthful of water while continuing to watch the house.

When the light went off, he gloved up and climbed out of the van onto the quiet residential Santa Barbara Street, where the sultry sea breeze caressed his face and set the palm fronds rustling. Their menacing shadows swooped and retreated on the lamp-lit sidewalk. He paused to wipe the beads of sweat from his forehead with a tissue and stuffed it in his pocket. Cautiously, he skirted the large oak tree beside the driveway.

The soft, flickering glow from a television seeped from under the curtains at the window as he crept across the lawn heading to the garage. Small stones scattered when he stumbled on the uneven pathway. Jesus, he cursed silently as he hesitated.

Thankfully, no dog barked. He pulled out a penlight, shone its beam low, until he reached the back entrance of the garage.

Once inside, hands trembling with adrenaline, he dropped the penlight. It clattered to the floor and went off. Cursing again to himself, he scrambled around in the dark until his fingers closed around it.

Opening the Ford, he leaned under the steering wheel, felt for the hood release and pulled it. Holding the penlight in his mouth, he lifted the hood and found the hydraulic brake fluid line. He pulled his wrench from his pocket, undid the nut holding line and eased it off with urgent fingers. Finally, he gently closed the hood.

Back in his van, he tried to still his trembling hands and ignore the nervous sweat soaking his shirt. He itched to rip the garment from his body.

About an hour later, the external house lights went on, and a tall, slim man and a boy carrying a stuffed animal appeared.

The father opened the garage door and secured the child into the Ford, went around and climbed in. He backed the vehicle onto the street and drove away.

He tailed them, keeping several car lengths away so as not to arouse suspicion, his heart thumping with anticipation.

The Ford picked up speed down the hill, took the first curve too fast and the next one even faster. It careened on two wheels at the next curve and flew over the embankment, tumbling end over end, tearing bushes and bouncing off boulders. Over and over the Ford pitched with bits of vehicle tearing away until it halted in the valley, wheels spinning. Breathing hard with pent-up pleasure, he stopped to see if the man or his son climbed from the battered vehicle.

When the Ford erupted into flames, he punched the air as the feeling of absolute power surged through him.

CHAPTER 1

Stephani Robbins looked up from the slides of tissue cultures she was checking for signs of necrosis. Her back ached. She leaned forward and rubbed it.

Nina Mumszuk, her friend and co-worker, set down the cultures she'd seeded on the white bench top and pulled down her face mask. "I spent the weekend looking at houses in Mesa. Vassily thinks we should wait 'till we have more savings, but I want my own place."

Stephani saved the results of the latest round of tests. "I should be buying, as there are still some bargains buys, but I'm not exactly sure where I want to live."

Three capped and masked heads turned towards them.

"People used to say that you couldn't lose with real estate." Richard Dixon, her colleague and head tissue engineer, said. "Coffee anyone?"

"Just what I need. I'll sort through the mail." Stephani said.

Fred Lincoln returned to calibrating the injection robot.

"I'll go," Nina said. She glared at Fred's back. "The usual, Richard?" When he nodded, Nina asked Stephani.

"Same here." Stephani bypassed bench tops and let herself into the glass corridor that led to three offices. They always reminded her of linked rows of goldfish tanks, like the ones she'd longingly pressed her face against as a small child at the local mall. She tugged at the face mask ties that had caught in her black hair as she strode to her office.

Her forgotten morning cup of coffee was on her desk. She started to sort the mail into two piles, one for Richard and the other for herself, until she came upon a pink envelope without a return address or company logo, addressed to her:

Doctor Stephani Robbins, Senior Tissue Engineer

Rigby Research Inc.

55-78 Desert Sun Drive

Scottsdale, AZ 85251

The envelope had an embossed edge like an invitation.

Richard strolled in with two coffees and paused when he spotted her abandoned cup. "You already have a take-out."

"That's from this morning. Thanks. Just put mine on the desk."

He took a sip and leaned over her shoulder. "Any of that for me, Doc?"

"Stop it. Just because I've got a few letters after my name."

"Just teasing." He grinned. "You're always so serious. I'd do anything for a smile."

If he could call her "doc" because she had a doctorate, then she could do the same for him. "Sure, Professor Dixon." That didn't come out the way she'd intended. It sounded like she was being sarcastic. God, she wished she could be glib like Iantha, her half-sister from her mother's second marriage, and get away with it.

"Now…now. I see you're still getting loads of stuff forwarded from our L.A. branch."

She took a sip of her coffee. The aroma reminded her of when her mom used to have one on the go as she got ready for work. Stephani had to be up and have her nose in her books.

"I'm not working two jobs for nothing. You'd better study hard and get a degree," her mother had always said.

Stephani looked up to see Richard rake his fingers through his unruly black hair. He was always trying to tame it. A Harvard graduate, Richard had been headhunted by Rigby.

His hands were large with prominent veins on the back and his fingers were almost squared off. And she remembered from when they'd first met, he had a handshake with a sure grip.

"I'm beginning to wonder if our suppliers bother to update their records. I emailed them two months ago when I transferred," she said.

"Obviously, none of them are as organized as you."

"It doesn't feel like that. After five years of research into healthy endothelial cells in stromal breast tissue, I should have made a breakthrough, not be agonizing that if I'd taken a different approach I'd be registering a patent for us now."

"Shoulda, coulda. You're too hard on yourself. We knew that finding a biological alternative to silicone wasn't going to be easy."

"Maybe I'm not committed enough." Her phone rang. The girl at reception told her that Jack Theed, the representative from West Labs Equipment, had arrived for their meeting. "He's early. Tell him I'll be down in ten."

"So after the fire at the lab in L.A. and having to move here and set up again, you still think you're not committed enough?" he said.

'Mm," she shrugged. She should be grateful that the project still had funding.

"How are the RT241 trials looking so far?"

"It'll be another thirty-six hours before we know anything." She opened the pink envelope and found a letter on matching embossed paper.

"What have you got there?" Richard asked.

"An invitation, I think." She unfolded the letter.

Dear Stephani,

You are my Princess,

My only Princess,

I'll make you happy,

When you are sad,

I'll always love you

And treasure you forever

Though others won't understand,

No one loves you more than I do,

So my Princess be true to me,

In your heart, you know I love you,

Soon, we'll be together,

And you'll be mine eternally.

No one loves you more than I do

No one!

Yours forever.

Who the hell's this from? She slumped into the hydraulic chair and edged backwards from her desk. Why would anyone send this corny poem to her? It wasn't even Valentine's Day.

"What's wrong?" Richard asked.

She shoved the letter back into the envelope. "Nothing."

"You sure?" Richard raised an eyebrow.

"How's the new iPhone?" She needed time to think this through.

"Still working out all those Apps. I tell myself it can't be that hard if a five-year-old can manage it." Richard glanced down at her quizzically.

She fumbled with the jumble of envelopes trying to cover the one with the poem inside, but everything cascaded to the vinyl floor. *Jesus, I'm a klutz.*

He gathered them up.

"I can do that." Dismayed, she watched him pile them onto her desk and swallowed as the letter fell out.

It was in his hands before she could reach for it.

"Mind if I take a look?"

Richard glanced at her. She found she had nowhere to hide from his searching gaze.

"Have a read and tell me if it's okay for someone to send this to me?"

He read the poem. "Is this from someone you know?"

She shook her head. "I'm too old for star-struck teenagers to be writing me a love poem."

"This is disturbing. Especially, since this guy thinks that you'll be his forever."

"Oh. Let me look again." This time, she took in each word.

"I can't think of anyone who would write this stuff."

"My conclusion is some weirdo's got a fixation on you." Richard frowned.

"No one's been following me. At least I don't think so. Maybe we're overreacting."

"Call security."

"But what if it's just a prank?" She'd had a couple of strange calls recently on her home phone even though her number was unlisted. Stephani picked up the phone, but put it down when she saw, through the glass wall, Nina leave Laboratory 1 and come along the corridor towards them.

Nina knocked on the door and entered. Strands of her blonde hair had worked their way out of the disposable cap and fell across her face.

"I've almost finished loading the incubator, and wanted to check you still want me set the timer for thirty-eight hours."

"Yes," Stephani said. "Let's see if the enriched mixture will improve the cell growth."

Nina glanced at the letter Stephani held. "Wedding invitation?"

"Someone's sent me this poem. It's not like the sort you'd get from an admirer, but from…." She let Nina read it.

Nina stared open-mouthed. "Oie Boczi. Sorry. That's 'Oh God' in Ukrainian. What is in their head? What are you going to do?"

"We're going to inform security," Richard said.

"Let's go talk to the staff and see if anyone's got any clues," Richard said. "You could have yourself a stalker."

Stephani, capped and gowned again, scarcely noticed the familiar smell of growth media and disinfectant as a moment of panic gripped her when two capped heads turned her way. She took a deep breath before she spoke. "Hey, guys."

She swallowed the hesitation welling in her throat. "Can I ask you something?" Why did she have to deteriorate into a nervous wreck when it came to something personal?

She turned to go when Richard gave her a look that said 'if you don't, then I will', so she pressed on, "I received a poem in the mail today. I don't know if this is meant to be a joke. If it is, it's not funny."

"What's the problem?" Melissa Toomey, the tissue-engineering graduate, closed the glass fume hood, peeled off her disposable gloves, stepped from behind the bench, and slipped down her mask to reveal a heavily made-up face.

"Have a read." She slipped the poem from the envelope.

"Do you think he's stalking you?"

"I hope not. Now I'll be looking over my shoulder every time I go out." She should secure the front door of her apartment at night. However, the thought of being in a locked space scared her more.

"Have you seen anyone suspicious, Fred?"

Fred added incubation media into an injection robot. A soft whizzing sound punctuated the air as a measured amount of medium squirted into test tubes.

Finally, he lifted his head and eased down the mask that covered his bulbous nose. "What?"

She repeated her question.

He raised his eyebrows. "As if I'd send you that! I'm here 'till eight o'clock most nights. When would I have time?"

A typical answer from someone who still lived with his mother and wore pants up to his waist with two pleats that were perfectly formed on each side.

"Can you glance at this and see if it sounds like anyone you might know?"

"Why?"

"Oh, why did I even ask?" She turned from him. Fred, the resident guru in cancer cell research, had an IQ that was probably off the scale, but possessed no people skills.

"Give it to me," Fred snapped.

"See the way he talks to me," she said.

"Fred, that was out of line," Richard said.

Fred flung the poem at her. "Let me get on with my work."

"I hope someone -"

"Stop your babbling," Fred said. "I can't concentrate."

"Richard, are you going to let him get away with that?"

"Quit it, Fred. We're adults and should behave as such."

"I apologize. Happy?"

Did he even realize that he'd upset her and pretended to be contrite?

"No," she said, knowing that it would have little impact on Fred. "Richard, how are the RT251 tissue cultures coming?"

"Promising. Still, it's too early to say for sure." He glanced at her with a questioning look.

"I'm fine."

Fred adjusted his mask and picked up the tray of test tubes partly filled with media and ambled, with a loaded tray, to the incubator. "Maybe, this guy's obsessed with you."

Her Mary Janes encased in disposable shoe covers made a shh shh sound on the floor as she followed him. "My God, Fred! What makes you think that?"

"The choice of words," Fred opened the incubator door and began to put the trays inside.

"Are you okay?" Richard asked. "You've gone very pale."

Clutching the poem, she rushed to her office, picked up the phone and realized she couldn't remember the number. She looked it up on the computer and dialed security. When someone answered, she told them about the poem.

After she hung up, she gulped some cold coffee, called the police and was told someone would be over that morning.

"I'm glad you did that. If you hadn't, I would have," Richard said.

"How long have you been standing there?"

"Long enough to see you make that call."

"I should be doing something." She left her seat and paced to the window, which gave a view of cacti and succulent gardens with a backdrop of cloudless blue autumn sky against a scattering of eucalyptus trees, and back to where Richard was standing beside her desk.

"Easy now. Just calm down," he said. "What did you plan to do this morning?"

She drew her palms up. "I don't know. I can't think."

Richard hugged her. "Let me get some photocopies of that poem so I can ask a few people."

"Thanks," she said. His aftershave smelled of musk, and his shirt had the scent of freshly washed laundry that made her think of her mother, who spent her nights doing washing and ironing for the extra cash. It was comforting. "I should get back to work."

Back in Laboratory 1, she picked up the slides and put them down, then picked them up again. Maybe, she was making too much of this, and it was just a joke. If that was so, then why did this poem make her feel uncomfortable?

After a few moments, Stephani tried to view the slides and discovered that the microscope wasn't working. She turned it off and on, to reset it. The images on the screen showed some minor bacterial growth. That was good. Two done and another twenty-two left.

God, the gloves felt wet on the inside from her clammy palms. Usually, she had no trouble concentrating. She forced herself to scan all of the slides and save them to the computer. She'd go back to them when she could focus.

Stephani deposited the slides into the refrigeration unit, binned the rubber gloves and face mask, and retreated to her office.

When her phone rang, she wrenched it from its cradle, dropped it and then finally uttered a flustered, "Good morning!"

She was told Jack was still downstairs at the reception waiting to see her.

"Shoot, I'd completely forgotten. Tell Jack I'll be down in five."

After a quick inventory check to see if the lab needed any more test tubes or other equipment that West Labs carried, she shrugged out of the lab coat and hurried into Richard's office. "Can you call me when security or the police arrive?"

"Where are you going?"

"Jack's waiting for me downstairs. Just call me when they arrive, and I'll terminate my meeting with him." She hurried out the door and was at the elevator when she remembered the order sheet and rushed back to retrieve it off her desk.

As she stepped back into the elevator, a chill ran through her. How long had this anonymous poem writer been stalking her?

CHAPTER 2

The latest photos he'd taken of Stephani were perfect. He pinned them onto the wall amongst the others of her. The angle of the sun lit up her face and gave her a, childlike look, and those full lips of hers—so innocent, yet sexy. Her hair fell like a satin black curtain almost to her shoulders. So often he wanted to reach out and touch the soft strands of his Princess's hair. "My one and only love," he whispered.

"Pud, you down there?" his mother called.

Her voice was like metal scratching on glass. At least she didn't call him 'Puddles' any more so anyone who heard would not make the connection to what his cruel nickname meant. Did she have to remind him that he had wet the bed until he was twelve? Nevertheless, who would hear nowadays? No visitors ever called. Besides, whenever he went to the shopping mall in Mesa, mother rarely tagged along. Many times when he'd been a teenager, he'd asked, no begged her, not to call him by that name. Cried, slammed his bedroom door, ran away a few times, and that whore had laughed in his face every time.

"I'm just finishing. I'll be up for dinner in a minute." He reloaded the color printer with photographic paper.

He stared at the collage of photos mounted on the wall. Moments in his Princess's life, captured forever on photographic paper. He reached out and gently stroked them one by one. His blood heated; he tingled all over and hardened instantly.

"I need you now."

The floorboards above him creaked. He could picture his mother's fat body, legs swollen from fluid retention, waddling from the kitchen and along the hallway towards the basement door. He hurried across the cement floor and started up the old wooden stairs. He did not want her poking her nose down here. "Coming, Mother."

The door opened as he reached the top step.

"What are you doing, Pud?" A jar of spaghetti sauce in her hand, she peered over his shoulder to the room below.

He felt for the switch on the wall beside him while staring at her and turned off the light to the basement. "Just looking at some shots I took of my snow globes and figurals." He moved forward, forcing her to retreat into the hallway.

"How many shots do you need of those fig…somethings anyway? How anyone can be interested in that useless stuff I don't know! Why do you need them displayed in the showcase anyway?"

"They're mine, and don't you ever open that cabinet and touch them."

Beads of perspiration glistened on her flushed face. Just the walk from the kitchen was enough to make her sweat with the effort and the heat. Her fleshy arms stuck out of a sack of a dress that strained across her ample bosom, and folds of wet stained fabric bunched under her armpits. She was always like that.

"What do you want?"

Hertha pushed the jar at him. "I can't get this open."

After a couple of tries, he went to the kitchen to find something that would give him the traction he needed to remove the lid. His mother trailed behind him. Faded peeling wallpaper embossed with daffodils and daisies brightened the drab room. Even the view from the window above the sink depressed him: a single velvet mesquite tree, some cacti, and the odd clump of yellow–brown grass that had died in the summer. "Where's the dish towel, Mother?"

His gaze took in the once white bench top and the old fifties cabinets painted bright orange, the paintwork chipped and marked from years of use. "I need a towel or something to get a grip on this."

"Don't know what I've done with them."

The stupid whore probably left them in the washing machine days ago. He wrapped the edge of the stained blue plastic tablecloth around the lid and unscrewed it. "Here."

He watched her add the sauce to some ground meat in the saucepan. A plastic strainer with cooling spaghetti was on the sink. "Why'd you cook it first? How many times have I told you I like spaghetti served hot?"

"So, you want it hot. It'll heat up when the sauce gets poured over the top."

"I hate cold spaghetti under hot meat sauce. The damned stuff tastes awful that way."

"You're too fussy. No wonder you can't find a gal." She added some salt and pepper to the mixture.

"Just shut your mouth about that. How can I bring a girl home with a mother like you, huh? Look at this place. You don't clean. You don't iron. This whole place is like the inside of a dumpster."

"Now listen here, boy. I raised you on my own. You don't know what that was like."

"Don't ever bring that up again! You hear!" *I hate you… I hate you,* he said to himself.

She jabbed the ladle into the sauce. Splatters of tomato sauce ran down the tiled wall and then pooled on the bench top. "Don't talk to me like that! You should show me some respect."

"Look at this. It's stone cold." He tipped the spaghetti into a bowl. "This isn't cooking. Just once it would be nice if you did it the right way. You know that. Now I'll have to nuke it. You can have yours cold if you want. I don't care. I just don't care." He dumped her portion back into the strainer.

"That darned contraption! It's too complicated," Hertha whined. "I swear you need a goddamned license to use it."

"Stephani will use it." *When she comes to live with us*, he added silently. She would make him delicious meals. Roast turkey, even when it wasn't Thanksgiving. Roast beef, with stuffed pumpkin. Home baked apple pie. He salivated at the thought. "Contraption? I don't know why I bother."

"Who's Stephani?"

"None of your damned business." He would get rid of the damned awful wallpaper when his Princess came to live with him. It should have been replaced when they first moved in ten months ago.

His mother was loath to spend a cent on this place. When she sold their last shack of a home and moved here to be nearer to him, the termites had chewed the floorboards in the third bedroom, but it wasn't obvious at the time. Two of the windows were taped over to keep the broken glass from falling out, and the roof leaked in four places. It was ready to be pulled down, and that's what the developer who purchased it planned to do. So long as the ground in the vacant lot behind their place remained undisturbed, his secrets would be safe. Hurried burials in the dark of the night carried out in silence were a thing of the past. He would not do those evil acts any more, he was almost sure of it.

When his Princess came to live with him…he saw mother stir the mixture. The fat from the beef formed pools around the edges of the pot. "Skim the fat off, Mother. You know how I hate greasy food."

Hertha scooped up some of the glistening mixture with the ladle. She tasted it. "Mm. Fat never did me any harm." Then she scooped some of the fat away with a spoon and splashed it into the sink.

"I hope it tastes better than the last time you made it."

"Listen here…you've been eating my cooking since you were a baby."

Spending more than a few minutes in her company made him angry. Why did she have to move here anyway? The distance had kept him sane. She'd kept saying that she was old and sick and needed to have her only son to look after her. "You need a wash."

She lifted her arm. "Had a wash the day before yesterday, I think."

"Well, have one today before you go to bed…and for Christ's sake, use deodorant. God, a man could keel over from the smell."

"You think you're a man? Don't make me laugh."

"You fat whore. No wonder father left you." His hand ached to strike her. But he remembered what she used to do to him when he was naughty when he was little, and shuddered.

"He died in Vietnam."

"That's a load of crap. He didn't want to come home to you!"

"Shut…your mouth."

He'd hit the target. "What did you say?"

"Your father didn't want you."

"I know he loved me, but couldn't stomach seeing you again."

"Love? He never loved you."

"Stop it! Stop it! Fuckin' shut up, shut your fuckin' mouth, Mother. Hear!"

"Get the plates, Puddles."

"Don't you ever call me by that name again! Hear!"

CHAPTER 3

Dionne Sarlos rose from the blanket that was spread under a group of mesquite trees and pointed. "Mommy, Auntie—did you see that?" she said. "Look, there's an eagle."

Stephani, in jeans and T-shirt, pushed her sunglasses up and stared into the azure-blue sky. She was struck yet again by how different Arizona was from smog-laden Los Angeles, where she'd worked and lived so much of her life. She watched the eagle circle over the Canyon Lake picnic area where scattered groups of families had set up their lunch at wooden park tables. The stillness was broken by laughter from children playing and parents chatting as they sat in easy chairs with platters of dips, cheese and crackers, nuts and other snacks.

The bird dove into a clump of rabbit brush. Moments later, it ascended.

"Did you see? He caught a lizard," Dionne said. "Where did he go?"

The other side of the lake was more or less flat, dotted with Joshua, mesquite, cottonwood, and the occasional ironwood tree. Stephani watched the bird's flight to the steep rise of the surrounding mountains. She pointed to a high ledge across the lake where sheer walls of rock rose to meet the cloudless sky. "Up to his nest."

Her half-sister, Iantha, retrieved cans of soda from a cooler bag and set them down on the rug. "Don't you wander off! Snakes and wild animals are out there. Remember last year that boy from your school was bitten by a rattler out here somewhere." Iantha turned to

Theo. "Can you get the chairs out?"

Theo, her husband, deposited the picnic basket on the blanket. "Sure."

"You've already told me a thousand times. Don't touch this, don't do that," Dionne said. "I'm not a baby anymore, Mom." Dionne glared at her mother. "Maybe that eagle will carry me away too." She stomped off, her black ponytail swinging, past other picnickers toward the water's edge.

"Don't get too close, or you'll fall in. What about your hat?" Iantha called after her. "You'll get sunburned."

Stephani smiled. Iantha had given the child numerous warnings since they'd set off from their home.

"Dionne's nearly ten."

Iantha sighed. "I'm sorry. I don't know what's gotten into me."

"It's okay." Stephani bent down to give her younger sibling a hug and found herself squashed against Iantha's large breasts.

"I think I've got PMS today."

"What would men do if they had to go through this?"

"There would be no end to their moaning and complaining."

Stephani laughed and laughed. Then she stopped abruptly. It felt strange.

"Welcome back. It's been hard for you, what with losing Allan in that car accident, having Henry in an institution and moving." Her sibling gazed up at her.

"I still think about Allan every day." *Would losing the only man she'd ever loved ever get any easier?*

"I'm glad you've returned to the living."

"I know I've been on auto pilot, but with Allan gone and Henry in that place..." Stephani shrugged. Her son was unconscious in a hospital bed and the heartache, every time she went to visit, grew worse. "I still keep hoping… that the last five months were just a bad dream, that Henry will wake up and be okay."

"You know that won't happen. I'm so glad you moved here."

"Selling the house and moving Henry had been all too much at first. I thought I'd made a big mistake leaving Allan behind."

"He'll be with you here, always." Iantha put her hand on her chest.

"I can't help feeling what I feel."

"I wish mom could have come. But she never wants to leave that place. Just the thought of going somewhere unfamiliar makes her nervous," Iantha said.

"I guess we have to accept that she'll never be her old self again.

"Sometimes mom doesn't recognize me when I visit."

"When did this start?" Stephani asked.

"A few weeks ago." Iantha pulled out a blue-checkered tablecloth and laid it in the middle of the blanket. "She asks about you all the time. I was beginning to think you'd forgotten about her."

"I will go see her. It's just that I've been busy with the move, seeing to Henry, the job and all."

"You've been here two months now."

Stephani glanced away, ashamed. "I don't know if I could take it if she didn't recognize me. I think about her all the time." When she was a child, she believed her mother would never grow old. Though her mom had been tough on her, she was still her mom and she loved her.

"Sorry. I didn't realize how much that upsets you. And I shouldn't get too heavy. After what you've been through… I don't know how I'd be."

Stephani reached down and touched her half-sister's long black hair. "I should be apologizing. I always have excuses."

"When the vacancy first came up at Rigby in Scottsdale, you wouldn't even consider moving. I can't imagine how hard it must have been packing up your life like that."

Stephani said, "You're right…the leaving…."

"There was nothing left for you there. Surely, you're not thinking of moving back?"

"I want my husband back."

"If I could do that for you, I would."

"Sorry. I didn't mean…."

"I was surprised when you sold your piano. You used to love playing it."

"Afterwards, I couldn't bring myself to touch the keys," Stephani said. "The piano reminded me of the happy times."

"He was a good man."

Iantha turned to Theo, though not fast enough as Stephani saw the tears in Iantha's eyes. *Breathe*, she told herself.

"Just put these chairs here beside the rug," Iantha said to Theo as she set down the plates and flatware.

Theo moved the basket closer to his wife. "Does that make it easier, darling?"

As he bent, his tall frame, Iantha straightened to kiss him and ruffle his receding grey-black hair.

Stephani watched them wistfully. Allan's image was fuzzy. How could she have forgotten his smile, the sound of his voice? Her throat constricted. She picked up a dry twig and broke it. Would the heartache ever ease? A child called her name…Henry.

She swung round expectantly. It couldn't be. She blinked to refocus her gaze.

"Mom, sorry I meant you, Auntie Steph. Come take a look. It's so pretty. Come on." Dionne started toward the lake edge.

"Give me Dionne's cap," she said to her sister. "I'll take it to her." Since moving to Scottsdale, this was the second time she thought she'd heard her son's voice. It had a similar tone to Dionne's. Their oval faces and long black lashes were similar too, although her niece had Mediterranean, honey-colored skin, and her son had inherited his fair skin from his father. She had held on to the hope that Henry would wake from his coma soon. At the moment, his life consisted of a feeding tube and various machines that kept him alive.

***

He smiled to himself from his hiding place behind an ironwood tree. His Princess walked down to the water's edge with her niece. He adjusted the telephoto lens on the camera, and then clicked again and again. Their features were so similar. Even though the niece's body was immature and her breasts had not yet began to bud, her slim build and the way she carried herself showed the pledge of a fuller figure in the years to come. The splendor would be sullied when the flower of womanhood fulfilled its promise, the buds became large, and the body, more like her mother's. However, that would take years.

Someone stepped on a twig nearby, and he looked up to see a fat guy in beige shorts and a busty blonde in brief jean cut-offs. They were holding hands. The blonde laughed. The fat guy probably cracked some stupid joke. She seemed to be in her early twenties. He did not like blondes and the woman was in his line of vision. He waited until she moved and took another shot and another.

They must have heard the clicking because they both turned to stare at him. The guy let go of the blonde's hand and trundled towards him. "Hey. Listen, jerk. You're not taking photos of my girl."

"I'm taking shots of the wildlife." Pud picked up his backpack.

"Don't look like that to me, buddy. You leave my girl alone or I'll have a piece of you."

The fat guy made a grab for the camera, but Pud jerked it out of reach and pushed him hard.

The fat guy groaned as his face hit the dirt.

"Fuck, look what you've done to Rick." The blonde bent over her boyfriend. "He's bleeding. I'm calling the park ranger. And, I'll bet you've got something you shouldn't in that bag. I'm sure he'll be interested in what you're hiding." She pulled out a cell phone.

He wrenched it from her and flung it as far as he could. The woman screamed.

He ran. Ran to where the flat ground gave way to the steep rise of the Superstition Mountains. He kept on going until his legs were shaky and he was out of breath. He wanted to sit down in the shade of the mesquite tree, but his jeans would get dirty, so he stood. The sweat from his body was staining his cotton shirt. Christ, he hated that. When his breathing returned to normal, and he'd waited a sufficient length of time and checked that no law enforcement officer was in the vicinity, he made his way down the slope of earth and rocks. He wanted to get just one more shot of his Princess.

***

Stephani stepped over patchy rye grass and uneven rocky ground to where her niece stood on the bank staring at the blue water.

Dionne leaned over and pointed. "Look at that rock on the bottom. Isn't it pretty?"

Stephani eased the baseball cap onto the child's head. "It's deeper than you think."

"But I'm starting a rock collection. Look, there's people swimming. It's safe enough for them." Dionne started rolling up her jeans.

"Don't even think about it."

"She treats me like a baby. And it's not that deep here."

"It would take one second for your mom to notice your wet jeans. Remember when you were four, you fell into a pool and nearly drowned? Let's go for a walk."

"Sort of do, but that was so long ago. Mom made sure I had swimming lessons."

"She was so upset. I don't think she's gotten over it." Stephani clasped Dionne's hand.

Henry's hand used to fit into her palm with barely a finger showing when she curled her fingers around it. He'd been five when.... His smile used to light up her soul, and the four words he spoke in that little boy voice nearly every day made her stop whatever she was doing. *Mommy, I love you.*

Her niece's voice drew her back to the present, but the sadness remained.

"Did you see that squirrel, Auntie Steph? He's so cute. I want to take him home." Dionne tugged her towards the animal.

"You've got too many pets already. Anyway, the squirrel might have a family." However, she only had memories of the happy times.

They followed the lake edge where tufts of grass grew here and there. Dionne let go and skipped ahead, then ran back to grab her hand again.

"Watch out." Stephani jerked Dionne out of the way just in time. "Ants' nest."

"Eek! They're big ones. How is Henry?"

Stephani's stomach contracted into a hard ball. "He is doing as well as expected."

"When will he come out of the hospital?"

"I don't know."

"Never mind, you can be my other mom." Dionne clutched her hand tighter. "Then you can get to do those things you miss with me."

She missed that funny little way Henry would crawl out from behind the sofa with his toy dog and 'surprise' her, shower her with wet kisses, and show her the stick figures he drew of daddy, mommy and himself. She swallowed the lump that had formed in her throat and blinked away tears that she didn't want her niece to see.

"That sounds like a great idea."

Dionne stopped to stare at the water. "Auntie Steph, Bree won't talk to me anymore. And she's my best friend."

"Maybe you should ask her why."

"I want to, but she might be awful to me. Auntie Steph…look." She pointed toward a clump of greasewood bushes, about the length of a football field away. There the ground rose steeply to the mountains.

"I can't see anything. What did you see?"

"A man. I think he was holding something small. Maybe a cell or a camera? I'm sure there was a man there. Can we go look?"

Stephani caught her niece's arm. "We should be getting back. I'll bet lunch is ready. Your mom and dad will send a posse out to find us if we don't show." Even if Dionne had seen a stranger, the thought of going to investigate did not strike her as a good idea.

"Look…there. Over there," her niece pointed.

"I can't see anyone." If she called the ranger and said what…that her niece thought she saw someone, he'd probably say, how does she know that the guy's not a picnicker? "Tell you what, I'll race you back."

"Okay," Dionne said as she took off with Stephani at her heels.

They skirted a family playing catch and children playing ball. Stephani, legs pumping, tailed her niece.

Dionne slumped down onto the blanket beside her mother. "I won. I won."

Breathless, Stephani stopped beside them, clutching her sides. "I had no chance."

"Yeah! You said it." Dionne punched the air with her fists. "I'm too fast."

"Glad you're back, I'm hungry," Theo said, eyeing the picnic table laden with cold chicken, beef, olives, three different salads and sliced sourdough bread.

"You're always thinking about your stomach. The buttons on your shirt are ready to pop," Iantha said.

"And you're always cooking such tasty vittles. Can I help it that my shirts have shrunk in the wash?"

Iantha started to laugh as she pulled the bottom of her skirt in, so her husband could move closer to the food. "Vittles? Don't try too hard to be an Arizonian, dear."

"Got to start training again," Stephani said between gasps for air. "Then I'll beat you…no problem." She sank onto the blanket.

"Training? You're going to join a health club again?" Iantha's look spoke the real question she asked.

"I know what you're going to say; it's time," Stephani said.

"Then I won't," Iantha said.

"I've got to make the effort."

Theo nodded. "Just remember, no matter what, we're here for you."

"Thanks. You two are my rock," Stephani said.

Iantha gave her an intense gaze as if she knew that no words could convey the depth of emotion that linked them as sisters.

"When can we start eating, Mom?"

"Where did you go?" Iantha handed out the plates and flatware.

"I saw a stranger, Mom. He was hiding behind some bushes watching us."

Iantha, eyes widened in alarm, held Stephani's gaze. "Who was the man? What the hell was he doing?"

Theo, about to pour a glass of red wine, set down the bottle. "What happened?"

"I didn't see anyone," Stephani said. "That's not to say there wasn't someone there. It was too far away to tell for sure. I thought about contacting the ranger, but...I really didn't see anyone."

A "I'll take a look-see while you three stay put," Theo said as he grabbed a chicken leg and a napkin. "Save me some food," he said as he turned to go.

Iantha watched him walk away with a worried look on her face.

"Do you think I'll get into the team, Auntie Steph?"

"You give one hundred percent every time you go out to play, so I can't see why not?"

She ate some potato salad and then leaned over to her sister. "It could have been nothing more than someone taking a walk. Remember the story she made up when she was five?"

"Yep." Iantha put down the rest of the flatware that she'd been clutching.

"She convinced her teachers at school that you were having a baby, remember, Iantha?" Stephani said.

"How can I forget?"

"Baby boy? I don't remember that," Theo said as he rejoined them.

"On parents' day at school…Iantha was complimented by a couple of teachers on how well she'd looked considering she'd just had a baby boy," Stephani said.

"You're not making this up, are you?"

"They stared at me like I was making it up when I denied it. Dionne told the teachers about this baby and had even given him a name. I probably didn't tell you because you were away on some job at the time. Dionne was desperate for a baby brother."

"Stop talking about me," Dionne said. "Can I have some of that chicken?"

"Sure," Iantha said. "So what happened?" Iantha asked Theo.

"I looked around. Asked a few people if they'd seen anyone suspicious. No one had. I called the ranger, and he's going to take a look. Said he'd call if anything turned up." He sat in a folding chair.

Theo leaned down and helped himself to potato salad and some peppered beef.

"Help yourself. I know you don't like chicken. Though for the life of me, I don't know why," Iantha said.

"I just don't." Stephani opened a bottle of soda and poured herself some. "I miss mom's dolmades yalatzi and stuffed zucchinis."

"They were the best," Iantha said.

"I used to make them for Allan and Henry. Allan didn't like them much at first…" She stopped to get a lid on the emotions she'd stirred up at mentioning their names. "Mine were never as good as mom's."

"How can you say that? They were great."

"The way that man was looking at us was creepy," Dionne said.

"Don't worry, pumpkin. The ranger will call us if he finds anything," Theo said between mouthfuls. His cell phone started to ring. "Hello. Oh, yes. Nothing there...no sightings. That's a relief. Thank you for your trouble." Theo disconnected and told them what the ranger had said.

***

It was late afternoon when the four of them packed up and headed back to Scottsdale.

"Can we stop at the gold mine, Dad?" Dionne asked as the ghost town came into view. "It'll be fun. The sign says there's tours,"

"Not for too long. I've got some work to finish off for tomorrow."

"But Dad, can't they get someone else to make some plans so you can have some fun?"

"Sorry Pumpkin, I have to keep us fed, and sometimes I have to take work home when there's a deadline."

"But they only put old people in the places you design."

Stephani glanced at her niece beside her. "Your dad's designed condos, too."

"Your nana's an old person," Theo said. "If she wanted to live there, you wouldn't deny her that, would you?"

"Sorry, Dad, I guess old people need somewhere to live."

"And your poor nana's got Alzheimer's and not able to look after herself any longer." Theo turned off Highway 88 and stopped in the parking lot near the mineshaft. The timber tower above it, a weathered grey-brown square structure, looked like the ground was slowly sucking it in.

"Does it hurt her?"

"No, Pumpkin, but her memory's bad."

"What's that tower thing near the mine?" Dionne asked.

"A water tower."

Then he went on to explain in detail its use when mining for gold, but Stephani could see that her niece wasn't paying attention.

"Hey. The sign says they have tours that go down into the mine. Can we go, Dad? Please, pleease."

Theo drove into the half-full parking lot.

Dionne reached for the door handle as her father turned off the engine.

"It'll have to be a quick walk around."

Dionne jumped out of the white Toyota and rushed towards the handful of buildings that made up the ghost town. She started up the timber steps of a reconstructed old saloon before her mother's feet had touched the dusty earth or Stephani had even opened the door.

"Hey, wait for us," Theo shouted to her.

Dionne scooted back to them. "Dad. Dad. Can I have an old-time photo with you and Mom?"

He sighed. "As long as we're quick."

"I might have a look in the museum," Stephani said.

"In a half hour we meet at the car. Okay?"

Stephani nodded. She went in one direction, and Theo and Iantha in the other with Dionne hurrying her father along to have their picture taken.

It didn't take too long to view the exhibits. As she exited the museum, she had an uneasy feeling that someone was watching her, and she looked over her shoulder. A few families were sightseeing, but no one appeared to be taking any notice of her.

Dionne came running towards her. "Come on, Auntie Steph. We're going to the zip line." She grabbed Stephani's hand and pulled her along.

"I thought your dad said-"

"Mom's waiting. Come on. We have to hurry."

"Okay."

Stephani jumped on a seat on the zip line, which was like a ski lift, with Dionne and Iantha and Theo behind them.

Dionne screamed and laughed when they took off. Stephani's stomach tightened with butterflies as the line moved faster. A small crowd had formed below to watch, and she noticed a capped man taking photos. She lost sight of him as they zipped along.

**

Iantha's family and Stephani climbed back into the Toyota and set off to Scottsdale.

"Did you notice anyone hanging around?" Stephani asked her sister.

"You're scaring me. You saw someone watching us?" Iantha asked.

"What the hell is going on?" Theo said. "Sorry darling. I didn't mean to cuss."

"I got a sensation that someone was watching when I came out of the museum, and I looked around but I didn't see anyone. Then when we were on that zip ride, I thought a guy was watching us. But now I think he was just watching his family," Stephani said.

"Dionne's fallen asleep." Iantha whispered. "She's plum tuckered out, what with all that walking and running. I didn't notice anyone unusual."

They passed ranch houses with chimneys set on dry cacti-ridden acres. "Maybe it's nothing." Stephani kept her voice low so not to wake her niece.

"You know that piano we got for Dionne last year?" Iantha said. "Well, she's stopped her music lessons, and it's just sitting there. I was thinking if you could easily fit it into your apartment that-"

"Nice try. Thanks, but no thanks," Stephani said.

At Apache Junction, they turned onto Main Street and headed back to Scottsdale. The shimmering black endless road divided acres of trailer parks and dry, rocky ground studded with the occasional tufts of brown grass.

Theo turned up the air-conditioning. He must have seen the two men sitting outside the local store in sleeveless undershirts soaked with sweat, Stephani thought.

Near Mesa, they passed rows of small boxy houses. Some needed a lick of paint, and some were littered with discarded objects. Others were barren structures with windows open and limp dusty curtains waiting for a breeze. These gradually gave way to stuccoed structures with neat pebble and cactus gardens as they traveled closer to Scottsdale. She was glad they were finally nearing Iantha's home, as she needed a coffee.

"Here at last." Theo pulled up in the driveway and buzzed the garage door and alarm.

The houses in this walled estate in Scottsdale, with a security guard at the main entrance, were all painted beiges and creams with small front gardens of succulents and other desert plants.

Dionne, eyes shut, rested her head on Stephani's shoulder.

"Time to get out." Stephani nudged Dionne.

Her niece stretched and yawned beside her. "What's for dinner, Mom?"

"I don't know. Something easy. Right now we'll have to help Dad unload the car." Iantha climbed out.

Theo opened the trunk. Iantha got the cooler bag, Stephani took the picnic basket, Dionne picked up the picnic blanket, and Theo pulled out the folding chairs. Iantha went first through the garage and opened the internal door that led to the house.

Dionne dropped the blanket in the kitchen.

"Dionne, don't leave it there," Iantha said as her daughter started up the stairs. "She ignores me. I don't know how I can get her to listen." She set the bag on the white streaked, grey, granite bench top.

"She's at that age. It's probably a matter of not giving up." It had been a good day.

"I guess. Want a drink, Stephani? I know it's been hot, but I still need my coffee. Do you think you could play a few notes on our piano? Last time Dionne played something, it made a funny sound."

"It might need tuning. Let's get this sorted first and have some coffee." Stephani set down the picnic basket, then reached over and pulled off the cloth that covered the dirty utensils. Two photos nestled in between the salt and pepper shakers.

Iantha put on the coffee maker and went to the bottom of the stairs. "Dionne. Come back down and put that blanket away."

As Iantha walked in, Stephani picked up the photo of Dionne and herself playing catch in the park. "How did...where did...did you...these photos?"

Iantha put down the bag of coffee. "What photos?"

Stephani showed them to her.

"Isn't that when you took Dionne to the park to get some catching practice in before the basketball tryouts?"

Her heartbeat upped its pace. "That's what I'm thinking too." She'd only played for two seasons when she was Dionne's age. Her mom wouldn't let her go anymore, as she thought that schoolwork came first and sports were a waste of time.

"And the other?"

"Taken in the company parking lot. Jesus, I wore that suit last week."

Iantha shook her head. "Who took them?"

"I wish I knew. You didn't see these when you were packing the basket this morning?"

"Not even when I put everything back afterwards. What's going on?" Iantha raised her voice an octave.

Iantha only did that when she was worried, Stephani knew. "I received a poem at work a few days ago. I thought it might have been some sort of stupid joke initially."

"What sort of poem?"

"A bit of a strange love poem. Someone declaring that they'd be mine eternally. Wait…I've got a copy in my handbag." She found it and gave it to her sister.

Iantha's brow creased. "You're right. It's creepy. Let me ask Dionne if she noticed anyone near our basket." She called out to her daughter. "Please come down. Stephani needs you to look at something."

"What's wrong, Mom?" Dionne clutched her Barbie doll.

"So you come down for your Auntie but not for me?"

Stephani showed her the photos. "I found this in the picnic basket. Do you know how it got there? Did you see anyone near our basket?"

Dionne shook her head. "But you sure look pretty in that blue suit."

"Are you sure you didn't see anyone?" her mother asked.

"What's this all about, Mom?"

"Just some photos your Auntie found."

"Do you think that man put it there?"

"What are you saying, Dionne? The ranger called Dad and told him that he didn't find anything out of the ordinary at that place where you saw the stranger," her mother said.

"I didn't want to say anything when I saw the same man at the gold mine, because no one believed me when I said I saw him hiding in the bushes at the lake."

"The same man?" Stephani and Iantha said in unison.

Theo walked in. "What's going on?"

"You should have told us. The same man you said?" Iantha said.

Dionne nodded.

"When did you see him?" Stephani sensed the hair on her neck tingle in alarm. Someone had been watching her. She wanted to go to the front window and check the street, but didn't want to panic Iantha.

Her sister bent down to Dionne. "What did he look like? Was he tall?"

"He was hanging around behind the museum watching you, Auntie Steph." Dionne started twisting the doll's hair nervously. "Is he a stranger, a pervert?"

"Do you know what that word means, Dionne?" Theo said.

"I think it's a bad man who-"

"Do they teach you that in school?" Theo raised his eyebrows. "What's happening, Iantha?"

"I'll explain in a minute," she said. "What did this man look like?"

Dionne shrugged. "He was tall with bulgy arms. Not fat, just bulgy."

"Like a body builder?" Stephani asked.

"Yup."

"What color was his hair?" Iantha asked.

She shrugged again. "He was wearing a baseball cap."

"What was he doing?" Stephani asked.

"Just watching you."

"Jesus." Stephani put her hands to her face in alarm.

"Did he hang around the whole time we were there?" Iantha glanced at Stephani.

Dionne twisted strands of her black hair around her finger. "I don't know."

"Can you remember anything else?" Iantha asked.

Dionne shook her head.

"Well, if you think of anything, come tell us. You've been a big help, thanks." Iantha pushed her long hair from her face. "How about you go and play in your room, Pumpkin? Stephani and I need to talk."

"Do I have to? Just when it's getting interesting."

"You've been a good help, but I'm sorry. This is for adults only."

Dionne stomped back upstairs.

"I found these in the picnic basket." Stephani repeated to Theo what Dionne had told them, and about the photos.

He picked them up and flipped the one of Stephani in the parking lot over, and expelled a long breath. "Mother of God, did you see what's written on the back?"

My Princess. My one and only love, the sticker label on the back read.

Her heart pounded. "What sort of deranged person would write this? I need a stiff drink," Stephani gasped. "Have you got any-?"

"No, you don't. You'll manage just fine," Theo said as he glanced at his wife.

"Dionne said she saw that man again at the museum," Iantha said.

"When would this…this…stalker have the opportunity to put these in the basket?" Stephani asked.

Theo and Iantha looked at each other. "It must have been-" Iantha said.

"When you were getting-"

"The other chairs, and I was talking to that woman who works at the local drug store," Iantha said. "That was while you and Dionne went for your walk. I was away from our things for only a short while."

"We must report this to the police," Theo said.

"I plan to go there on my way home." Stephani reached for the photo on the counter but didn't pick it up. "Have you got a small paper or plastic bag? Fingerprints."

Iantha got a plastic zip bag and edged the photo inside. "Do you want us to come too?"

"I'll be fine." Did this man know where she lived? Was he following her all the time or only some of the time? Why had he singled her out? Jesus, she would have to look over her shoulder everywhere she went.

"Let's get the police to come here. After all Dionne did see the man."

"I did see a guy with a baseball hat on when we were on the zip line, but I didn't get a look at his face. I don't even know why I noticed him. I didn't think anything of it at the time."

"Let's see what they say when you tell them."

Stephani tapped in the numbers.

CHAPTER 4

Stephani pulled on her black and purple edged spandex shorts and white T-shirt and then sat on the bed rubbing the sleep from her eyes. She padded to the closet and reached for her running shoes from the bottom shelf. She'd be damned if some stalker would stop her from running in broad daylight.

The phone rang on the bedside table. She let the answering machine kick in. The caller didn't leave a message. Probably some telemarketer trying to sell something.

Through the slatted blinds of her first floor apartment window, she watched the sun's rays push away the darkness. She slipped on her shoes and started tying the laces.

A thought that became a vision filled her head so fully that she stopped tying her shoes. The vision grew stronger with each intake of breath.

Dawn breaks. Sunlight penetrates the darkness inside through the uneven gaps in the wooden planks that make up the walls of the chicken coop. A rooster climbs onto the roof, and crows. Crows the new day into the wind, which whistles through the gaps so hard that the rows of hens fluff up their feathers as they sit on their nests.

Fear and bite of the wind keeps me here on my bed of straw. I pull a rough old blanket over my head and draw my legs up to my chin to try to keep warm and make myself smaller. The hens cluck and scratch about. Someone will be coming soon and I wish it would not be him.

Footsteps thump across the dusty earth and break through the farmyard noises. I close my eyes tight and hope he does not find me here in this darkest corner, and will go away.

The door creaks open, and he comes in.

I start to tremble and wish hard that my mommy were here.

He comes closer. I am scared, so scared I think I might wet myself.

Stephani blinked. The vision disappeared as suddenly as it started. She shivered with imaginary cold, bewildered that she had lost herself in this…this sort of hideous daydream.

She'd never, as far as she could recall, been on a chicken farm or stayed on any sort of farm. As a teenager, occasionally, this same image and other similar ones would enter her head, but this time the vision seemed so real.

Who was that ten-year-old boy that appeared to instill fear in the child?

Stephani finished tying her shoelaces as the phone rang again. She went into the kitchen to see if the caller would leave a message this time.

"I hope I haven't woken you."

She picked up. "Hi, Richard."

"You're up," he said.

"I'm about to go for my morning jog." She sandwiched the phone between her shoulder and her ear and finished tying a double knot.

"When did you start this?"

"Yesterday. But I sort of decided about two weeks ago."

"Daily, huh?"

Running was a cop-out, but it gave her time to think about whether she had the courage to join a health club again. "I'm determined to go. I'm not going to stop doing normal things because some nut-case has sent me that poem and some photos. Besides, I'll be running in a public place with lots of people around."

"What photos?"

She told him.

"This is getting out of hand. What did the cops say?"

"Not too much except that they'd keep me posted. Did you want something?"

"Don't tempt me."

From the light edge in his deep voice, she could bet he was smiling.

"Can you come in to work a half hour earlier today?"

"You don't give a girl much notice." Stephani smiled as she picked up her apartment key. "Any special reason?"

"Just a staff meeting about security."

"Any problems?"

"Ross suggested it, and I thought it was a good idea."

"I'll see you then." She hung up. Ross, the managing director wasn't usually involved with the day-to-day running of the company, but he had taken a special interest in their project of rapid fabrication of multi-layered human hepatic cell sheets primarily for mastectomy patients.

As Stephani started on her morning run, she couldn't help but eye every shrub and building warily. Perhaps she shouldn't have gone out running after all.

CHAPTER 5

Princie Younger picked up his car keys from between an open can of half-eaten baked beans and a discarded cheese wrapper on the kitchen bench. He glanced at himself in the mirror and saw a slim, fair-skinned male. He hated the flaky, scaly skin on his arms and in his hair. He fixed his blond ponytail. Sidestepped piles of old newspapers and magazines from which he had cut out female faces that he liked, two bags of trash that should have been taken out, but he couldn't be bothered and hurried down the narrow hallway to the front door.

Two days ago, he had watched Stephani buy a pair of running shoes and had hoped that she might start jogging in the mornings; but he had not risen early enough yesterday to see her. He didn't want to be late this time.

Princie eased the van to the curbside, and watched Stephani leave the apartment block.

He climbed out wearing the typical running outfit and kept a short distance behind. He liked to watch her firm buns and long legs as she ran. And he especially liked watching her pert breasts move up and down.

He followed her into the park, which was an oasis of green, and then he slowed a little to create some space between them.

A little way in, Stephani stopped to sit on a bench seat, probably to catch her breath.

Princie eased into the bushes that curved in a semi-circle nearby.

Her sweat beaded on her skin. It tantalized him. He wanted to kiss it from her skin everywhere.

Hunched over, he watched the rise and fall of her firm breasts against her T-shirt; his gaze touched her shapely legs from her narrow ankles to her curvy hips.

As he edged closer, a twig snapped underfoot. Startled, Stephani glanced his way. He froze.

The tightness of the leather collar he wore against his Adam's apple seemed suffocating. That bone was too prominent, and he hated when it bobbed up and down when he drank or spoke. However, the collar covered it and made him look sexy, and he liked that.

A bird flew out of a tree above. Stephani screamed, ducked, and jumped back, waving her arms. Then she ran.

Had she seen him? A frisson of excitement began somewhere deep in his groin. He trembled. Those nut-brown eyes had stared at him, and they liked what they saw. He was of a reasonable height and a little on the skinny side, but almost handsome if you did not look too closely at his flaws. Sometimes he wore tight jeans when he wanted women to look at it.

If only he were bigger down there. If only.

When the next jogger passed by, he crept from the bushes, and started after Stephani. He stumbled into an Irish setter and its owner. The man had tried to overtake him, and the dog had followed.

"Hey, watch it buddy," the man said.

He should have been saying that to the man, not the other way around.

Stephani disappeared around the tennis courts. He retraced his steps to her apartment and waited across the road for her to return.

A police car cruised by and he pretended to look in his pockets for keys while they were in sight.

Where was she? He shifted his weight from one leg to the other in agitation and started to wheeze. Damn it, he fumbled in his pockets for his asthma puffer.

Ten minutes later, she came into view, her olive-skin shiny with sweat. At the front entrance, she paused to catch her breath before she went in. Princie kicked the gutter, disappointed; she had not noticed him.

Now he had to go to work delivering the boring mail. He would be just in time for his shift. He hated his job, but it paid the bills and gave him a reason to stop and linger in places where attractive females lived. He'd spotted Stephani checking her mailbox a few weeks ago. The next time he delivered her mail, he took note of her name—Googled it and found her blog. It was as if she was writing to him. From this, he knew so much about her. That she liked going on picnics, shopping with her niece, green and mauve were her favorite colors, and she thought she was too skinny. Stephani was wrong on that count, he liked her just the way she was.

He did not have a blog; you never knew who was looking at it.

He recalled reading her latest post yesterday. The tone had changed, and she wrote that she was closing it down. He would have to resort to sifting through her trash if she did that.

What the hell was going on here! What was happening to him? He couldn't understand it. When he covertly watched women, he did not want them to know. It spoiled his fun. However, this one was special. She was so beautiful. His memories would serve him well tonight. It would be good.

CHAPTER 6

Stephani turned off the microscope and sighed, arched her back and stretched like a cat. Stiff from hours of looking at test results, she pushed her fingers through her hair while she tried to think. What was wrong? Was the mixture too rich? Had the cell structure decayed while being kept in the cryogenic freezer after harvesting? She discounted that; it had tested as normal and healthy at the start of the trials. When they seeded the cells, had the process somehow contaminated it? She must send a few samples to an outside lab for testing for mycoplasma and acholeplasmas.

The fire in the lab in L.A. had not stopped her from striving for her dream, nor would this.

She should have been glad to pack up and head for home, but no one waited for her there, no one to call her Darling or Mommy. Her heart heavy with an ache that the passage of time had not diminished, Stephani picked up a tray of test tubes that had been prepared for the next series of tests. "Richard, I've got my arms full, could you open the door for me, to Lab 2?"

Richard pulled down his mask and straightened his tie. "Oh, you mean scan my palm on the security panel?"

"That's what I said." Her voice was muffled by her mask.

"Anything for you." He grinned.

"Are you trying to tick me off, because if you are…"

"Just cheering you up a little. You look so serious."

"I'm tired. It's been a long day. We've sat in meeting after meeting today, and we're supposed to be scientists. I know we need the board behind us on this, but they just go on and on about totally irrelevant things. How can we get any work done?"

The glass door to Laboratory 2 closed slowly behind them. "Get used to it. It'll only get worse, the closer we get to our goal on this project."

"Are you telling me I have to grin and bear it?"

"Yep."

After she slid the tray into the incubator, she returned for another two trays and deposited them as well.

Richard followed her a second time to help.

"Thanks."

"Anytime." They exited Laboratory 2 together into the hallway to the first lab.

Richard returned to the microscope and she, to her office to pick up her cell. The phone rang and she pulled off her mask. "Hi, Jack. You're lucky you caught me. Another minute and I'd have been gone."

"Sorry to ring you so late, but I thought I should let you know that your order will be delayed at least another week. Half of the last shipment was broken. There'll be an insurance claim, but that doesn't help you, I know."

"That will leave us short of test tubes. What am I going to do?"

"I'll hunt around and see if I can source some for you. Will 300 get you out of trouble?"

"Yes."

"I'll be in touch. By the way, have you given any more thought about joining the health club? I think I told you that I've been a member for over a year. The facilities are nice and clean and they have all the latest equipment."

She took a deep breath and said, "I suppose I should go."

"Well, you did mention you wanted to join."

She didn't want to end up with a jello-belly. "Yep. Can't stand seeing my flabby self."

"What are you talking about?"

"Let's not go there."

"See you there tomorrow night," Jack said.

"I guess so." Stephani hung up, slung her handbag over her shoulder and went back to Laboratory 1. "See you all tomorrow," she said to Nina and Fred, who were busy collating the results of the latest round of tests on the multi-layering of endothelial cells after ten days' incubation.

Fred ignored her.

"Yeah. Poor us have to work overtime," Richard said without looking up from the glass slides.

"Will you be long?" she said.

"Have pity and cook me dinner. I'll be over later," Richard said.

His tone suggested that he wanted her too, even though he'd said it in jest. She pulled a face. "I'm buying Chinese on my way home."

"I love Italian. I'll do anything for a dish of pasta with a sauce of ground beef. Delicious…mm."

"I rang Chan's five minutes ago, and they'll have my take-out ready for me when I get there. I'll pick up after I visit Henry."

"How's he doing?"

"Same." "I'm sorry to hear that. Catch you tomorrow then," Richard said.

"Don't you like Chinese?"

"I didn't say that. Just don't feel like it tonight."

"Oh, come on, can't you admit to it?" She'd worked out weeks ago that he didn't like Chinese food as he'd declined every time one of them offered to get him some.

Nina, perched on a stool, closed the textbook she'd been reading. "Men, admitting to anything? Please…do not make me laugh! Do not worry about us having to work late. The timer is going to go off any minute. It will not take long to record the results. Then I'm off to the university. I've got a paper to hand in tonight."

"How long before you graduate and become registered as a doctor in the US?" Stephani asked.

"The end of next year. Then I have to do the internship over again. But it will be worth it as doctors do not earn much money in the Ukraine."

"See you later." Stephani walked into the changing room area and noticed one of the doors to the stalls was closed. She continued past to her locker, pulled out her handbag and the bag of groceries she'd rushed out to buy in her lunch break and said, "Anyone in here?"

"Only me," Melissa said as she emerged. She had changed from her white uniform into a burgundy sleeveless number.

She sighed, relieved. "Going out?" Stephani brushed her black hair. "Boyfriend coming over?"

"Not tonight."

Stephani shrugged out of her lab coat, threw it into the trash and picked a white thread from the skirt of her black dress. "Someone else then?"

"No." Melissa opened the door, and they both went into the corridor.

"I read in the paper that Macy's is having a sale. So I'm going down there tomorrow to buy that dress I was telling you about. That's if it's still there," Stephani said. "I probably don't need any more clothes, but I can't resist a sale." After only wearing hand-me-downs when she was growing up, she tried not to pay full price for anything even though she could now afford it.

Melissa remained silent while they continued past locked storage rooms and other research laboratories.

Finally, her co-worker answered. "I've had a fight with my boyfriend."

"Nothing too serious, I hope."

Melissa shrugged.

"After I pick up some Chinese, I'm going to eat dinner, curl up in front of the TV and not move for the rest of the night." Stephani once had a family to enjoy the evenings with. She could hear herself playing "The Pink Panther" tune on the piano for Henry and Allan. All the things that reminded her of Allan were gone: sold or donated. Their absence, a constant reminder that her negligence was the reason he was dead.

Stephani scanned her palm on the panel near the elevator, and then pressed the down button.

The doors opened, and they stepped in.

"Say, did the police find out who sent that poem to you?" Melissa asked.

"They're still investigating was the reply I got. They probably don't know. I haven't received anything else since the photos I found in the picnic basket on the weekend."

"What?"

"Sorry. I thought I told you." Stephani told her about it, but did not mention the guy that Dionne said she had seen. It gave her the creeps to think about it, but the main reason: if she didn't talk about the sightings, the police might find a perfectly acceptable explanation; and if she did, well, it might somehow make things much worse. Her adult mind told her not to be so superstitious, to be logical about it.

"So far, the police aren't convinced there's a connection between the poem and the photos," Stephani said.

"You're kidding me, aren't you?" Melissa said as they went outside through the staff entrance.

"It seems so obvious to me. I can't figure out why they would think otherwise."

Melissa glanced at her as they crossed the almost empty parking lot.

"I'm sure glad it's not me." Melissa let out a sigh. "Whoops, that didn't come out too well. Sorry."

"It's been worrying me ever since I got the poem. I keep hoping all this will just go away."

They said their goodbyes.

Stephani slid behind the wheel of her car and tried to place her handbag on the passenger seat beside her, but it slipped to the floor. A splash of red caught her gaze.

What the hell! A red cellophaned rose lay on the floor. She jerked away.

Where had it come from? She had not noticed it when she'd gone shopping on her lunch break or when she'd returned to work. Jesus.

She blinked, hoping that it would disappear like those visions she'd had recently. With trembling fingers, she picked up the single stem encased in the cellophane wrapper. It would have wilted if it had been there for hours, and it looked fresh. Then she noticed that the stem was in one of those small capsules with water crystals inside. A small pink envelope was attached to the cellophane.

She dropped the rose back on the seat beside her. "Jesus."

Her hand shook as she called Richard. "Somebody's left a rose in my car. It was locked."

"What? How?"

"I wish I knew. I'm almost sure it wasn't there when I returned from the shopping mall after lunch."

"Where are you?"

"Parking lot."

"Lock yourself in and stay put. I'm coming down."

"Okay." She checked her back seat for any more unpleasant surprises—found none—and glanced around. Melissa had driven away and she was all alone in an empty parking lot. She wrapped her arms around herself even though the heat of the day had not eased. *Hurry up...where are you, Richard?*

Stephani screamed when someone knocked on the driver

56

window. A man's face looked down at her.

"You okay, ma'am?" the security guard said.

She buzzed down her window the slightest bit. "Haven't seen you before. How do I know who you are?" She wasn't about to trust anyone that she didn't know by sight.

"I'm with the security company. I'll show you my card. Okay, ma'am?"

CHAPTER 7

The high-energy beat of music mingled in a sort of discord with the rhythm of a half-dozen men and women running on treadmills. Stephani wanted to turn from the counter and run outside as those once familiar smells of sweat and machines assaulted her.

A blonde in black and yellow spandex gym gear approached Stephani as she stood at the health club reception desk. The blonde looked like an overgrown bee. The name tag on her yellow midriff top identified her as Trainer Jenee. "Can I help you?"

"No." She needed a strong drink, not this. Stephani held her gym bag in front of her as if it were a shield.

Jack was supposed to be meeting her here.

"Your first time here, huh?" Jenee said.

"I haven't been to any health club for about five months." Those words reminded her just how long it had been since her last workout in Santa Barbara. That was the day Allan...

"Keeping fit is the greatest. Bet you've been missing it?"

"No." Her heart pounded like the lost, frightened kitten she'd held in her hands as a teenager that her mom had not let her keep. She swallowed and took a deep breath. Painful memories committed to the recesses of her mind flooded in. Her car not starting when it was time to go home, her subsequent phone call to Allan, to pick her up, the endless waiting, and the unanswered phone calls to his cell when he failed to show. Two police officers had approached her. The way they'd spoken in subdued tones with that air of authority and seriousness alarmed her. Then they had said, "We are very sorry, your husband's vehicle burst through the safety rail, plunged down an embankment and burst into flames. Your son has been taken to the hospital." For a moment that had seemed to go on forever; she thought that she still had Allan as well because it was too horrendous to consider the alternative. "Allan, he's okay?" she had asked.

The officer had shaken his head. "I'm sorry, ma'am."

Jenee's voice brought her back to the present.

"You know they discovered that women who do weight-bearing exercise have much less incidence of osteoporosis in later years, they show their age less, and even enjoy sex more. Yep…I'm for that, aren't you?" Jenee said.

"Yes, I know a little about the first two, but about the sex, I'm a little skeptical."

"We have an excerpt from the article published in a medical magazine in our brochure, and it's been written by a leading doctor…see here." She shoved it towards Stephani. "Maybe you're wondering how to use some of the equipment?"

"Oh…I…." Stephani continued thinking about the event that had altered her life forever. The overwhelming guilt that it had been her fault had never left her. Why had she forgotten to book in the car for a service? She shouldn't have let it break down, should have called for a cab, not Allan. The police asked her all sorts of questions even though the finding, of why the vehicle had careened down the slope, was inconclusive due to the damage caused by the fire. Was their marriage a happy one? Did she know how much life insurance Allan had and so on? Her own vehicle was impounded and inspected to see if her car had been tampered with. They had not been able to find anything that suggested it had. Her mechanic had been questioned as well as her friends and colleagues. At that point, she was beyond caring about anything else other than her son hooked up to machines in that hospital bed.

"Let me explain how our system works, then I'll take you over and explain each piece of…"

Stephani took a backward step as she lied to the woman. "I don't…I don't have the time today. Maybe later."

"You're here now. These are the forms you need to fill out."

"I need to think about it."

"Sure. Then let me show you the equipment, where the changing rooms are and where you can stow your gear. Our membership rates are very competitive."

Stephani swallowed down the sadness and grief rising in her like a volcano. Her palms were clammy with fear. "I don't want to join just yet."

The woman smiled. "Sure. No problem. Then you'll need to sign a disclaimer before I can show you the set up. It's for insurance purposes and let us get your details for our records."

A vast array of equipment arranged in groups on industrial carpeting was almost the same color as the walls, gunmetal grey, and huge plate-glass mirrors hung flush with the walls. More than ever, Stephani needed to see a familiar face.

She saw a hand wave to her from under a set of barbells. Jack Theed. Thank God he was here. He racked the equipment and eased himself out, and with a sure-footed stride, crossed the expanse of carpet towards her.

"I've got more to show you," Jenee said.

"I've just seen my friend. Can I finish the tour later?"

"Sure thing. If you change your mind, just remember, the first workout here is free. We have great membership rates. Three months-"

"Hey, Jenee, can you help me?" an overweight male asked as he struggled on a stepper.

"Just give me a holler when you're ready," the blonde said to Stephani as she went to help him.

"Hey there." Jack, in white sleeveless top and black shorts, muscles gleaming with sweat, smiled. "Glad you could make it."

Stephani shrugged. "I nearly chickened out."

Jack ran his fingers through his thick dark hair. "You've been to a health club before, right?"

She nodded.

"Did you have an accident on one of the machines?"

She shook her head.

"That look. It's so serious. Want to share?"

"It's nothing really," Stephani said.

"I'll show you where the ladies locker room is." He briefly touched her arm.

She hesitated.

"Come on. I'll stay with you when you exercise if you like."

"No need for that. Lead the way."

***

After six sets on her biceps and triceps, then leg extensions and leg curls, abs, and lower back, her muscles ached and her skin was slippery with sweat. Stephani headed for the locker room. She showered, slipped on her jeans, and shrugged on a button-up white blouse. As she brushed her hair, she began to tremble. Scared that something terrible would happen when she left, Stephani sank onto a bench seat and told herself to breathe. The ghosts of the past still haunted her.

"You okay?" a woman asked as she passed her on the way to the showers.

"I'm…just fine."

Jack, his hip against the reception counter, was talking to Jenee as Stephani approached.

The trainer laughed. "Oh, Jack. You know I'm a single gal again."

"So, how do you feel?" Jack asked Stephani as he turned to her.

"Tired and out of shape. I'm probably going to be sore tomorrow."

"Jenee, can you show me how to adjust the seat?" a client said from the leg curl equipment.

"See you next time, Jack." She pushed a slip of paper into his hand as she said, "My number if you want a little company."

He let out a sort of embarrassed laugh. "Thanks."

Then, without a word to Stephani, Jenee marched off.

"Sorry. She's never been like that before. I don't know what's gotten into her."

"Forget it." That was minor compared to the demons in her head.

"So, did you enjoy that?" Jack asked.

"Got the blood pumping again. I needed that."

He glanced at her. "How about we go for coffee? I know a great little place just half a block away."

"Thanks for talking me into this."

He raised his eyebrows in query. "I hardly twisted your arm. So, about the coffee..."

"Sorry, but I've had a busy day and the workout has plum tuckered me out."

"Maybe, another time." He looked crestfallen.

"Look, okay. Let's make it a quick one," she said.

"Just forget it. You feel sorry that you let me down and I don't need that. I've got plenty of women to go out with."

"I'm sure you have." She nearly said, 'you're a nice-looking guy' but thought better of it because he might get the wrong idea. "Sorry, but I am tired. I plan to hit the sofa when I get home."

CHAPTER 8

He unwound the length of cord from the neck of the young female just into her teens. Her wide-open sightless eyes stared up at him.

Their stark message...You... taker of lives...taker of selfish pleasure that was not freely given.

His stomach contracted and he felt he might throw up. This would pass, he knew from previous occasions.

Her blue skirt was torn and twisted up around her waist. Her once smooth firm flesh bruised and bloody from the rocky ground.

He leaned against the Joshua tree to gather his thoughts and to decide how he would cover his tracks. The hot dry scent of the desert flora at Salt River crowded him, sucked the breath from his lungs.

He rubbed his palms on the sides of his navy chinos, trying to wipe away her indelible imprint on him. He'd been doing it for so many years that he couldn't remember when the habit had started.

She was dead. He knew she must die from the moment he bundled her into his van. She had stared at his face, stared into his eyes, had seen his innermost thoughts.

No, she would not tell anyone what he had done. He brushed off stray twigs from his sports shirt and chinos, and buckled up his leather belt.

He promised himself that in future he would only drug them. He'd not meant to take her. If only she had not been walking alone in the parking lot at the local mall in Mesa, and had not struggled so much. Why did she tempt him with her Stephani-like face, and her smile? Yes, the black-haired female had practically asked for it. How could his lustful body resist? After all, he was only flesh and blood.

Deep breaths to quiet his agitated state did little to help. He closed his eyes and bent his head to stop the build-up of intensity inside him. It seemed to rise and rise in him like a tide.

"It's too dangerous. It's madness. Stop doing this. Stop it. Stop it. Stop it now. Do you hear?" His scream broke the silence, zigzagged off prickly tall cacti, and died.

In California, the police had visited his mother's home a few times. Each time they were more and more suspicious. They had forced him to move. His mother had not wanted him to go. The whore of a mother had no idea why he had to leave or why it had to be so far away. When a developer had offered his mother twice the amount the old dump was worth, she had finally relented and moved as well.

Enough of that stupid reminiscing, he told himself. Think. Had anyone seen him grab that girl in the almost empty parking lot? Perhaps that fat cow busily packing her groceries into her trunk had seen something. The fat cow might have heard the single cry the female emitted before he bundled her into the back of the van, and taped her mouth, taped her hands and legs to stop her struggling. He always worked quickly. There was never much time.

He would sell the van after he changed the color, and get something else. You could never be too careful.

The flies buzzed around the female. He looked for anything that he might have dropped, anything that might blueprint him.

What he noticed was a memento.

A hair clip. He reached down and pocketed it, then went back to the van and pulled out some old sacking from the back, and then looked around for some twigs and branches. After he gathered an armful, he threw the sacking over the girl. It partly covered her. He followed with the twigs and branches. However, her head remained exposed. He turned from her and broke more branches from a nearby creosote bush scratching his hands on its thorns in the process. As he bent to cover her face, again her sightless accusing eyes caught his gaze.

Finally, he broke free of her gaze, and threw the bundle of branches over her face. He turned away…his body shining with nervous sweat.

His mother's scratchy voice started up. That whore's voice was in his head.

He screamed into the hot dry air. "Shut up, shut up. Shut up, biiitch!"

The stillness enveloped him again.

He took a last glance at the untidy mound of twigs and branches that covered the body. It should do if anyone wandered past and didn't look too closely.

He started down the track and walked for a while until it petered out, stopped and retraced his steps a few times until he finally located another that led back to his van.

The intense blue sky seared his eyes. He felt his pockets for his sunglasses and found them missing. Frantic that he'd left a clue behind, he hurried back. He scanned the area where the temptress had writhed and cried out.

Nothing.

He couldn't bring himself to go near the body. Now that it was over, he wanted to be gone from here. A long breath escaped his lips.

Where were they?

Relief flooded him when he saw them lying upside down on a rock where he had broken off a few branches earlier.

He picked them up and hesitated. The inner voices started again. Taunted him, told him how useless and stupid he was.

He pulled out a thick-knotted rope from his back pocket, kneeled and removed his shirt. He leaned over, began to flagellate his back, and uttered the incantation that had been drummed into him.

"You stupid,"…whack…

"Stupid,"…whack…

"Stupid,"…whack…"stupid."…whack.

"Stupid, stupid"…whack…"stupid…bed wetter,"…whack.

The rope was slick with sweat and blood.

"Noooo," he screamed. "No more, mother. You made me like this. It's your fault. All your fault." He closed his eyes and waited for his breathing to return to normal.

The first time he had taken a life many years ago, he recalled cutting himself too but it hadn't been enough to ease the logjam of pain. He knew he needed something better and this agony was infinitely more satisfying.

Slowly, he rose as the voices subsided and the silence enveloped him again.

As he began to walk, he whispered over and over to himself. "I'm better than you, you stinking fucking whore. Better, you hear!"

He retreated along the winding rock strewn track. A cholla cactus attached itself to the side of his boot. He tried to kick it away but its thick cover of creamy hook spines held fast. He tried again and again.

"It's your fault, mother. You made me this way." He glanced up sensing her watching him. He stared hard at the mesquite bush expecting her to appear from behind it.

Finally, he continued along the dusty red earth. When he reached his van, he brushed the cactus off on the tire and it attached itself there. He guessed it would fall off by the time he reached the city limits.

Some of the spines had worked their way through the leather and were starting to prick his skin. It was enough that his back was aflame and at first, he ignored the needle-like pain, but it got worse. He bent down to rub the spot, and a hook spine still attached to the leather pierced his finger. "Son-of-a-bitch." He screamed shaking his hand.

He spun around when the whit-whit call of a thrasher nesting in the cholla branches startled him. He held his breath as his gaze darted across the flat cactus-ridden plains.

Nothing.

Why had he let that stupid bird spook him? He opened the van and reached for the bag of salt. When he dusted his back with it, he screamed in pain. The pain was good. It sharpened his mind. It cleansed his soul and healed.

He gingerly toweled his bloody back, and after the bleeding had stopped, slipped his shirt on and climbed in, carefully pulled his boots off, and put them in a plastic bag together with the towel and the knotted rope on the passenger side. His hands were bleeding where the thorns had torn through his disposable gloves. From the glove box, he pulled out a container of moist baby wipes, and cleaned the scratches as best he could. It would have to do until he could have a hot shower to erase the imprint of this deed from his flesh. He started the vehicle, and then drove along the rocky track past catclaw, and yucca until he reached the macadam shimmering like endless flat-black licorice in the sun, and then followed the road until it reached the highway.

He turned for home. His mother would be waiting for the groceries and angry that he was so late. He'd spin her some story. He glanced at the two shopping bags. One was soaked at the bottom with the frozen pizzas he'd bought for their dinner. In this heat, they would have thawed ages ago. It didn't matter. He'd dispose of them and buy some more. His job paid well enough for him not to worry about that sort of thing.

CHAPTER 9

Stephani held Henry's hand and spoke about the times they used to play hide and seek and other games. All the while she watched to see if there was any sign that he was listening. He didn't stir. The only sounds were the constant beeping of monitors and the machine helping him breathe. She opened a book, yellowed and stained from constant use, and read it aloud. It had been his favorite.

"Goodbye, my baby. See you tomorrow." She leaned over and kissed his cheek.

He looked to be sleeping. However, she knew better. "I'm going to the movies to see Jackie Chan. Daddy loved his moves. When you grow up, you'll probably like them, too." She stared at his pale face and long lashes and pushed his wavy hair from his forehead. Just wake up, she whispered, turned and left.

***

Stephani got in line outside the movie theatre to buy tickets to see a rerun of a Jackie Chan movie. It appeared half the male population of Scottsdale thought this was the best thing to do on a hot Saturday afternoon.

Martial arts movies were not the sort of thing she usually watched, but Allan had loved them. Now, every time one of these sorts of movies was released or they had a festival of them, like today, she couldn't help herself. In some small way, it made her feel close to him. She knew she shouldn't put herself through that pain over and over, but she couldn't help it. After she bought her ticket, she waited at the counter for a drink.

"What'll it be?" the shop assistant asked in between chewing gum.

"A small soda and popcorn, please."

"Stephani?" a deep voice called.

She swung round and saw Richard, in casual jeans and sports shirt, pushing through the crowd towards her. "Hey, Richard."

"Hey to you, too," he said.

"What are you doing here? I didn't think you'd be into martial arts movies," she said.

"As a matter of fact, I reached the Judo Association junior brown belt stage. I started my black belt but didn't complete it. A Raspberry crush please and popcorn," Richard said as the girl placed Stephani's purchases on the counter.

"Why didn't you keep going?" she said.

"My studies got in the way and I thought I'd pick it up later but never did. I think I should be more surprised that you're here."

She smiled. "I could be a black belt, you know."

"I just can't see you being the type, but you can never tell these days."

"Mom thought sports were a waste of time when we could have been studying." They often went without breakfast, because her mom had to pay the rent, so there wasn't money for any extras.

"You're kidding me." He pulled out his wallet. "Let me get this."

"No, you don't." Since her first job where she'd worked in the local mall while in college in L.A., she'd paid her way. "Bread and water for me next week."

Richard laughed. "I'll bet." He picked up their drinks and Stephani took the popcorn.

They settled down and ate popcorn while they watched Twin Dragons and Rush Hour 3.

***

The first time he'd entered his Princess's apartment was two months ago, right after she'd moved in. He'd waited until someone punched in the code to get inside. Earlier, he'd positioned a pin camera on the wall adjacent to stream on movement to his cell.

After the resident entered, he'd limped over and entered the code. Once inside, he'd crossed to the elevator, punched in the security code again, and pressed the button for the second floor. He'd noted the security cameras positioned in strategic spots in the common areas, but his disguise of a mustache, glasses, grey wig and false limp would have made it hard for anyone to recognize him.

This time, he put in the code and let himself in. He knew she wasn't home as he'd seen her drive away. He had the elevator to himself. With a set of bump keys at the ready, he was about to try the lock when he tried the handle and found that the door opened. His princess was careless, however it was to his advantage.

Now this would make it the second time that he walked right in. His princess still didn't lock her door.

Nice décor, he thought as he strode through the living room and down the hallway to the bedroom.

After he had gone through her closet and taken what he wanted, he pulled out the present that had taken the two months since he'd visited last time, to find.

He pulled out a pin camera, positioned it in between two petals of some decorative metal wall art in her bedroom and checked that the camera was working via the stream on his cell.

A little while later, he exited the apartment block.

***

It must have been because Richard was there beside her in the theatre that she didn't feel lonely; she didn't feel that ache inside and that longing for Allan's touch.

When the credits rolled and she had not shed any tears of loss for her husband, she knew that she was finally accepting what had to be. And it scared her. Stephani wanted to remember every line, every freckle on his face, and she couldn't.

As they walked out with the crowd into the foyer, Richard asked, "Do you have any plans for tonight?"

"No."

"How about going someplace around here?"

"There's a place round the corner that I've been to a few times with Iantha and her family."

A guy pushed past, and she was flung against Richard.

It felt good to be close to him. "Sorry."

"I'm not." He stared into her eyes and smiled. "Did you see that studded leather collar he's wearing around his neck?"

"Think he's a biker?" She saw his back as he disappeared in the crowd. "Or maybe just weird."

"Don't know and don't want to know."

They went outside into the hot night air. Street lamps threw pools of light into the darkness.

A hooker on the street corner in tight-fitting skimpy dress and killer heels smiled at him.

"Get off the streets and find a decent job," he said.

"Maybe they can't," she said.

"They're in it to get money for drugs."

"Maybe not. Maybe, they're in dire circumstances." What would he think of her if he knew what she'd been doing to fund her last year of college?

"Stop feeling sorry for them."

"Don't tell me how I should feel. Maybe, I should go home."

"Please don't. I didn't mean to upset you," he said.

He just didn't understand. Stephani stepped over a crack in the sidewalk, a childhood superstition via her best girlfriend that it was unlucky to step on a crack. Her mother noticed and made her promise to stop. Since then she'd forgotten about it until Allan's death resurrected this and more.

She shrugged out of her jacket. It was hot out and she didn't need it. "Here's a bit of trivia for you that I read somewhere. Jackie Chan's broken a bone in every movie he's been in."

"I didn't know that. So, how are you settling in?"

"Still getting used to the heat. Otherwise, great. And the people are much friendlier than in L.A."

"'Course we are. Well, after nearly five years here, I consider myself one of them now."

"What's this…of course we are? And you're so unassuming, humble and what's the other word?"

"Conceited?" he grinned. "A little facetious, aren't you?"

"All in fun," she laughed. "Where are you originally from?"

"From the West Coast, too. I promised my high school sweetheart we'd get married when I finished Harvard. She waited for me. It was a huge mistake for both of us. We'd grown in different directions. The only good thing that came from our marriage was our daughter, Belinda."

"Do you see her often?"

"Once we broke up, she went back to California and took Belinda. My baby stays with me during the school holidays, twice a year. It's not much, but I take what I can get. I'd see her more if she didn't live so far away. I miss her."

"So you're on your own?"

"My mom lives with me. After Dad died, she came for a holiday. My ex had been gone for a while by then. Mom's still here. Not that I mind. She ought to find a place of her own, but I haven't the heart to tell her. At least I get a break every summer when she goes to Orlando and holidays with Brad, my little brother."

"You've never mentioned a brother before. Here it is." She opened the entrance door to The Ranger's Cabin. Waiters were carrying trays of meals to tables, and the inviting smells of roast garlic, fries and spices teased her senses.

"He's a high flying corporate lawyer. We're not that close, but usually manage to get together at Christmas."

Walls lined with split logs; sawn pine tables and varnished wooden floors completed the décor.

"We'll be lucky if we get a table," Richard said.

The maître d' approached them. "Nice to see you again, Ms. Robbins. I haven't seen you here before, sir."

"Richard Dixon," he said.

"You're lucky you came in now as we have only one table left."

"I see more folks have gotten to know about this place," Stephani said.

"Can't complain. We're busy most of the time now."

He led them past a well-stocked bar with patrons drinking and talking, to a table at the far end of the room and pulled out their chairs. "Our specials tonight are...tender filet mignon with shrimp served with béarnaise sauce, scalloped potato and asparagus, or there's the honey-butter glazed pork spare ribs, served with hand cut fries and salad or maybe the buffalo might be more to your taste and...Here. Allow me." He picked up the napkins and placed one on Stephani's lap, then on Richard's, who was sitting opposite.

"Same as last time for me," she said.

"Certainly, Ms. Robbins. Mr. Dixon, would you like more time?"

"I'll have filet mignon." Richard studied the wine menu and selected a red wine.

"I'm impressed," Richard said to Stephani when the maître d' left.

"He remembers everyone and what they ate last time they were here. It must be a great sales point," she said.

After their glasses were filled, Richard said, "Let's toast."

She didn't voice what she'd rather toast to…that for the first time since Allan had died, she had not cried at a martial arts movie.

"I've just thought of one." Richard held her gaze for long moments.

Her stomach tightened. She hurried to fill the silence between them with a jovial brightness that she didn't feel, "To seeing more martial arts movies."

He raised his glass and tapped it against hers. "To enjoying life and many more dinners together."

"Enjoying life again." The words seemed hollow.

"You haven't been, I know, with your son in critical care."

She shrugged. "How can I?"

He looked into her eyes until she turned away. She didn't want sympathy, it would break down her defenses and she wasn't ready for that.

"Ask and you shall be served. Here's the waiter with our meals now."

"I thought that when I grew up, I'd be a fireman." Richard said. "Our cat was stuck in a tree and my mom got the firefighters to come and get Mopsie down. That was until I went to middle school and found out how much I loved science." He cut up his meat.

"Yum, I love fries though I know they're bad for you." She

forked one and ate it. "I had dreams of working in the local ice cream shop when I left school so I could eat all the ices I wanted. In the last years of grade school, I worked there, but you know what, you quickly get sick of eating all that stuff."

"You're kidding me, right?" Richard said.

She shook her head. "I'm into natural foods, except for the fries."

"So what made you want to become a tissue engineer?" he asked.

"I could see that there was no future in working in a shop, and my mom would've been upset if I didn't go to college. She said that she had not sacrificed herself for my sister and me not to study hard and make the most of ourselves. I did science, and I decided to major in molecular biology and sort of fell into this."

After they had eaten and finished off the wine, Richard said. "Where to now, pretty lady?"

"It's home for me."

"But the night's still young. What about some boot scootin' line dancing? It's great fun," he said as they went outside into the breezy night air.

"You, dancing? Well, I've been surprised twice in the same day." The breeze tugged at the jacket she had slung over her arm.

"I like to keep everyone guessing," he said.

Richard's long strides had her hurrying to keep up, but when he noticed, he slowed his pace. "Sorry. I tend to forget that some people have shorter legs than me."

"What's wrong with my height? Well, I'm here to tell you that I'm not that short."

"Hey. Some of the best things come in medium packages."

She didn't know how to take that. "You're really into line dancing? From the way you are at work, I expected you'd be studying the latest textbook. I can't figure you out."

He looked at her quizzically. "No one's ever said that about me before. But I've got a confession to make. I can't line dance. I've never been. But I'm up for it."

She paused in her stride. "Thanks for the offer, but I'm a little tired, busy week and all…I'd just rather go home. Can I have a rain check?"

"Hey. There's a karaoke bar across the road."

"What? No," she said.

"Hey, come on." He took her hand.

As she started down the stairs to the bar, she heard some guy singing "Moon River" out of tune.

"Drink?" Richard asked.

"Wine, please."

Stephani edged through the crowd and found them an empty table while Richard went over to the bar.

"God, isn't he awful?" she said when he returned with their drinks.

Richard laughed. "But he's enjoying himself."

A few people had joined in. "They probably feel sorry for him," she said.

When the bald guy finished, Richard got up.

"Sit down. Please, don't do this, Richard. Jesus, what's got into you?"

He grinned and kept walking. "Have you got...'Getting To Know You,' by Oscar Hammerstein please? I know it's corny, but my dad used to sing it to my mom."

"That's an oldie. Just give me a minute," the DJ said.

She should have stopped him. The song started playing and Richard joined in.

A fish in a goldfish bowl was how she felt, with people looking at her, and Richard singing to her. He was sweet, and most of the time he was in tune.

Then he climbed down from the stage and walked over.

"Come and help me," he said.

She shook her head and sipped her drink until he took her hand. "No," she whispered, though he'd put the microphone towards her, and the crowded room heard this too. They urged her to join him.

Reluctantly, she rose. At least no one would remember her.

"She's great. What do you think, folks?"

The crowd cheered and clapped.

He looked into her eyes as he sang the last stanza.

By the end of the song, they were both laughing, and Richard had his arms around her waist.

"I haven't had so much fun in I don't know when," she said as they sat down. "I can tell you, that this is so unlike me. I've never sung in public."

"Good thing we came in then. It's time you loosened up and had some fun." Richard finished his glass of wine. "Do you want another?"

"Sorry, but I am tired."

"Home then. Now where did you park your car?"

"First level, parking lot."

"I'll walk you there." He took her hand in his large one.

It felt nice, and he had done what no one had done since…since…. A weight had lifted from her chest and she could breathe easily again. "Sure."

Leaves and dust sailed through the air. They walked past a shopping mall, closed for the night, its neon signs lighting up the lonely sidewalk. For the first time in five months, she wasn't alone and feeling lost.

"What are you doing this weekend?" he asked.

"I was supposed to be going on another picnic with Iantha and her family, but after what happened the last time we decided to cancel it."

"Did the police get any prints from those photos?"

She shook her head.

They rounded the corner where the steps led to the parking lot.

He shook his head. "What about on the cellophane from the rose you found in your car?"

"It's a 'no' on that one too."

"This is adding up and I don't like it one bit. Maybe, we should get a private investigator on the case."

A scraping sound came from somewhere behind them.

Unnerved, Stephani let go of his hand and swung around. A short distance away, a couple crossed the road, but otherwise nothing moved. "Did you hear that?"

"Maybe, it's some trash being blown about by the wind," Richard said.

They continued walking.

The noise sounded again, and she swung around again to see a figure about one hundred yards back on the opposite side of the road. The person darted into the shadows.

"I'm sure someone's there," she whispered.

"I can't see anyone."

"There was a guy back there. I'm sure of it. Now I know how Dionne felt at the picnic," she said. "I'm sure it was a man, I could just make him out in the dark."

"Could be some drunk? All the same, we shouldn't take any chances. Let's go." Richard clasped her hand, and hurried her up the parking lot steps to the first level.

When they heard a noise that sounded like footsteps, Richard released her hand and turned. "Who's there? I know someone's there!" His voice echoed as it bounced off the concrete floors and ceilings.

The parking lot was quiet, suddenly threatening, shadows...everywhere.

"I don't like this one bit. Get your keys out now so we're not standing around near your car. I'll hitch a ride with you to my car." He clasped her hand again. "Come on."

"This is making me nervous." She was sure Richard would try to protect her if necessary. However, she'd rather it didn't come to that. The back of her neck prickled with dread.

They hurried by several vehicles, and stopped by her silver Honda. She unlocked the door and had the car started by the time Richard had gone around to the passenger side and opened the door.

"I hope this isn't the guy who left the photos in the picnic basket and left the rose in my car." She accelerated down the ramp, and through the ground level towards the exit. "If it's the same guy on each occasion, then I have a stalker and it's freaking horrible."

"This is serious. Here's my car."

"Sorry." She jammed on the brake.

"I'll follow you home. Just to be sure you're safe."

"Thanks." She glanced in the rear-view mirror, glad that she didn't see anyone.

"When we reach your apartment, give me a call when you're inside. That way I'll know you're okay."

"How about coming up for a coffee?" She didn't want to be alone right now.

"Then I can make sure you're safe." He closed the door and climbed into his Lexus.

All the way home, she kept checking her rear-view mirror to make sure no one was tailing her, besides Richard.

She drove into the security parking lot, which was full of owners' cars while Richard parked outside. She rode the elevator to the first floor, and let herself in. By the time she had turned on the lights, he was buzzing on the intercom.

"It's Richard."

"Come on up." Stephani pressed the button to the street-level entrance door.

A few moments later, he let himself in.

"I don't think we can call the police over that guy you saw because nothing happened. Anyone can walk the streets at night," Richard said.

"I know. But these incidents are adding up."

"I'd feel better if we hired a private investigator," he said.

"That's a great idea. Let's talk about that on Monday. Make yourself comfortable while I change my shoes." She stepped out of her kitten heels one at a time, picking each one up as she went across the beige tiled living room and into her bedroom.

She smiled when she caught sight of her old jointed teddy, Mr. Ted, sitting in the middle of her bed on the white, black and purple hand-woven cover. She picked up Mr. Ted and kissed him on the nose. Mr. Ted smelled a bit musty, but who wouldn't? He'd been with her since she was two or three. His eye hung out a little. One day she'd fix it, but then maybe she wouldn't. The five of them had moved a lot. Usually when her step dad lost his job again and occasionally because he'd had an argument with the boss. Other times she would come home from school with her sister to find her mother packing because the rent was months behind and they had to move. The first thing she'd pack was Mr. Ted. They'd been together through so many changes, so much sadness...She put him back and slipped on her flip-flops and hurried along the tiled hallway to the living room.

He stood by the cream leather sofa. "You've done a great job decorating this place."

"Thanks. I didn't bring much with me from L.A…just clothes, a few bits of crockery and mementos. The big stuff, I sold. So this is pretty much all new."

"Are you…maybe I shouldn't ask?" He stared through the window at the streetlights. His tone suggested that his usual confidence was temporarily absent.

"What's wrong?" Stephani asked.

He swung around, hands in his jeans pockets. "I want to ask you something. Are you seeing anyone?"

The shrink back in L.A. had said talking about it would help. So when was she going to do that? Before she could think any more about it, she said, "I'm still getting over losing Allan."

"It must've been hard for you. I can't imagine what it would be like."

"Every time I try to move on…I just can't seem to…" She turned from him, took a deep breath and closed her eyes for a moment. All tense and knotted up inside now, she went past the dining table and into the kitchen. She picked up the water-well that fitted into the espresso machine. "I'll get the coffee going. On the other hand, would you prefer something stronger? I've got whisky, rum, wine or Ouzo."

"A closet drinker, eh? Just coffee for me."

She sensed he was trying to lighten the atmosphere, and she appreciated it. "Ouzo. It's for special occasions or for when I want to relax after work. I couldn't imagine not having some in the house. It's a Greek tradition."

"I've never tasted the stuff."

"Take a seat and I'll pour you some. And I might have one

myself." Or two, she added to herself.

Richard took a few steps towards the kitchen. "Need help with anything?"

"I think I can manage. Sugar, milk?"

"One and yes." He watched her move about in the kitchen. He appeared to be deep in thought.

She got out the mugs, sugar and spoons, and the Ouzo.

"You're not seeing anyone then?"

Why did he have to know? Her bed was lonely but she had not looked at another man in that way since she'd married Allan. He'd been all she wanted. She missed rolling over in the morning and having him beside her. Just lately, she missed the lovemaking. "You mean boyfriend?"

"Forget it. That was out of order, and I wasn't meaning to pry." Richard sort of laughed and ran his middle finger along one eyebrow, as if he wanted to say more.

He wanted to know—it was something to do with the way he touched his eyebrow—and now she wanted to keep him guessing for a bit. She had not dated since she'd started dating Allan. He'd bought flowers for her every week until she said she'd go with him. Even after they were married, he often came home with a bunch of roses. They were her favorites.

"Have I mentioned my mom's in a nursing home now. It broke our hearts to put her there, but she's got Alzheimer's." No matter how tough her mom had been, she still loved her.

"That's sad."

She poured the coffees. "She was living with Iantha, and one day she started a fire on the stove because she totally forgot about something she was frying for lunch. The house was full of smoke, the fry pan had almost melted, and the flames were leaping up the kitchen cupboards. She was outside staring at the sky. That's when we realized that there was something more seriously wrong with her than her just being forgetful all the time. We had her assessed and put into care."

She poured the Ouzo and downed a shot while he wasn't looking. That felt good.

"My mom, tries to boss me around at times, but I'm grateful that she's in reasonable health. I wish she'd find a place of her own." Richard said.

She carried in the hot beverages: two shot glasses and the Ouzo on a tray, and put them on the coffee table. She poured out a measure of Ouzo for both of them. Its strong scent was warm and inviting.

He reached for the liquor.

"Throw it down your throat," she said.

"You're joking?"

Allan had said something similar the first time, too. However, she didn't drink much then. "Do it. It's the only way. Like this." She gulped the fiery liquid, her second tonight. It was like lava slipping down her throat.

"Here goes." After a moment he said, "Wow. It warms you up all the way down." His cheeks reddened.

He reminded her of the time she had been caught out by her mom when she came home from the end of term party. No matter how hard she tried, she had not been able to stop laughing until she had collapsed into a heap on the floor. She smiled at the thought.

"Another?" She started to refill her glass.

"One's enough for me." He sipped his coffee.

She sat at the other end of the sofa, took off her flip-flops, and tucked her feet under the cushion. Another childhood habit that she couldn't seem to break. Nevertheless, it was also one that she didn't do unless she felt comfortable with whomever she was with. "I don't know how she'll be when I visit. Sometimes she's okay, but there are times when she doesn't recognize me, and I have to tell her who I am."

"That's hard to take."

Not as hard as knowing her son may never wake up. Stephani downed her shot glass, then went to reach for the bottle and stopped short. The urge to pour another shot was there, but with Richard sitting beside her, it was much easier to resist. Her phone rang and she got up to answer it.

There was no sound on the line. "Hi. Is anyone there?"

"Who's that?" Richard asked.

"Who are you?" Stephani asked too late as the caller had hung up.

"What did he want?"

"I don't know."

"Do you think it was a wrong number?"

"Not sure. Maybe it was random. I hope it's not one of those guys who...you know....gets their kicks out of this." She sat on the sofa.

"If it happens again, call the telephone company."

"I think I'll let the calls go to voice-mail and I'll pick up if I recognize the voice." She reached for the bottle.

"Good idea. Before we were interrupted you were going to refill my glass and try to get me intoxicated and have your way with me, weren't you? But your conscience stopped you?" He smiled.

"What? No, I wasn't." She flushed. He wanted to bed her and she wasn't at all sure what she wanted.

"I was going to put it away." Who was she kidding; she needed more.

"Now I'm a little disappointed. I wouldn't have been able to drive if I'd had another drink."

"How about another coffee?"

"Too much of that stuff keeps me awake half the night. Glad you joined us here. Collaborating face to face is far better than us talking via the net."

"I didn't know what I was going to do when our branch in L.A. burned down."

"Any other family?"

She tried to ignore the tenseness enveloping her at the mention of family: her husband gone, son gone, and her mother in a nursing home. "Henry, my sister and my mom, but you know that. There's my stepfather," she said. "He's overseas somewhere."

"You keep in touch?"

"I probably hear from him once or twice a year. He sent a sympathy card when I lost Allan…from Paris." He'd not made contact with her before that for over a year and a half. How he'd managed to find out what had happened was a total mystery to her. "What are your plans for the rest of the weekend?"

"I'm going in to the lab tomorrow. Did you have something in mind?"

"But it's Sunday?"

"I've got some reports to complete. Shouldn't take too long." He got up. "Can I help clear these things away?"

"They'll go in the dishwasher. Thanks for seeing me home."

"That was the least I could do. Thanks for the coffee, and Ouzo. I'm glad we ran into each other at the movies."

"Me too." She was talking like a schoolgirl.

He looked into her eyes, and her breath caught in her throat. Why did her heartbeat quicken when he looked at her like that?

"Are you in a relationship with someone else?"

"Goodnight, Richard," she said as she walked him to the door. "And, it's no."

"If you have any more stalkers or photographs turning up, call me," he said.

CHAPTER 10

After Richard left, Stephani went into the bedroom, picked up Mr. Ted and put him on her dresser. She pulled down the bedcover, folded it, and left it at the foot of the bed. She kicked off her flip-flops and yawned. Then she padded to the bathroom.

She turned on the water and stripped while she waited for the water to warm up. Richard had not kissed her good night. She suspected he had wanted to.

He deserved someone ready for a relationship. She wasn't.

Would she ever be? The memory of that funeral still haunted her. Her mom and Iantha had been busily making sandwiches for each wake while she went through the motions of getting ready. It was as if it was happening to someone else.

It wasn't until she saw the coffin near the altar that she'd felt the finality of his death in the form of a crushing black sorrow that rose and rose inside her. She'd wanted to hug him one last time. She'd worried that he would be cold and so alone.

It felt like someone had wrenched her heart from her breast.

That grief companioned her now. However, it wasn't as raw and she was able to manage it better, if nothing else.

When she'd heard heart-wrenching sobs echo through the church, she'd looked up to see who had been making that noise and had realized she had.

Was she entitled to enjoy life after what she'd done to her family? Eyes shut, she slumped against the bathroom wall, tears building, unreleased.

Finally, she slid open the glass door and stepped into the shower. The stinging hot water cascaded onto her skin, temporally washing away those ghosts of guilt.

Without meaning to, she began to think about Richard again as she soaped her arms and shoulders. He wasn't good-looking in the conventional way. Although, she liked the thing he did with his eyebrow when he, in a roundabout way, asked whether she'd had any boyfriends. Heck, he couldn't even cover up a white lie. She wasn't good at that either.

The first lie, at least it was the one she remembered best, was when she told her mom that she lost her field trip money. All of eight years old she had been, and the money spent at the local drugstore on two little dolls, one for herself and one for her best friend. Her mom had guessed right away that the story she'd told about it falling into a drain was just that. Then her mom explained to her how little money they had. At that moment she understood people bought new clothes and furniture, not just made do with hand-me-downs from used-goods stores.

Skin waterlogged and hair dripping, she stepped from the shower and toweled herself. She slipped on her mauve top with spaghetti straps and matching bed-shorts, brushed her teeth and applied moisturizer to her face.

The phone rang. Was that Richard? She hurried to answer the call.

"Someone is watching you," a male said.

She slammed the phone down. She would have to be more careful and let the answering machine screen her callers.

She took two steps inside the bedroom before she noticed the bedside lamp was on and she couldn't remember leaving it on. She folded back the bedcover and opened the closet door. As she dropped it inside, something caught her eye.

She picked up the cover to get a better look.

Mr. Ted.

She spun around. The other bear was still on the dresser where she'd left it.

"Holy shit!" It was as if the floor was moving beneath her feet. The cover fell from her grasp.

Hands shaking, she picked up the soft toy and stared at it, turned it over. "Holy shit," she said again, feeling as if she was going mad.

The left eye was hanging out of the teddy. "Okay, okay. Just pull yourself together and work this out," she said aloud.

She smelled it. Dusty, mixed with the scent of Chanel No 5, her favorite perfume.

Then she took it over to the other bear on the dresser, the one she'd thought was hers. He was still sitting exactly in the middle, just where she left him before she showered. This one had a musty stale odor and no hint of scent.

One bear had its right eye hanging out and the other had its left eye hanging out.

She stared at the two bears and knew the one she'd found in the bottom of her closet was hers. Her hand shook. God, the one on the dresser was almost identical.

"Jesus, this is blowing me away."

Someone had been in her room while she was in the shower.

CHAPTER 11

Stifling a scream, Stephani dropped the soft toy and backed away.

Suddenly aware that an intruder might have disturbed something, she scanned the room, taking in the armchair in the corner, the painting of a desert rose done by her sister a few years ago and her mom's dressmaker's dummy dressed with a shawl, hat and beads. She listened for any sound that would betray an intruder. The silence held no comfort for her.

Had the person been waiting for an opportunity to attack her? Had the intruder been watching her while she undressed?

How did this intruder know what Mr. Ted looked like? When had they been in her room previously?

Each thought heightened her alarm.

Stephani ran to the front door, hesitated for a moment and opened it. No one lurked in the hallway. There were only two apartments on this floor, and the sounds of a TV playing were from the neighboring apartment. She went inside and got the key. She had to lock the door and got as far as putting the key in the lock, then with a shaking hand, withdrew it. "Oh hell."

She had not been able to lock her home back in Santa Barbara either and Allan had installed an alarm so she could set it to perimeter so that he wouldn't have to worry when she was home alone with the front door unlocked. She slammed the door and ran into each room, checking that each window was locked even though she was on the top floor of a two-story apartment block. Nothing appeared amiss.

After another sweep of the second bedroom she realized that an intruder could have been lurking the behind any door waiting to attack her.

Her mouth dry, she hurried to the phone. About to call 911, she stopped when she noticed the voice-mail machine blinking red. She played it.

"Some bad dude broke into your apartment."

She gasped and went to play it again, but touched the delete button. "Damn."

She picked up the phone again to call 911. What was she going to say? That someone had put an extra teddy in her apartment and someone had left a warning message that she'd deleted?

She found herself calling Richard instead.

"Did you call the police?" he asked, after she told him in a tumble of words what was wrong.

"I started to, but then didn't. I can't prove that someone left that message now after I deleted it. Wait...I'm not thinking straight. The letter, photos and that rose...they would, at the very least, have to take the two bears seriously. I'll call them now."

"Be careful, please. Are you sure the intruder is gone?"

"I did check the apartment."

"Stay put. I'll be right over," he said before he hung up.

Her next call was to the local police.

"You're talking about teddy bears, not grizzly bears, are you?" the police officer said.

"Yes! A teddy bear just like the one I already own."

"Ma'am, are you sure?"

"Someone's broken into my apartment, and what's more, I think it was while I was in the shower. And someone left a warning about the break-in on my voice-mail machine."

The cop sighed. "Do you suspect someone's there now?"

"I've checked every room."

"All the same, I suggest you go to a neighbor's home where you'll be safe. Just leave a cell number where we can contact you. We'll send out a patrol car as soon as we can."

"Hell. I haven't looked outside. It's dark...Just a second." Stephani dashed to the balcony. The street below was bathed in moonlight. "It's deserted out there. I don't know my neighbors. I've only been here a short while. I've asked a friend to come and stay with me."

"We'll get a patrol car over as soon as we can," the officer said again.

She hung up, pushed a chair against the front door and went back to the window. The street still looked empty. At eleven, most people were in bed.

Maybe Iantha...only she knew about the teddy. No, her sister would never do this, would never try to surprise her like this? She'd call her anyway.

"Iantha," a sleepy voice said. "Do you know what time it is?"

"There's another bear."

"Stephani?" Iantha's tone was more alert now, and incredulous. "Couldn't this wait till the morning?"

"Someone's given me another bear, not given but just...it's a bear just like mine."

"I'm happy for you. Can I go back to-?"

"You know the bear I've always had. I found him in my closet."

"Good. Now-"

"An intruder's put a bear on my dresser. I don't know when-"

"Intruder? Steph? What's going on?"

"I don't know how it got there. Did you buy one the same and want to surprise me?"

"You really think I'd do this?"

"No. Sorry. It's a stupid thing to say."

"I'm so glad you've thought this through."

"They're identical except for the wrong eye hanging out of one. Now I don't even know which one was on my bed before I went to the movies. I suspect someone was in here while I was in the shower. The whole thing's got me spooked."

"Woo now. Tell me again."

So she did.

"You think it could be connected to the photos?"

"I don't know? I've called the police and they're coming over. So is Richard."

"I should come over, too."

A bang startled Stephani, and she nearly dropped the phone as she ran to the balcony. The street below was empty except for something that looked like a cat running across the road.

"Steph. Stephani, are you there?"

"I heard something and went to have a look. It was only a cat. I'm sorry I woke you."

"Woke me? Now I'm freaking out. You sure the intruder's gone?"

"I think so. Sorry about what I said."

"Forget it. I'm getting dressed and coming over right now."

The intercom buzzed and Stephani jumped at the sudden noise. "Just a minute. Let me see who this is."

"Who's there?"

"Stephani, don't speak, don't let anyone in. It could be a trick. Wait for the police. Wait for me," Iantha said.

"It's me, Richard."

"Thank God you're here." Stephani buzzed him in and pulled the chair away from the front door.

"Don't worry about coming over, Iantha. Richard's here now. I'll call you later."

"Don't even think about what time it is. Just call. I don't think I'm going to be able to sleep much now anyway."

She hung up as Richard came in.

He put his arm around her shoulders in a protective gesture. "Are you okay?"

"Of course I am." She sounded better than she felt.

"Sure?"

She nodded. "I'm a little shaken up."

"I'm going to check the apartment for intruders."

"But I-"

"Just to be sure." He went through to the hallway, opened and closed doors while Stephani tailed him.

"All clear," he said after he checked each room. Then he came and took her into his arms. "I drove over here sick with worry. This made me realize just how much I care about you." He pushed strands of her hair from her face and kissed her.

She resisted for the briefest time and gave herself up to the sensation of his lips against hers, his body fitting against hers in a way that felt good and temporarily it held her unease at bay.

No man since Allan had shown her this tenderness, this concern for her wellbeing. "I can't do this. I haven't since Allan…"

Richard ran his hands down her arms. "I'll make us some coffee while you go rest up."

"Don't baby me. I'm not falling apart." Just because she'd sunk into a depression after the death of Allan and Henry's being in critical care didn't mean that she'd fall apart now, did it?

"Then let me help you. Come and stay with me until this is sorted out."

That was too big a step for her right now. "Let's see what the police say when they come."

He followed her into the kitchen. "You locked the door after I left, didn't you?"

She looked down at the floor. "I can't stand the thought of having to lock myself in. I just can't."

"You don't lock your apartment door?"

"The street entrance is secure. You need a security code to get in."

Richard shook his head. "You've got to lock your door, especially now. You can't be claustrophobic or you couldn't work in the lab."

She grimaced. "At work, it's different and doesn't seem to matter." It was something she couldn't explain, let alone understand.

"Do you have a phobia about that?"

She shrugged. "Just the thought of not being able to get out terrifies me. I've had some therapy, but it hasn't helped."

"Do you have a burglar alarm?"

She nodded. "Sometimes, I forget to turn it on."

"What about your neighbors? How well do you know them?"

"Hardly at all. Do you think one of them…?"

"No point in guessing. Do you have a bathrobe? It might be a good idea to put it on, or get some clothes on before the police turn up." He pushed up one of the straps of her mauve pajama top as it had slipped off her shoulder.

She suddenly felt awkward. "I'll be back in a moment."

***

It wasn't until after she'd changed into a T-shirt and shorts, shown Richard the two bears and had shared a second coffee with him that the police finally showed.

The tall one spoke first after he flipped his badge. "I'm Officer

Kennelly and this is Officer Zamoloski. Can I listen to the message?"

"Sorry. I deleted it, accidentally. I did report that when I logged the call."

Zamoloski, the taller of the two, raised an eyebrow and it seemed that he doubted she'd actually had a message.

"I see. Now, could you tell us about this intruder?" Kennelly, balding with the sort of chameleon face that an actor might have—that you didn't know exactly what he was thinking—stood before her.

She handed over the counterfeit bear. "I didn't see him. I can only tell you that he left this bear. The scary thing is that it's almost identical to the one I own. How did he know what the one I owned looked like? The one that's mine has a damaged left eye, which happened when our dog Hobo got it hold of it and I tried to pull the bear free.

Kennelly glanced at his partner.

He didn't believe her, she could tell from the look they shared.

Kennelly went over to the front door and felt the wood around the lock with his fingers. "No signs of forced entry. You're on the second floor. How do you think the intruder got in?"

"I don't lock that door. No one can get in downstairs without a security code."

Kennelly expelled a short breath. "It's easier than you think."

"I thought it was secure."

"Ma'am, nothing is secure."

"So the perp walked in." Zamoloski rolled his eyes. "Show me your bear."

His attitude was beginning to irritate her. She took the officers to the bedroom. She opened the door to the closet. "My teddy, I found in here. And the imposter was sitting on the dresser just about here." It was when she turned back to the closet that she noticed something else was missing.

"My blue suit! It's gone. It was hanging just here." She pointed out the empty space where the clothes had been pushed apart. "I know because I picked it up from the dry cleaner's yesterday."

"You'd better check everything, Steph," Richard said.

She moved aside more of her pants and dresses. "I can't tell if anything else is gone. I'll have to go through them all thoroughly."

"So the bear's okay. It's just some of your clothes are missing?" Kennelly appeared puzzled.

"Aren't you following what I'm saying? Hold on...neither of you believes me. Officer Zamoloski, the bear you're holding isn't mine. And the suit, well, I've only noticed that it's missing. Jesus." This was too much.

Officer Kennelly pulled out his notepad with a bored expression on his face. "Okay. Can you describe the suit?"

"You're not taking this seriously. Someone was in my apartment, and I'm worried they might come back."

"Sure. Now about the suit..."

"Didn't you hear?" Richard said.

"Well, yes, we'll need the details of what was stolen."

She gave him a description.

"Is there anything else?" Zamoloski asked.

What made her open her panty drawer she didn't know. She stepped back, stunned. "Huh?" Someone had separated the colors from the whites. They were still in neat piles, but separated. "He's...he's...he's been through my...my...."

"What?" Officer Kennelly said.

Distraught, she jerked open other drawers in the closet. Her bras, her socks and her camisoles: were color separated but still in neat piles. She pulled open the panty drawer again and started going through them. "What the hell? He's taken some of my underwear. The pink satin G-string and the mauve lace ones." The heat rose in her cheeks with embarrassment when she realized what she'd said. "It gives me the creeps just thinking about it."

"Something you should know. Stephani's received a letter in the mail. And two photos of her and her niece were discovered in a picnic basket after she returned from Canyon Lake with her sister last weekend. It's been reported. Oh, and she found a rose in her car. The police checked the car and couldn't find any forced signs of entry. I'm told you can buy one of those universal keys off the Internet."

"Yeah. Makes our job all the harder. Let me call the precinct," Kennelly said.

She stared at the officer while he made the call and asked about the case.

"I see," Kennelly said into his cell phone.

"Now do you believe me?"

"Calm down, ma'am."

"I am calm! Are you going to investigate this?"

"Do you have family?"

"My husband was killed in a car accident just over five months ago. What has that got to do with this?"

"Would you submit to a psychological evaluation just for the records?"

"I'm not the perpetrator but the victim."

CHAPTER 12

Princie's shoulders slumped in disappointment. Stephani had not gone for her run this morning. He'd waited and waited for over an hour at the park entrance.

Was she unwell? If she was, he wanted to go look after her the way his mother had done for him when he was little. But, when he became a pimply teenager and had gotten asthma, she'd said he was dirty, that he didn't wash enough, that's why he was always shedding flakes of skin all over the place, that he was strange; and she didn't know where he'd gotten all that from, and that she couldn't stand his wheezing. Maybe, it was that bad dude that had snuck into her apartment yesterday. After about forty minutes, he came outside carrying a bag and hurried to his vehicle.

He'd tried to warn her that she had to be more careful because some bad dude was following her. He couldn't tell the cops because they'd be asking too many questions.

Yesterday, when he saw Stephani, wearing black and purple spandex shorts and a white T-shirt, it made his mouth water. Often now, he let his imagination loose on how she'd look naked and spread eagled on his bed. After a few moments of heightened sexual excitement, he got sort of worried that he wouldn't be able to bring himself to touch her if that happened. That he would watch her reveal her inner self and he would just sit and chew his nails and have an asthma attack.

She'd run her usual route in the park, and for the first time he'd managed to keep pace behind her without someone passing him and getting between them. Her hair had been loose and her silky black bob had swayed in rhythm with each step.

Now he glanced at his watch and grimaced as he walked to her apartment block. Another ten minutes and he'd have to leave or he'd be late for work.

A blonde ran past. But, she wasn't as special as Stephani.

Diagonally across the road, the roller-door to the underground parking went up. Stephani drove out in her silver Honda. She must have been on her way to work, he guessed.

Why hadn't she gone jogging this morning? Would she go tonight? He planned to come back after his shift and see. The glimpse he caught as she left wasn't enough to satisfy him.

Princie raised and focused his binoculars at the open blinds on the first floor window: Stephani's bedroom. Not that he could see much, but the thought of spending time in her room taunted him. He longed to linger there, to touch her things, to smell her scent, to bury his face in her intimate clothes. It was driving him mad.

No, he shouldn't go there, should he?

He adjusted his black leather collar, studded with micro silver cones. It made him look macho; of that, he was sure.

The urge was stronger now…but he fought it. He knew from past times, the aftermath of self-contempt rose up in him when he weakened.

When he was sure no one was watching, or was coming past, he crept out of the bushes, and slunk to his van. He got in, had a last glance at Stephani's apartment, and then he drove away.

CHAPTER 13

Richard opened his locker, the second in the row just outside the urinals. He pulled out his soft sole work shoes, slipped off his Oxfords and closed the grey door with a clang. Fred was here. He could tell because Fred had left his loafers by his locker. Fred was always the first employee to arrive for work in this section. It was rare for anyone to be here before him. Richard shrugged into a disposable lab coat. The silence in the building was welcoming. He was glad to escape his mother. She never stopped talking to him while he was at home. He should get his mom to move into a place of her own, but he knew she'd be lonely, and he couldn't bring himself to do it. Last night he'd bunked on Stephani's sofa. He didn't want to leave her by herself after what had happened.

The coffee machine beckoned him. As he went along the corridor, he could see it through the picture windows, waiting. Fred was in the kitchenette emptying the old residue into the wastebasket, and then he filled the water well with fresh water. "Good morning. I'll have some too, thanks."

"What's good about it?" Fred opened the bag of ground coffee.

"I've been talking to the Ross. He said we should receive delivery of the first of the new microscopes next week."

"It's fine for the CEO to say that, he doesn't have to use them; we do. We should have had some training." Fred stared out of the window.

Richard joined him. "It can't be that hard. Anyways, two instructors are coming in on Monday." Except for the cacti garden, the occasional tree and a green quarter acre surrounding the building, the rest of the back lot was sunbaked brown clumps of grass and red earth.

The brew started to boil and the aroma teased his senses. He breathed deeply, savoring the scent as he poured Fred and himself a cup; added milk, and then took a sip even though it burned his lips. Addicted to the stuff he was, he never cared about what people said caffeine did to you. "Don't forget that meeting's on at one thirty today."

"I noted it on my computer!" Fred picked up his cup and without a word of thanks hurried out.

Boy, that didn't go down well. What's eating him? Richard wondered, as he was following Fred to the entrance to Laboratory 1 that led to three glassed offices. He pressed his palm to the scanner and entered. He stared into the laboratory as he walked along. The autoclave was on timer; two packs of petri dishes and a rack of unused test tubes had not been put away. He made a mental note to remind the staff to tidy up before they left for the night. It may have been Melissa, but he couldn't be sure, and it wouldn't go down well if he singled her out without any hard evidence to back him up.

Fred was already tapping away on his keyboard. Richard glanced at the wall clock as he went to his office. In thirty minutes, the rest of the staff would arrive.

He put down the cup on his desk beside the unfinished report and turned on the computer.

He re-read what he'd written so far, made a few changes here and there, and started to type.

Stephani pushed the glass door and entered. "Hey. What's happening?"

"Are you okay?"

"I managed to fall asleep sometime around two in the morning." She yawned. "You didn't wake me."

"I thought you needed your rest. Don't forget the meeting's on at one-thirty."

"No problem. I've had someone contact me from a group that's doing research similar to ours. I'll tell you more at the meeting. I'd better get my report finished, too. Otherwise, I'll have nothing to present."

"What are you doing for dinner tonight?"

"Probably rustle something up."

Richard had to smile. Nina had told him that Stephani was a great cook. "Would you like to try that new restaurant on Pasadena Street? It's called Giovanni's. I hear they make great pasta."

"I have to call in to the local precinct later this afternoon. They have some mug shots of likely suspects for me to look at. I'm not looking forward to it."

"Do you want me to come with you?"

"I'll be okay."

"It didn't seem like that to me last night." He was about to continue when he heard raised voices through the metal grill above the door that opened onto the corridor.

"I told you I don't want you coming round," Melissa said.

"Don't do this to me. Please." The male cajoled.

The voices got closer.

"Call me on your cell when you're just about done with the cops and I'll meet you there," Richard told Stephani.

"Let go of my arm," Melissa snapped.

"I'll meet you there, but I'll be in my work clothes, though," Stephani said to Richard.

"I can live with that," Richard smiled. Anything she did was fine with him. "I'll stay tonight as well if you want."

"Iantha might be coming over. I'll let you know."

"Sorry. I'm so sorry babe," the male out in the corridor said.

"You promised to give back the money you borrowed three weeks ago. I had to go and draw on my savings to pay the rent because of that," Melissa said.

"It sounds like that security guard, Jagger," Stephani said. "I thought there was something going on when Melissa had words with him the other day."

"Sorry, babe, I'll give it back. I just need a little more. I'm on a sure thing this time. How about I call round tonight for old times' sake."

Richard shrugged. "He sounds like a real jerk. Why would an intelligent woman like Melissa bother with a guy like that?" The guy appeared to have a problem with money, and that didn't make for a good security guard.

They were rounding the corner now and would see Stephani and him at any moment.

"So you can soften me up for another loan? And, fuck me. No way," Melissa said.

"Oh, babe-"

"Don't you babe me! You still haven't cleared out all your stuff. I'm going to throw it out with the garbage if you don't come and get it soon."

"I'm going to fix myself some coffee. Do you want a fresh one?" Stephani said as she moved to the door.

"Thanks." Richard watched Stephani's shapely legs as she strolled away. He sighed, wishing those legs would be wrapped around his hips soon. When she disappeared from view, he stared at his handwritten notes. He had to finish putting these on the computer and make the presentation look professional.

Peripherally, he saw Melissa passing. She was wearing that short red number again.

The security guard stopped abruptly and stared at him.

Richard turned the page of his handwritten notes and tried to concentrate on finishing the report. The man didn't seem her type. Nevertheless, how would he know? He'd made a mess of his relationship with Ellen when they'd been married. He'd been too busy being involved in his work to spend enough time with his family. When he'd pleaded with her to stay, she'd said, "I might as well be single. You're never around enough for me or Belinda to know what's going on in our lives." He prayed he didn't mess up with Stephani.

He heard the guard stride away.

Melissa put her head through the doorway into his office. "Hi. I hope you don't think that something's going-"

Richard shrugged. "What did you say? I've been trying to get this report done before the meeting with the members of the board." He pushed some stray strands of hair from his face. "I feel I've missed something. I wish I knew what it was. What were you saying?" It all came out in a rush, and he was trying to act natural.

"Nothing. You didn't hear me talking to someone, did you?" She fidgeted with her keys.

"Sure, I heard voices."

"I hope you're not going to say something to-"

"I don't plan to say anything to management. I don't think HR would enforce employees not being allowed to date anyway." After all, he was seeing Stephani. Both Stephani and he were critical to the project, and there was no way Rigby could impose the no-dating policy on them. "You're a big girl and you should know what you're getting yourself into."

"I'm getting some coffee."

Melissa turned to go, but paused in her stride when Richard said, "Don't waste your time with guys that aren't worth it."

She closed the door and went into the corridor without looking back.

His phone buzzed and he picked up the receiver. "Good morn-"

"Hey, you haven't called me. I thought we were going to get together," a female said.

"Is that...?"

"Abby."

"I've been busy."

"I cook a mean roast. Come over for dinner tonight?"

Stephani burst into his office carrying his coffee and a magazine. "Did you see this article in The Scientist?"

He smiled at Stephani. "Thanks for the offer, Abby, but I can't tonight."

"Aw, come on, Richard. We had a nice time…who's that?"

He mouthed thanks. "Stephani. She's working on the project with me."

"Aw, come on say yes. You won't regret it."

"Sorry."

"You gave me the come on and now…you think I'm not good enough? Is that it?"

Richard sighed. "I'm so busy with this project."

She hung up. He sighed again. "Sorry, what were you saying?"

Stephani slapped down the magazine on his desk. "Have a look at this article, if you can tear yourself away from the line-up of females calling you." She headed for the door.

"Hey?" He jumped up and crossed the room. She tried to shut the door, but he caught it. "What's upset you?"

"Nothing." She continued to her office.

"Hey. Talk to me." He tried to look into her eyes, but she wouldn't meet his gaze.

"Some scientist in Sweden is saying that he's been successful in the forceful contraction of fibroblasts when they formed cell sheets—a new method for the rapid fabrication of multi-layered human hepatic cell sheets. No need for a layer-by-layer deposition. It's all in the article."

"He could be bluffing. I still think the direction we're heading on breast tissue is the right one."

"I get worried that someone will beat us, and I don't want all our efforts wasted."

"Me either. Are we still on for dinner tonight? And let me know what's happening with your sister," he said.

"You should have gone out with Abby. Now let me get back to work."

"You can't be jealous?'

"Don't flatter yourself." She sat down at her desk. "And close the door on your way out."

"I'll call later to see how you did and we can talk about tonight." He nearly added, 'when you've calmed down', but he thought he'd better not.

CHAPTER 14

"Thanks for coming, Jack." Stephani stood up from the round table, which was in one of the downstairs Rigby meeting rooms. "You really didn't need to call in today. We don't need much. I could have emailed you our order." She closed the catalogue of scientific instruments he had given her.

Her white lab coat hung open, and the soft pink knit fabric of her blouse molded itself around her petite breasts, which were just about eye level. "But you're my favorite customer." Jack pushed back his chair. "You should get your order sometime next week except for the glass measures." He stood, and then straightened his tie. "We won't have them in stock for another month. They'll have to be reordered. If you like, I'll put them on back order for when they come in." Jack started to key in the order into his iPad.

"Don't worry. We should be able to manage for now," Stephani said.

He slammed the iPad onto the table. "I'm just trying to make it easier for you."

She edged back in her seat. "Jack, I do appreciate that you are trying to help, but I find that I can get a double up on the order if I do that."

"I was just doing my job. Don't worry about it!" *How dare she! Did she think that he did this for all his clients!*

One look into her eyes made his anger disappear. He loved gazing at those hazelnut eyes. The feeling it gave him was like the luxury of swimming naked at night and not caring if someone caught you. "I wanted an excuse to see how you're doing, and to tell you that I'm going to the health club tonight. I thought you might want to join me."

His lips turned up at the corners, but he wasn't going to smile; he was taking it slowly.

She yawned. "I'm tired and I've got to go to the police department later this afternoon."

"Something wrong?" Jack asked.

She told him about finding the extra teddy last night. "I called Richard and he came over and bunked on the couch. Neither of us really slept. I kept thinking someone's going to creep in when my eyes are shut, even with Richard there. I can't work out how the intruder could have gotten in." She sat back down and stared at the cover of the catalogue.

"Did they take anything?"

"They took my blue suit and some underwear."

"Just theft. It's probably some guy who gets kicks from taking women's clothing. My guess is that they won't be back. Probably didn't find anything else they wanted to steal."

"But the bear…how did it get there? How did they know what my bear looked like? What sort of person…."

He stared into her eyes. "You didn't take the suit to the dry-cleaner's and forget about it, did you?"

"I took it to the cleaner's a week ago and I picked it up a few days ago."

"Have you considered that the suit could have been taken days ago, and you didn't notice until after you saw the extra bear?"

Stephani shivered. "Jesus, this is getting worse by the moment."

"What are your neighbors like? Could it have been one of them that left the bear?"

"I've hardly met them. Anyway, how would they know what it looks like or that I even have one, unless they've been in the apartment before?"

"Good point. Who had the unit before you? They could still have a key or have given a key to a neighbor or friend?"

"I should ask the real estate agent. I'm going to have to have new locks installed."

"Call the agent first. No need to go to that expense if it's not the case."

"I'm not some dumb broad. This person would have needed a key or a security code to get in the front entrance."

"Just maybe, you didn't close the entrance door properly when you went out. Or if not you, then one of your neighbors."

"I just don't know anymore. The thought that some creep's been through my things makes my skin crawl."

"You're certain you didn't have two bears? You could have forgotten-"

"I only have one...I can count. I'm not stupid."

"I'm sorry. That's not the way I meant it. Some people have a lot of soft toys and...well...can't remember."

"I've had this bear since...since I was two or three. My father gave it to me for my birthday just before he left us. I don't know where he is or if he's still alive." She looked dejected.

"That's sad about your father." He reached over to touch her hand, but the cedar table was too wide.

Stephani frowned. "I don't know why I'm telling you this."

She must have been angry with him. He shouldn't have said that or the stuff about the bear. "Hey, if it helps, talk away. My father died the year I started school. I missed him for ages. It must be hard for you."

"I accepted that he didn't want to see me, or my mother years ago. But I do care when you imply that I don't even know if I own one or two bears."

"Hey, I'm sorry. Next time, remember you can call me. By the way, I know a locksmith. So if you want to get them changed and the agent doesn't mind, I can give you his number."

"I don't know why I've told you about my father."

"What friends are for…what about the health club?" When she frowned again, he said, "Don't worry." He pushed back his chair, stood and then picked up his iPad. "I thought it might help take your mind off all this."

Stephani rose. "You're probably right. Iantha's coming over tonight, but I can work something out with her."

"Great. See you about seven at the health club." He smiled. The elation was equally inward as much as it was outward for the first time since he could remember. As he walked outside the building, he tossed his keys into the air and caught them, again and again.

CHAPTER 15

He picked up the two photos. One was her leaving her apartment to go jogging and the other, his Princess with her niece at Canyon Lake. He would send the one taken at the picnic grounds to his Princess.

He stared at the next shot of her with her niece at Canyon Lake. He'd wanted to take more snap-shots, but her niece had noticed him so he'd hidden behind a creosote bush. That young girl looked so like Stephani that she could have been her daughter, but he knew she was not.

The heavy tread above him came closer to the door that opened into the basement. He put the photos down, and hurried across the concrete to the stairs.

"Pud. I need you."

The muffled screech drifted to him.

He ignored her and continued to admire his handiwork.

"Pud."

He gently placed the photos on the bench. "Coming, mother." He bounded up two stairs at a time. The hall light outlined the woman who stood in the doorway, and made her look even more repulsive.

That nosey-assed whore: she opened that door and looked in. He must have forgotten to lock it. Had she seen what he was doing? He stood to his full height and blocked the entranceway. "What do you want now?" He reached across and turned off the light to the basement.

"What are you doing down there?"

"Can't you stop asking me that?"

"I need more pills. I haven't got any left."

The fat whore couldn't have seen much in those few seconds, but she was getting more curious by the day. He would have to do something about that soon!

"Why didn't you remember to tell me when I did the shopping the other day? Are you sure you haven't got any?"

Without saying a word, she turned and trudged along the hallway to the kitchen.

Pud tailed her.

She picked up two empty pill bottles from the windowsill. "See. I ran out two days ago. You think I'm stupid, don't you. Don't you?"

When he did not answer, she added, "Just get them, or do you want me to get sick? Huh? Then you'll have to nurse me."

He wanted her to get sick, real sick. "You're always doing this to me. Go here. I need this. Go there because…because…because. I'll go to the drug store later." Did she think he was her servant?

"I need them fluid pills and the heart ones too. I can't seem to get my breath lately."

Wet rings circled the armpits of the dress his mother wore. Holy shit, how she stank. He wrinkled his nose. God, he had to get away. "Where's the prescription?"

"In my handbag. Go to my bedroom and get my bag like a good boy, and I'll get it out for you."

"You are so god-damned lazy. Get this…get my that. What do you think I am…your slave?"

"Listen boy. You think life was easy for me raising you without a father? I could have spent money on myself if I didn't have to constantly feed you and put clothes on your back. I had to find ways to get food in the house. You think I wanted to be tied to you? You sniveling…dirty…little…bed-wetting-"

"Just shut your mouth before I shut it for you. Who keeps you now? I should let you starve. It would do you good to lose some of that weight. And, you should wash more often. You stink. Don't you ever dare remind me again, of what I used to do when I was little! You hear! Do you hear me?" Would he ever be free of the whore?

Hertha laughed. "You'll never get a gal to marry you when they find out. Who would want a bed-wetter like you? Not a nice girl, that's-"

"Whore! Whore! You fuckin' whore." He stomped outside and slammed the back door. For long moments, he stared at the dried-up stalks of grass as if they could solve his problem. Then he paced up and down, thinking over how he could rid himself of the stinking whore, and finally, when a solution started to crystallize, he stormed back inside. "You get your own medicine from now on. My girl is beautiful and she's…." Shit. He'd said too much.

His mother pressed her lips together in a sort of smirk as if she knew things about him that he didn't want anyone to know: things that lived deep inside him that no human ought to have there. These things and more, that he couldn't bring himself to think about, tied him to that whore.

He should wipe that look off her face; his hand itched to lash out. He turned from her, side stepped the kitchen table, strewn with cuttings. She was always collecting recipes and other useless stuff.

She never looked at any of it again, just stashed mountains of the rubbish in boxes in the attic. Even when she moved from L.A., she had to bring it all with her. The stupid whore couldn't part with a single thing.

"Stop that nonsense. I could have let you to die like your brother but-"

"What did you say?"

"Nothing."

"You just said I had a brother! That's what you said!"

She turned away. "I had no choice. He was a cripple and we-"

He slapped her hard. He wanted to keep hitting her until she was dead. Something about the look in her eyes stopped him even though his fingers were balled into fists. "What did you do?"

Her cheek was red and started to swell, but she didn't put her hand to it. "When he slipped out of me with those slant eyes and flat nose, and didn't cry like babies do, I knew something was wrong. One in the litter is always defective. You watched while I drowned him in the river. Weighted him down with rocks, and he never made a sound."

"I had a brother. When? Tell me, when," he screamed.

"You were still little, 'bout four."

"You piece of shit. You heartless murdering whore. How many more sisters or brothers did you kill besides the sister, that you had to God knows which client? I still remember you made me put her in the chest freezer straight after she was born. I looked at her little frozen body every day 'till I buried her."

"None." She looked away.

"One, two or three?"

She shook her head.

"Tell me! Now!"

Hertha's voice came out in a whisper, "Another sister."

His fingers were balled so tight that his short nails dug into his palms and he thumped and kicked the wall, again and again.

"Stop it." For once, his mother looked nervous.

"You asking me to stop?"

"Please," she said.

When had he ever heard her plead? Never! The thought swelled inside him.

He turned from her and walked along the threadbare-carpeted hallway and upstairs to her bedroom. She never opened the window in that room. He turned on the light, and then held his breath as he rushed in, and picked up her bag from the cluttered dresser. Hesitated for an instant when he saw a bottle of face cream, then picked it up and smashed it against the wall beside her bed. Let the whore clean up the mess or leave it, he didn't care. Just let her try to scold him for this.

As he hurried downstairs carrying her handbag, he imagined sweeping up all those face powders, lipsticks, creams, hairpins, brushes that she rarely used anymore, and the piles of used tissues, into a trash bag with one swoop of his arm.

A few minutes later, he grabbed the proffered prescription from her hand.

"Don't take too long. I have to have them pills right after dinner."

He slammed the door as he left.

Let the fat pig wait. A gust of wind stirred a tall clump of bamboo muhly grass that had survived the summer, and it cast moving shadows against the darkening sky. He started up the van and accelerated down the driveway.

***

After he had the prescription filled, he went to the library in the hope they were open late Friday nights. Fortunately, they were. He didn't want to browse the Internet from his own laptop. That was too dangerous.

He went up the steps to the entrance, and pushed through the heavy doors. Books catalogued in neat isles lay behind the librarian's desk. He asked where he could find medical books, and she directed him to the reference section a couple of floors up.

He stepped from the elevator into a cavernous room of orderly rows of books and a few people walking about.

There were some students studying in the cubicles. With an armful of books, he sat down at a desk and spent a few hours flipping through them and then another hour or more searching the Internet as well. All the while, he made notes when he found anything of interest.

Finally, he shut the volumes and returned them to the shelf.

As he went outside and down the front steps, he started to hum some song that he'd heard on the radio earlier that day. Life was going to turn out just the way he planned.

CHAPTER 16

Stephani locked her silver Honda as she juggled her bag of groceries against her spaghetti-strap white dress. Even in the underground parking lot, the overheated dry desert air seemed to suck the moisture from her lungs.

She rode the elevator to her apartment, let herself in, kicked off her sandals, put down her purchases on the kitchen bench-top and turned up the air conditioner.

After she put away her groceries, she started to make a tuna salad for lunch. While she was slicing a cucumber, she thought about her conversation with Jack last night.

"How about we make meeting at the health club a regular thing? Say once a week?" Jack had said.

"I've started going Monday and Friday mornings. How about Wednesday night?" she had replied as they parted.

Jack agreed. He'd wanted to hire a tradesman to come and change her locks, but she'd put him off with a story that she'd had them changed already. The police had taken that teddy but had not found any decent fingerprints on it. You couldn't get decent prints from fur, they told her.

The photos, the duplicate teddy bear and the persistent caller were enough to put her on edge constantly. She had not slept well since the first photos turned up. She pulled out the Ouzo and poured herself a shot.

She put down the knife and rinsed the lettuce under the faucet.

As the water swirled down the drain, her thoughts spiraled to some alien childhood, but the images were so vivid that they seemed to be happening at that very moment.

"Mommy, Mommy, I don't want to stay here." My mommy has her sad face on as she opens the front door.

"Don't leave me. Please. Please." I start to cry. Then my mommy starts to cry too. I grab her hand. "I'll be a good girl. Pleeease."

"Hush sweetheart." Mommy wipes her eyes. "You are my best girl. I love you so much. I explained to you that I have to work. All our money's all gone. I have to go to work so we can eat."

"But I'm not hungry. I don't have to eat," I say.

"Sure you do, to grow up big and strong." My mommy kisses my cheek. "Bye-bye, my best girl," my mommy whispers.

She gets up, and lets go of my hand.

I don't want her to let go. "Mommy...mommy," I sob. "Please take me too."

Just before she goes out the door, she says, "Now don't forget, I'll be back to pick you up at the end of the week. Friday night. That's just like I taught you. Monday comes first, next is Tuesday, then Wednesday, then Thursday, and then Friday. Okay."

I wipe my tears and then hiccup. "Okay."

After she closes the big door, I thump my fists on it until they hurt. More tears wet my face and I swipe them away. I should be brave for my mommy, but I can't stop the tears.

The fat lady stands and watches me with her arms folded.

The house smells funny. It makes my nose wrinkle. The same as when my mommy found that dead cat behind the dumpster near where we used to live.

I wonder how long a week is. It has those days my mommy talked about. It must be an awful long time. I miss my mommy so much already.

I stare at that door and wish hard it would open again and my mommy would be here to take me home.

The fat lady trudges down the hallway. "Get away from there, kid."

I do not like her. She only gives me bread with peanut butter to eat. I told my mommy but she said I had a good imagination. Whatever that was? When my mommy asked the old lady, she said that she gave me chicken and vegetables. That fat lady lied.

Now Stephani blinked and stared at the water cascading from the faucet over the lettuce she held in her hand. She turned it off. "Shit," she said aloud. "What's happening to me?"

These images couldn't have been from her childhood. So where were they coming from? Was it from a movie she'd seen years ago? She had no answer.

She reached up into the cupboard for the bottle of Ouzo. Just one small glass would settle her down. The buzzer downstairs rang.

Stephani flicked the intercom. "Who is it?"

"Hey, Stephani. Are you ready to go?" Richard said.

"I'm running late. Come on up. I'm just about to eat lunch."

She put away the alcohol.

Richard let himself in. "Was your front door locked?"

She shrugged. "It is when I'm out." At least it had been since finding that teddy. "I've tried to lock it, honestly I have."

"Then try harder. I don't want anything to happen to you. Maybe you should see someone about this?"

"Leave it be. I'm just fine." She wouldn't tell him about the visions she kept having; he'd think she definitely needed help. How could she explain them to any shrink?

He put up his hands in surrender. "Just a suggestion."

"Have you eaten?"

"I had to call in to work to check on the last round of RT282's and then I came straight over."

"And?"

"Just as we expected, unfortunately."

"It was the layering, right?"

"The molecular structure broke down."

"Damn. Not the news I wanted. Tuna salad okay?" she said.

"Yep. How about I make us some coffee?"

She continued preparing the rest of the salad, opened the can of corn, and tuna and forked it through. "The cups are in the cupboard above the microwave and the sugar is on the third shelf in the pantry."

He put on the coffee and sat. "Delicious," he said after his first mouthful. "I can't cook."

She rolled her eyes. "Oh, come on. You're kidding me. There's nothing to cook in this."

He set a coffee beside her. "I guess I'm spoiled with mom living with me."

"So where's this antique fair we're going to?"

"Just north of Phoenix." He took a sip of coffee and ate some more salad. "I got interested in the old wind-up watches when my mom gave me my grandfather's after he died ten years ago. I have five in my collection now." He held out his arm to show her his wristwatch. "This is a gold-cased vintage automatic Omega Seamaster DeVille I got at a flea market two years ago."

"I've seen you wear that before." She ate some tuna. "Iantha and I didn't keep much of mom's stuff. Not that there was much anyway. My step-dad left us when I started junior high. He just said that he'd gotten a job on a trawler and…well, never came back. I think, looking back now that he and my mom sort of agreed that he would go."

"That would have been hard. Has he kept in touch?"

"Occasionally. But not for the last few years now. I don't know where he is. I didn't tell you this to get some sympathy."

"Sorry."

"Yeah, well. That's life." Why was she getting these visions? What was wrong with her?

CHAPTER 17

Princie sat in his van opposite Stephani's apartment drinking his morning coffee. He watched her exit the building in her jogging gear. She crossed the road right in front of him, and started to jog to the park.

He tipped out the rest of his coffee into the gutter and threw away the cardboard cup. This was the best way to start a week. His mouth watered.

Princie, dressed in black shorts and T-shirt, followed a little distance behind. He passed some tall gay guy prancing along with his dog.

Stephani picked up the pace, and it was more of an effort for him to keep up. Nevertheless, it was worth it.

He loved the way her black hair swung so sensually in rhythm as she moved.

"Good morning," a male jogger called to him as he passed by.

He ignored it. Let them make an empty cheerful greeting to someone else. Hypocrites all of them, they probably didn't have anything to be happy about anyway.

When Stephani reached the middle of the park, she slumped down onto a bench seat. He couldn't hide as he had done other times; there were too many joggers here today. He kept on going. A little way along, he left the path for the grassy area, and then circled back, taking a short cut through a clump of fan palms.

He sighed with relief when he saw her. She had stopped to retie her shoelace. A hobo with shoulder-length hair and a beard came and sat next to her. The hobo spoke to Stephani and she looked tense. He got ready to cover the distance and protect her if the guy got ideas. However, the hobo got up and walked away.

Relieved, he allowed himself to enjoy the gift that was Stephani. He drank in her lithe grace as she rose. She was so different from other females he'd followed in the past.

Something glinted in the early morning sun. When it happened a second time, he noticed it had come from the bushes somewhere behind Stephani. Camera lens, he was sure of it now.

He caught a glimpse of an adult male moving at a crouch. He knew right away that this man was taking photos of Stephani. The same guy he'd seen enter her apartment block. He did not like it one bit.

Some creep had invaded his girl's privacy. He wished he could do something about it.

After Stephani had started running again, he watched the man step from the bushes with the camera. He sensed that the guy was a real bad dude from the first time he'd noticed him. He couldn't work out why he felt this way, but his gut feeling had never let him down.

Princie turned and followed his girl. He wanted to protect her, but he didn't know how he could do that without being discovered himself.

CHAPTER 18

"These aren't the pills I was taking before. They're the wrong color," Hertha whined as she turned from the kitchen sink, tablets in one hand and the glass of water in the other.

He wrinkled his nose in disgust when he saw how grubby her fingernails were.

"How would I know? Maybe the doctor changed the strength of those fluid pills. If I don't go now, I'll be late for work."

He buttoned the sleeves of his white shirt and then shrugged into his navy jacket. A mountain of crumpled women's clothes and sheets lay in the corner of the room. The old sixties wood veneer table was stained with coffee and food. The dirty dishes piled in the sink since yesterday, he'd washed this morning. It didn't matter how often he cleaned up after her. The next time he came home, the place would be in a mess again.

"Those other pills were pink, these are white. Maybe the drug store made a mistake." She finished off an iced donut and then wiped her fingers on the side of her faded brown sack of a dress.

"Never have before. I'm sure they were white. You've just got your colors mixed up."

"I was up with the water four times last night. I hope these don't make me go more."

"I just told you. They're the same ones you were taking."

"I don't know." She shrugged.

"If you're worried, don't take them."

"Easy for you to say. I'll get sicker if I don't," his mother said.

"Take them, goddamned you. I'll see you in three days." He picked up his black overnight bag.

"I don't want you leaving me anymore. What if I get worse? You've got to find another job. One that you don't have to work weekends and doesn't keep you away for days at a time. I don't like you going away."

"It pays the bills, doesn't it? I've left my cell number by the phone if you need me. But don't call me unless it's important."

"Are you going to give me a goodbye kiss?"

"Christ, you stink. When did you have a shower last? Holy shit, mother, and you expect me to get close to you?"

"I can't remember."

"Well, make sure you have one before I get back." He'd put an extra lock on the basement door, as the whore was getting nosier by the day. The last thing he needed was her poking about down there and interfering with his plans.

CHAPTER 19

Stephani walked down the stone-grey vinyl covered corridor in the reception area of the nursing home and caught the sour odors of old people as she passed their rooms. In the common room, wizened men and women slumped in armchairs, some in pajamas, drooling or dozing off. A few were dressed in street clothes watching some soap on TV. She hoped her mother was more alert today.

She had all the excuses in the world not to visit, because she wasn't over the loss of her husband and son, because she was too busy... because it distressed her to see her mom who had been so active sit in an armchair and stare out of the window at nothing.

A nurse strode towards her. "Can I help you?"

"How's Mrs. Giannopoulos today?" When she was a child, she believed her mother would never grow old. She'd finally come to terms with how hard her mother had been on her and knew now that it wasn't because she had not cared for her; it was just her mom's way.

"Oh. You're her other daughter, aren't you! I can see the resemblance. Why don't you go see for yourself? Letha's been good today. She's just down the hall, third on the left. And she'll be so happy you've come." She smiled.

Stephani continued past other patients' rooms. Some were self-furnished, others were just hospital-issued, and some smelled of urine. *Please recognize me, Mom. I don't know if I can take that vacant stare that Iantha was confronted with,* she said silently.

She stopped at the doorway and took a sip from her water bottle.

Seated in an armchair, her mother was drinking coffee, and the smell of the brew wafted in the air. No one could have guessed just by looking at her why she was here. The hairdresser must have been in today and had tinted her soft grey curls black. She was wearing her favorite dress—a small white polka-dot print with a green background. Stephani recalled the shopping trip with her mother when Letha purchased it. Her mother had tried on a few dresses and when she had found one that fitted and looked nice on, her mother had tried to give the sales woman two dollars for a fifty-dollar dress. She had thought then that her mother was just getting older and a little senile, but now she knew better.

Her mother looked nice, even if she didn't know it. "Hi, Mom."

Letha looked up and smiled. The color had returned to her cheeks.

Thank God. Stephani rushed past the bed and kissed her on both cheeks.

"Careful. You'll make me spill my coffee." Her mother put down her hospital-issued plastic mug and tried to get the lid back on.

"Let me do it for you, Mom." Iantha had told her that last time she had visited a week ago, it had taken almost a half hour before her mother recognized her.

"So, how's your job?" her mother asked.

"Great. We're getting closer to perfecting that formula." In her late fifties, her mother should have still been enjoying life. It wasn't fair.

"They take real good care of me here. But, I don't understand why they haven't let me go home. I feel so healthy. It's been years since I had a cold or anything."

Iantha had explained to their mom why she had to stay, but none of it had sunk in. In the end, her mother had gotten more and more upset.

"Mom, it's because you're losing your memory," Stephani said.

"So I'm getting forgetful. At my age, who can blame me? I'm entitled, aren't I?"

"Nobody's blaming you, Mom." Stephani drank some more spring water.

"And don't drink from that bottle. It's unladylike."

This disease had changed her mother's nature and she'd become more aggressive. Stephani gritted her teeth. However, this part of her nature had not changed. "Everyone drinks from bottles now, Mom."

"Not my daughters," Letha said.

She took another defiant sip as her mother glared at her and then slowly put it in her handbag. *What am I doing,* she said to herself, *fighting with mom as always.* This had to stop, her mother was sick.

"Would you go talk to the manager and find out when I can leave this place? It's full of old people. I don't belong here." Her mother leaned forward and whispered, "You know, some of them are so crazy, they don't even know their name or what day it is...come to think of it. Some of them stink 'cause they wet their pants."

"I'm sorry, but you have to stay."

Her mother was silent for a moment, and then an intense look crossed her face. "Don't you ever come to this!"

Oh God, she knows...how could she know and stand it, thought Stephani. The unfairness of this tore at her heart and she looked away so her mother wouldn't see the tears in her eyes. Now she was mothering her mother. It was a huge shift, one she didn't know if she'd ever get used to. "Doctor's orders, you know."

"Well, what are you still standing for? Pull up a chair. Do you want these cookies? Put them in your bag. They're wrapped in cellophane and will keep. I've got more in the first drawer just next to the bed. Reach over and take as many as you want. The nurses never take any notice."

Stephani breathed a sigh of relief. Her mother had forgotten what she'd said earlier and accepted that she couldn't go home this time. She'd have to remember to say 'doctor's orders' next time, too. "No thanks, Mom. I'm not hungry. I'll put them in with the others, shall I?" She opened the drawer and saw it was stuffed full of packets of salt and pepper, sugar, cookies, small medicine cups, and lots more. When Iantha and Stephani were growing up, her mother had been particular about keeping everything in its place and never hoarding rubbish. Well, the cookies weren't rubbish, but the rest of it was. "It's not going to fit, Mom. Just leave it on the tray, and the nurses can have them."

"I'll keep them for later." Her mom squeezed the cookies into the drawer.

Stephani wanted to tell her to leave them on the tray again, but couldn't bring herself to do so.

When she heard the opening notes of 'Nothing Compares 2 U,' she reached for her cell and realized it was ringing in the next room. It was strange to hear that someone nearby had the same ring tone.

"So how's that hard-working husband of yours?"

Stephani's stomach contracted as if she'd been punched hard there. She blinked back tears; shocked and vulnerable, she searched for some morsel of inner strength. "Allan was killed in a car accident five months ago."

"You should have told me. I would have gone to Allan's funeral."

"But you did go."

"How could I have? You didn't tell me 'till today."

Her hands clenched into fists and her nails dug into her palms. A sob rose from deep within. Her mom looked at her quizzically.

Stephani closed her eyes and concentrated on her breathing to bring some stillness back to the crushing emotions her mother's words had stirred up. "Mom, I'm trying to forget."

"Well, I can't understand why you kept it from me?"

It was hard enough without this. However, it wasn't her mother's fault. "I've started going to the health club again."

"I don't know why you gave it up."

She shrugged…no use explaining. "I don't know if I mentioned Jack last time I came? He works for a company that sells us laboratory equipment. He calls in to work once a month. Anyway, he talked me into going again."

"Is he good-looking?"

It was hard to keep up with how her mother changed from one thing to the next. "Oh. I guess…. He's super fit."

"Has he got nice buns?"

"Oh, Mom. We're just friends."

"Well, has he? You have to notice these things. You don't want to be alone forever."

"I'm not ready…never mind. He has. Okay?"

Letha started to fidget.

"Something worrying you?"

Letha looked down at her hands, and then shook her head. "I know I ought to remember something, something I promised myself I would tell you when you were older." Her eyes filled with tears. "It was something you once asked me about and...and I couldn't bring myself to tell you the truth." She tugged at the button-down dress she was wearing. "I know, it was after your dad left us and...."

While she waited for her to continue, Stephani stared at the framed family photo of her sister, her mother, Henry, Allan and herself, taken just over six months ago. Letha was laughing then. She didn't laugh anymore.

She glanced at her mother. The frown was replaced with a serene smile. Maybe next Saturday when she visited, her mother would remember whatever it was she wanted to tell her. "I love you, Mom."

"I'm so glad you stopped by."

"I love you," Stephani said again. Letha didn't react, as if a fog had drifted across her brain.

Stephani leaned over to kiss her but her mother pulled away.

"Iantha's coming by later," Stephani said.

"That's nice. Who is she?"

CHAPTER 20

Pud walked inside and dropped his keys, the hot chicken and fries on the bench-top. He'd been away for a day longer than he'd expected, but he'd gained some new accounts. The company should have been pleased.

However, his mother would be angry that he'd stayed away the extra day, but he didn't care. "Hi, Mother. I'm home."

The TV was blaring. How could anyone hear over that racket? She must have been going deaf. He passed the Formica table with the four metal chairs with vinyl cover seats and backs, to the sofa. She wasn't asleep on the sofa. Where was she? He called out from the bottom of the stairs and thought he heard her answer but he wasn't sure.

"I've got take-out for dinner." Was she sick?

He bounded up two stairs at a time. "Mother? Where are you?"

"In here. Don't feel so good."

As he stepped into the stillness of her bedroom, he could smell her body odor and the unwashed sheets.

His mother, flat on her back, had her arms out of the blankets, which covered the rest of her fat body. "I'm feeling weak. Get me some water?"

"How can you stand it in here? It's so hot." He opened the window, put his head out and took a big gulp of fresh air before he turned to her.

"I got take-out chicken and fries for us."

"I'm lying here sick, and my son's cruising around the country."

"Hey, you didn't call, and I'm not a mind reader. How can you stand it under those blankets?" If she'd not killed his siblings, she'd have them to take care of her.

"Told ya I was sick."

"Well, dinner's downstairs." He made for the door. He'd spent long enough in this goddamned room.

Not a moment longer could he stand that noise on the TV, so he flicked it off.

After he'd eaten and washed up, he went up to see how she was doing. He kicked aside some dresses, tops and underwear she had piled on the floor. He didn't know if they were dirty and didn't care. No way would he wash her stuff. "You'll have to come down to eat. I'm not bringing any food up."

"Listen…you should look after me."

"So what's wrong with you?"

"I don't feel good, and I'm thirsty."

"Can't get the doctor out for that. You'll have to be more specific."

"Just lemme alone." She turned away from him and stared at the wall.

"Suit yourself. Go hungry, for all I care." This was so unlike her. She was always ready for an argument. He could get used to this. He turned and went downstairs, slipped out the key to the basement from its hiding spot at the back of his display unit and hurried down to look at the photos of his Princess.

The next morning, he rose, ate breakfast and got ready for work. He didn't look in on his mother before he left.

When he came home that evening, he opened the back door to silence. He didn't dare hope that his solution had worked so quickly. Nevertheless, he made himself some coffee and went upstairs to change into his gym gear.

Pud went into his mother's room first. "Are you okay, Mother?"

His mother didn't stir. She was still facing the wall. The window was still open, and it didn't look like she'd moved since he'd seen her last night. He approached her cautiously. He'd learned from previous times that if she was in a mood she'd swipe at him without provocation. "Mother? Hell, are you playing a game? Cause if you are, I'm not interested."

Her cheeks were greyish, her eyes were open, and she appeared to be staring at something beyond the wall. He leaned over and touched her cheek. The skin was just warm. He felt for a pulse on her wrist and couldn't find one.

Finally, he located a weak pulse at the side of her neck.

"Can you hear me, Mother? I think you're dying, and I'm not calling the doctor or an ambulance."

Hertha blinked, he thought, but he couldn't be sure.

"I'm going to the health club." If she recovered, no one would believe that he had not tried to do all he could for her. Another coffee stop sounded good on the way home from the club.

Pud pulled off his suit trousers all the while humming 'Nothing Compares 2 U'. This was his Princess's and his special song. Then he went downstairs, picked up his keys, left through the back door and locked it. Then he jumped in his van and drove away.

Hours later, when he returned to his mother's place, he whistled as he unlocked the door. "Mother, I'm back."

All quiet inside.

For the first time that he could remember, he turned on the TV, got himself a glass of wine and slumped on the sofa to watch another rerun of 'I Love Lucy'.

A few hours later, he climbed the stairs slowly and went into his mother's room. "Mother, are you awake?" He leaned over and touched her hand. It was cold.

"I can't forgive you for making me go with those men, Mother. You shouldn't have made me do that. It hurt so much and I hated you for that for as long as I can remember. You made me what I am! You made me what I am!" he snarled.

"I used to be scared of you, but not any longer. If I could kill you all over again, I would for my brother and my sisters who never got to grow up. But maybe they were better off dead than living with you."

He retreated from the room and went downstairs.

"I'm so upset. My mother's in bed. She's not moving. I don't know if she's dead. She was sick but I didn't think it was serious. She meant the world to me. I loved her. I don't know how I can go on without her." He said this repeatedly, each time evoking more emotion into those words refining his delivery. By the time he had picked up his cell, a tear had slipped down his cheek.

CHAPTER 21

"I am sorry, we did all we could, but it was too late," the doctor said. "Her heart just stopped beating. Even if Hertha had lived after the cardiac arrest, she would have had a difficult life." The doctor touched his shoulder. "At least, Hertha is at peace now."

He stared at the laminate hospital floor as if engulfed with grief. "Thank you for all you did. I don't know how I'll ever be able to carry on without her." Even to him, he sounded genuine. He should have been an actor.

Settlement on the property that he'd spent months looking for in Camp Verdi was tomorrow. It would be a push to get it ready for his Princess. But it would be worth the effort.

A beeper sounded somewhere, and another white-coated doctor rushed by.

"We have a resident grief counselor you can speak to. It might help. I'll give you her number."

He shrugged. "I don't know."

"Think about it. Okay?" The doctor reached over the half wall separating the nurses' desks from the area, picked up the counselor's business card, and handed it to him.

"I guess there are things I should organize." He wanted to get out of this place of noise and antiseptic.

"Before you can set the date for your mother to be laid to rest...I wish there was another way to tell you but there isn't. By law we must perform an autopsy because of the suddenness of her death."

The doctor was a gullible idiot. "I'd rather not. She's been through enough."

"I don't know if we can allow that. I'll have to check with the registrar."

"Maybe it's better to know. Do whatever you have to do." They would only find she'd taken too high a dose of those fluid pills and had not kept up her potassium levels. She'd had heart problems anyway. As soon as he got home, he would change the labels on her drugs. The original ones he'd carefully peeled off and replaced with his own self-printed drug store label. No one would ever find out.

"Why don't you go home and try to get some rest. It's been a long night for you. I'll prescribe something so you can sleep."

They could always be handy for any number of things. "Sure. And something for my nerves?"

The doctor picked up a pad and wrote out a prescription. "Here. Take one when you can't sleep and the other, once per day. And don't forget to call the counselor."

"Sure." He glanced at a nurse wheeling a patient on a gurney down the corridor as he summoned whatever sad emotions he could. He thought of his dog. His whore of a mother had drowned it when he was twelve just because the animal barked in the mornings. He suppressed his anger. His performance had to be convincing. Think of the poor dog he loved, its droopy ears and soulful look. As he lifted his gaze to meet the doctor's kindly one, he said, "Thank you. I know you did your best for my mom." He blinked away a tear. God, he was good.

"I shall miss her always. She was a wonderful mother." He nearly choked on those words. "Thanks for this." He held up the prescription. "Good bye."

"Remember to call the counselor."

He nodded and walked with a measured tread to the lift; pushed the button and waited. He didn't dare turn around. The doctor would have seen the smile he couldn't stop from appearing.

He was free. Rid of that whore. He wanted to jump and shout: to proclaim how happy he was, but instead he joined the other people waiting for the elevator. The doors finally opened and he stepped inside.

He would never need to endure her insults, her bad cooking, her filth and her disgusting habits. A laugh erupted from somewhere inside him and the other occupants stared at him. They didn't know the hell he had endured with her. The laughter still bubbled up. He tried his best to stifle it and look serious. When the doors opened, he hurried down the corridor. The urgency to get home and dispose of her things nearly overwhelmed rational thought.

Then he remembered the autopsy. Her pills, and a few other things, would have to stay just in case of an investigation. He would leave a few photos of the whore to look as if he loved her, the rest would go into the dumpster at the shopping mall.

He passed the café near the entrance, and the newsstand collared his attention.

'Half naked girl found dead at Falls Creek.'

He paid for the paper and glanced at the article as he strode outside: 'Grief-stricken mother appeals to public for help in finding her daughter's killer. Police comb the area looking for clues.'

He tucked the paper under his arm and unlocked his van.

CHAPTER 22

Stephani slipped into her burgundy evening dress. Last night Iantha had stayed over. When the burglar alarm went off early this morning, Stephani had jumped from her bed, still muddled from sleep, to see if there was an intruder. But it had been Iantha who'd set off the alarm when she'd gotten up and padded to the kitchen without thinking. After breakfast, she'd told her sister to go home, as the alarm gave her a degree of security.

She pushed up the spaghetti-straps of her dress, staring at herself in the mirrored closet doors. She turned this way and that to gauge how her new shorter bob looked. Cheekbones hidden by longer hair now seemed to be more defined. Her nose was just a little too big, but not enough to consider a nose job. Moreover, just the thought of that unnecessary pain made her wince.

A chain would be perfect for this dress. She padded in her stocking feet across to the dresser and opened a Chinese black-lacquered jewelry box. There, amongst the few pieces she owned, lay a platinum chain with a one carat diamond pendant.

Allan had given her this on their first wedding anniversary. She slammed the box shut as tears welled in her eyes.

Don't think about Allan…just wear it, she told herself. *Don't let his death keep upsetting you.* She tried to secure the clasp around her neck, but her hands shook so much the chain slipped from her grasp and clattered to the dresser.

Stephani blotted her tears as she remembered. Allan had taken her to Suttons by the Bay for their first anniversary, then they'd strolled in the moonlight, and when they'd stopped, he'd told her to shut her eyes and had slipped the chain around her neck. Afterwards, they had kissed.

She couldn't recall how it felt to have his lips caressing hers...to have his body pressed against hers...to have his hands touching her where she wanted. "It's not fair, Allan," she said aloud.

She balled the tissue in her hand and threw it in the waste paper basket beside the dresser.

The front door buzzer rang at the same time as the phone.

She hurried to answer the buzzer and picked up the phone on her way. Maybe it was Iantha.

"Hey, it's Richard."

"Come on up. I'm nearly ready." She buzzed him in and let the call go to voice mail, but the caller didn't leave a message this time.

Was the caller the one who had told her to watch out for some bad dude? She poured herself a shot of Ouzo.

Stephani put her head back, gulped the fiery liquor, and then replaced the glass in the cupboard as Richard came through the door.

CHAPTER 23

He pulled up across the road from Stephani's apartment.

Great. The blinds were open. He grabbed his binoculars and stared at his Princess's silhouette. She was brushing her beautiful hair. Then he looked harder, shocked. *When did she cut it?* His hands clenched the binoculars and then he threw them on the seat beside him.

Ruined. Those beautiful black silky tresses. He thumped the cabin door with his fist again and again. *How dare she?*

She was a real princess. His Princess!

Finally, he reached for the binoculars again and stared at her once more. She was still the most beautiful female he'd ever laid eyes on. He grabbed his camera, adjusted the telephoto lens and started clicking. He couldn't see past her waist, but that evening dress, the way it clung to her breasts.... She looked sexy even with her shorter hair.

Someone entered his vision. Who was that man kissing her? He flat-palmed the steering wheel when he recognized the rat she worked with, Richard. When had he arrived? He'd been too busy trying to catch a glimpse of her to see any vehicles pull up.

When had this guy made a move on his girl?

The lights went out. Moments later, he saw her exit the front entrance with him. *How dare that rat keep company with his Princess?*

Stephani's hair was spun silk; even though it was short...and he decided…it wasn't too bad after all. He ached to touch it, to run his fingers through it.

Head held high, with a slim shapely figure and pert breasts beneath burgundy silk caught at the waist with a neat bow at the side, his Princess waited on the sidewalk while that rat opened the vehicle door.

He took another photograph of her just before she climbed into the rat's Lexus and salivated, drinking in every nuance every curve right down to her slim ankles.

He didn't like his Princess soiled by other men. He would have to make her pure again for him. His plan was ready. When the time was right, he would make his move.

CHAPTER 24

"Welcome. How are you?" Ross Grenfeld, the Chief Executive Officer of Rigby asked first Stephani, then Richard.

"Well, thank you," they replied in unison.

Grenfeld introduced them to his wife, Sue. The woman was as tall as her husband was, but where he was dark, she was fair.

"Pleased to meet you." Sue leaned forward and air-kissed Stephani on the cheek. "We've been looking forward to this. All the money raised tonight will go directly to those poor homeless people. That tornado demolished everything it touched. Houses, trees, apartment blocks-"

"Dear," interrupted Ross, "they know all of that."

"Yes, yes, I'm sorry. I'm not myself tonight. Melvin, our terrier's gone missing."

"I'm sorry to hear that," Stephani said. She'd rather not have come, but Ross had personally given out the invitations, as Rigby was one of the major event sponsors.

Another couple had entered the ballroom, and Ross introduced his wife to them.

Stephani turned to find a flash going off in her face. Someone was taking photos of Richard and her.

"Don't." Stephani jerked backwards feeling as if that stalker was taking them and she'd find them in her mail the next day. "I don't want my photo taken."

151

"Sorry, ma'am. It's for the Rigby staff newsletter."

"Thanks, buddy. Sorry to cause a problem," Richard said.

"I'll delete the ones I've taken. Didn't mean to cause offense. Next time I'll ask first."

An usher walked Richard and Stephani across the ballroom past clusters of dark suits and ball-gowns to their table. The ceiling above them, festooned with billowing lengths of white silk radiated towards the center where a huge black silk rose hung upside down. Rows of black bows secured the fabric to the corners of the room, where it curtained the walls in white.

When they reached their table with seating for ten, the usher pulled out their chairs. After kisses and handshakes with the other couples, Richard and Stephani sat down.

"My dog Howie went missing when I was in the tenth grade. I spent every spare moment walking the streets for weeks looking for her," Richard said. "Finally, some neighbor had found Howie caught in a rabbit trap down near the river. She must have yelped for days until she'd starved to death. I was so angry that I put signs all over the town, telling people to spring any traps they found or more pets would get killed."

"That must have been awful to find her like that."

"Yeah. They should ban those traps," Richard said.

The band began to play a waltz. A few couples started to dance around the clusters of people talking.

A waiter appeared. "Drinks, sir?"

"Martini for me, and what would you like, Stephani?"

"Do you have Ouzo?"

"No, ma'am."

"Then I'll have the same as Richard." She had to stop drinking that stuff. One and a half bottles a week was far too much. "I'm so excited, Richard. Finally, the multi-layered human hepatic cell sheets using pre-cultured fibroblast monolayers as a feeder layer on a culture dish are doing well. No problems this time with-"

"What a nice surprise to see you here. Hello, Stephani, Richard."

She looked up. "Hi, I didn't know you were coming tonight."

Jack, his black hair parted to one side, smiled as he bent over to kiss her cheek. "West Labs is one of the sponsors, and I was given a couple of tickets because I had record sales last month. In fact, my sales have been consistently high for the last six, so I earned it. Hey, you look lovely in that dress."

"Thank you," Stephani said.

He smiled, shook hands with Richard, and they exchanged small talk.

The waiter brought their drinks.

"You don't mind if I steal her, Richard?"

"Be my guest."

"Would you like to dance, Stephani?"

"I'm not very good," she said as she stood.

"Follow my lead, and you'll do fine." Jack escorted her to the dance floor and took her in his arms. "What have you done to your hair?"

"I needed a change."

"It suits you."

More couples joined them as they circled the dance floor.

"What's this baloney that you can't dance?" he said.

"You make it easy. Did you have lessons?" She was enjoying herself.

"When I was about twenty-two, I wanted to get involved in ballroom dancing in a serious way, but at the time the newspapers were writing about some companies swindling their customers so I didn't."

"I can't think of the name of that tune they're playing, can you?"

"It's a waltz." He smiled.

"Know that. It's…it's from Swan Lake, Tchaikovsky. I'm sure of it."

"Where did you learn such things?"

"I love listening to classical music, and I always wanted to learn to play the piano and finally did after Allan suggested I take it up when we were married."

Jack moved easily and drew her around other couples until they were near the point where they had originally started.

She glanced at Richard and their eyes met. He smiled and winked.

As they danced, she felt the slight pressure of Jack's arm around her waist and his thigh rub against hers. At his quickening breath, she realized just how close they now were.

Stephani eased backwards to create some space between them. Her step faltered and she kicked someone behind her.

"Sorry." She slammed against Jack as they turned and crashed into another couple.

"Whoa. Are you okay?" Jack apologized to the woman.

Stephani drew back and Jack gave her a puzzled look. The music stopped. "See, I'm a klutz."

Another blinding flash startled her. She addressed the photographer. "I told you I don't want my photo taken. You were told to ask."

"Sorry, ma'am."

"I asked him to take a couple of photos. I thought it might be a nice memory of tonight," Jack said.

"You didn't ask me. Just for the record, I don't want to have my photo taken."

He pulled out some bills and gave it to the guy. "Please accept my apologies."

The guy nodded and went in search of other quarry.

"Let me apologize to you first. I've upset you, and it wasn't my intention."

"Accepted."

She didn't want to go into any further details with Jack. "Our first course is on its way, and I'm starving." She wasn't that hungry, but after that photographer taking more photos, she was tense and wanted to get off the dance floor.

"Another dance later on?" Jack asked.

"Thanks for asking, but I'm not sure I want to get up again."

"Wine for you, ma'am?" the sommelier asked as Stephani sat down.

She nodded.

Marcel, seated on the other side of her, started to tell her all about his little hobby that had grown into a multi-million dollar business.

She had finished her entree of crabmeat while still listening to the ins and outs of how the man had turned making and selling computer accessories into a big business, when Richard offered her a reprieve.

"The band's playing again. Dance?" Richard asked.

"No, thanks," she said.

"You're young and only live once. Go on," Marcel said.

Richard winked at her. "Listen to him."

"But that photographer was taking more-"

"Then I'll be sure to wave him away if he comes close." He took her into his arms. "I should have had dancing lessons, but I didn't get around to it."

"You're doing just fine." His steps were jerky, but she didn't mind. "I'm not much of a dancer myself," she said, as she began to relax.

"I spoke to Belinda today. She's coming to stay with me during the school holidays. While she's here, I thought I'd take her for her first visit to the Grand Canyon. Then I want to take her to Disney World for a few days. I would like…would you like to come to Disney World? She's a little older now and…it's just easier with another female." He hesitated and pursed his lips as though considering his words. "Let's rewind on this. I want you to come so that we can spend some time together too. And I've been worrying about how to ask-"

"I'd love to tag along." It was, after all, just to help with his daughter.

More dancers joined the floor. He held her closer. "We'll have a great time."

Every breath drew in the scent of his aftershave and his freshly laundered shirt. The thud, thud of his heartbeat kept pace with hers. His breath fanned her hair as her cheek rested against his jaw.

They were dancing slowly, and when he kissed her earlobe her stomach fluttered. She wouldn't mind staying in his arms all night. *Whoo, girl*, she said to herself. *That's not going to happen.*

"You're doing great." She smiled.

"Shucks…a compliment. I think it's a lie as well. Our dinner's coming."

He led her to their table as waiters served steaming plates of roast duck, fluffy mashed potatoes and honeyed baby vegetables.

"When I told Ross about the latest results, he said we should consider doing a press release."

"It's a bit premature."

"I'd rather be sure and wait 'till all the trial results come in, but he said that if we don't make an announcement soon, then someone else will beat us to it. He found out about a third group doing similar research," Richard said.

"I see what he means. I don't want to be red-faced in front of the media if there are any problems. When I think of how frustrating it was in the early days of this project… You know I came close to giving it up. So much went wrong, and I just didn't see how we were ever going to get there," she said.

"You…giving up? You're kidding me."

She laughed. "I guess you know me."

"Not as much as I'd like to."

She liked Richard, but she wasn't sure if she was ready for that.

Richard finished his meal and said, "Do you mind if leave you? I need to speak with Ross."

"Business tonight?"

"Can't be helped."

The moment he left, her neighbor, Marcel, started talking to her. It was all she could do to stop yawning.

Someone tapped her on the shoulder. She turned. "Jack."

"Dance?"

She couldn't think of a plausible excuse and her neighbor wouldn't stop talking. Who said men can't talk. "Sure."

As Jack led her to the dance floor, she noticed Richard squeeze past a group of people and proceed towards their table. She sighed, wishing that Richard had come back sooner. Thank goodness that annoying photographer had gone.

Jack began to waltz her around the floor. She stared at Richard. Her neighbor had moved closer to Richard and was talking to him.

Richard met her gaze and winked.

"So what do you think, Stephani?"

"Sorry Jack, what was the question?" A couple laughed as they danced by.

"I said…it doesn't matter. You weren't listening." Jack stiffened.

"The music's too loud. Let's move away from the band."

He swept her further down the ballroom. "Can you hear me now?"

"Could you repeat what you said?" She glanced at Richard again and saw that he was watching them.

"Forget it."

She didn't think it was such a big deal.

"No more security problems in your apartment?" he asked.

"There's been a burglary in the apartment below mine," Stephani said.

"When?"

"A couple of days ago."

"You haven't had any more photos or bears, have you?"

"No, but I can't get over that someone was in my apartment while I was in the shower. I still can't get over that intruder knew about my bear and left an identical one in my apartment. It freaks me out."

"Maybe, the guy got lucky."

"You're making a joke of this," Stephani said.

"I'm sorry. I didn't mean it that way."

"I need to freshen up."

"Thanks for the dance." Jack did a sort of little bow with his head.

She grabbed her purse. "Back soon," she said, as she edged by Richard.

When Stephani returned to the ballroom, the band was playing the Macarena. She skirted the crowded floor and made her way back.

"Dance?" She mouthed the word to Richard as she approached their table.

He nodded, excused himself, and then came towards her.

"I'll try anything once," Richard said.

"I'll bet, after having your ear talked off. This is one of the few dances I can do. Allan taught me."

He looked so awkward; the harder he tried, the funnier he looked. She tried hard to stop herself from laughing. Then he fell towards her.

She caught him as he grabbed her shoulder for support.

"I've got two left feet." He straightened and then drew her to him.

A laugh rose in her throat and died as he stared into her eyes. She could drown in those hazel eyes.

***

His smile turned to a snarl. His Princess was leaving with that man; he could hardly bring himself to say his name, Richard.

A woman brushed past him as she walked up the steps to the tall glass entrance doors. "Sorry."

He stood and watched that man take Stephani's hand across the paved plaza to the parking lot. He had to find out where they were going.

"How rude. I did apologize," the woman snapped.

He was rushing towards his van before she had finished speaking. By the time he had strapped on his seatbelt, Richard had pulled out onto the road.

After speeding out of the lot and careening around the corner, he caught up with them but kept his distance. Then he realized that someone else was following them, too.

***

Stephani turned to Richard as he eased into a parking spot outside her apartment block. "Would you like to come up for a nightcap?"

"I thought you'd never ask." He turned off the engine.

Stephani stepped from the air-conditioned car into the hot breeze. "I still haven't gotten used to this constant heat."

"You will." He waited until she unlocked the entrance door and followed her inside.

He stood so close to her that they were almost touching. As they got into the elevator, Richard bent his head towards her. She knew he wanted to kiss her, and she tilted her head towards him.

As the elevator doors began to close, a grey-haired man jumped in. "Just made it."

They moved apart and looked at each other in the mirrored wall of the elevator.

He smiled back at her as he held her gaze that seemed to say, 'I want you'.

"Been to a party?"

"Charity ball," Stephani said. She'd seen the guy a few times in the building, but this was the first time he'd spoken to her.

Richard took her hand in his as they got out. "Keys?"

"I didn't lock it." She opened the front door.

"After what happened with Mr. Ted, you didn't think it was something you should do?"

"Don't tell me. I'll get us some drinks."

He gently put his hands on her shoulders and turned her to face him. "That can wait." He drew her to him.

Her heart thudded. His body pressed against hers. He pushed his fingers through her hair. She longed for his lips to touch hers and when they did, a fire of longing traveled from her head to her toes and settled in her core.

He finally drew away, leaving her lips tingling. She wasn't going to overthink this and spoil it.

He kissed her again running his hands along the curve of her hips.

Her heart upped its beat in time with his when he pulled her against him.

Richard groaned as she melted into him and ground her hips,

wanting more.

She took his hand and led him to the bedroom.

"I don't want to rush you," he said.

"Really!" She kicked off her shoes and turned on the bedside lamp. "Unzip me, please?" She turned around so he could help her out of her dress.

"Well. Maybe, that's a little lie."

"A big whopper."

"You got me there," he whispered into her ear.

She felt a little shy in her bra and panties until he kissed her shoulders and slipped off her bra. He turned her toward him, kissing first one breast, then the other, increasing her longing for him.

"This isn't fair. You're still dressed," she teased.

"Do you want to undress me?"

"With pleasure." She unbuttoned his shirt and pulled it free of his trousers. She slipped it from his arms, feeling his heated skin as she did.

"I thought you were the prettiest girl I'd set eyes on when you presented your approach on cell sheet engineering at the Rigby gathering in L.A."

"That was so long ago. I was a new recruit and married."

"I know. So I never made a pass."

"I don't remember you."

"Will you remember me now?"

He kissed her hungrily, his fingers trailing desire across her flesh.

"You bet," she whispered and threw back the bedcover.

He undid his belt, unzipped his trousers and let them fall, his growing need for her evident.

Richard crushed her to him, trailing more kisses on her neck. "I want all of you."

He eased her onto the bed and scattered kisses across her stomach as she moaned with desire. Richard drew her panties down, going lower.

As Richard drew her to a climax, he called her name.

Afterwards, they lay spent in each other's arms.

"Thanks," Richard said.

"Why?"

"I didn't think I could…"

"It's been a while for me too."

He kissed her shoulder. "I don't want to go home."

"Then don't. You can stay here with me forever."

***

He stared at the live feed in disbelief. The pin camera in his Princess's bedroom disguised behind the beads on the dressmaker's dummy was so he could watch her undress, be close to her and imagine her removing her clothes for him, not see some dirty filthy man have sex with his Princess.

He thumped the desk in anger and jumped from his seat, hot and sweaty with need. He needed to seek relief from his pain. He picked up the car keys, stalked upstairs.

He slammed the front door behind him. He'd find a teenager who'd drunk too much and was looking for a good time. But, he'd give her more than a good time. This was the last time he'd need to do this. Soon his Princess would be his all his. He couldn't wait.

Richard would pay for defiling his Princess. He would pay soon.

CHAPTER 25

"Hey, Jack," Stephani said breathlessly, as she turned off the treadmill and toweled her face. "Sorry about not making it last night. I had to work overtime."

"Hey, you already apologized. When did you get here?" He put down his backpack and leaned over to kiss her, but she shrank back.

"I'm all sweaty." She pushed back a few stray strands of hair that had fallen across her face.

"It doesn't matter to me."

"Don't be silly. I came early because I'm seeing Richard later." There she'd said it. There wasn't anything between Jack and herself, but for some reason it made her feel awkward. "Did you have a good time at the charity ball on Wednesday night?"

"The food was great and I enjoyed our dance. I thought the plan was we'd have coffee after the gym."

"Next time. Okay?" He reminded her of the boy who always tried to sit next to her in the biology tutorials at college and often asked her for a date. He would limp in early carrying a stack of textbooks. It wasn't the shorter leg that put her off, but rather his skewed attitude towards life in general. Not that she knew what Jack's thoughts were on that. He was good-looking enough, but she wasn't attracted to him.

"Look, if you'd rather not, it's okay." He reached for his bag. "I'm going to change."

"See you soon." Stephani started on her abs and after she'd done the circuit, she picked up her towel and headed for the change rooms.

Pumping weights—Jack's angular face grimaced with the effort, his biceps bulging—as she passed by him. "I'm heading for the shower, and I'll see you next time."

"Catch you later," he said between lifts.

The women's lockers were separated from the men's by way of two open entrances that curved right or left depending on whether it was the male or female area. Stephani pulled out her things from the second locker and went through another doorway to the showers. She stepped into a stall, closed the door, stripped off and turned on the water. The hot spray relaxed her muscles as she thought about meeting Richard afterwards.

She toweled off, and from her backpack sitting on the ledge beside her, pulled out her bra and a fresh pair of panties.

What the hell? These weren't hers. These were white lace bikini panties. She put them back and dug around for the ones she knew she'd placed in her pack. Finding her familiar panties gave her some relief, so she pulled them out and put them on the dry shelf.

Maybe, just maybe, they'd been caught up with the other ones she'd packed this morning. Not that she could remember buying them. She pulled out the strange panties. They had a Chanel emblem on the inside. Never had she purchased any item of clothing by that exclusive brand.

A folded sheet of paper fell out. For the longest time, she stared at it in disbelief.

Finally, she reached for the paper, opened it and found a type-written note.

My gift for your sweet ass.

Wear these for me, My Princess.

They are fresh and pure as you soon will be.

"Oh my God." What sick fuck sent her this…this? Her hand trembled as she pushed the note into her pack.

Stephani scrambled into her street clothes fearful that this stalker might be hanging around the gym waiting to pounce.

All dressed, she began to stuff her sports gear into the backpack, but even with the worry of how that note and panties came to be in her bag, she couldn't leave them crumpled up. She pulled them out and quickly folded her black leggings and white top, zipped up the pack and hurried through the entrance with the back of her neck prickling with dread.

By the time she started the Honda, she was trembling all over. She should have told Jenee at the desk or at least someone who managed the place but couldn't summon up the courage to go back inside. That stalker might still be in there. Her gaze flitted from one car to another to see if anyone was in a vehicle watching her.

When did this sick guy get the opportunity to put those things into her pack? Was it a woman when she had been thinking it was a man? Hell, had he or she put their face to the panties first? What made her think of that? Fuck.

She turned off the engine, reached over to the passenger seat, grabbed her backpack, and drew out the message. Rereading it only scared her more.

She wanted to curl up and make herself small so she would…become invisible. She fought the urge as she gulped down the sob that threatened to surface.

Jack, he'd help make sense of this. He was so level-headed. She was inside the health club before she remembered that she had not locked her car.

Jenee glanced up from her cell phone and continued to key in a message to someone as Stephani hurried by her.

Jack waved from the treadmill. "Thought you were leaving?"

"I'm…was but…" Stephani said.

He stopped the machine. "What's wrong? What's happened?"

"I…" She couldn't get the words out.

"Can it wait till I've had a shower?" Jack said.

She nodded, and then blew her nose.

"Meet me at the entrance and then we can talk. Okay?"

She nodded again, and then went out.

Jenee looked up. "Need help?"

She shook her head and Jenee went back to her texting. Stephani paced on the tiled floor at the reception back and forth in agitation. Could she be sure that the stalker had put it into her bag while she was working out and not long before that? She should call the cops. She pulled out Kennelly's card and tapped in the number.

She asked for Kennelly, but was told he wasn't available. Kennelly would call back shortly, she was told.

Jack came over. He'd changed into jeans and a shirt. "How about we go for some strong coffee? You look like you need it." He hitched up his backpack. "Then you can tell me all about what's upset you."

They didn't talk while they walked to the deli next door, and it wasn't until he had ordered and the waitress went away that Jack spoke.

"Come on, spill it. You look so upset."

She pulled out the note from her bag. "This."

"Let me look." Jack stared at it. "Who wrote this?"

"I don't know. Oh, shoot. I forgot…fingerprints. Too late now."

"What's going on here?"

"I've been getting unsigned notes, like this one and photos from…I don't know who. It's freaking me out."

"I see what you mean." He carefully wrapped it in a napkin and handed it back.

The waiter brought their beverages.

"It was in my backpack, and it fell out of some…clothing when I was getting dressed."

"Maybe you picked it up when you were sorting through your sports gear in the change rooms."

"You don't believe me." She grabbed the note. "Jesus, you think I'm being a hysterical female." She jumped up and slung her handbag over her shoulder.

"I'm sorry. I didn't mean it like that."

"So how did you mean it, Jack?"

"Sit down, please. You're all upset."

"Wouldn't you be?" She went to leave.

He rose, and caught her arm as she started for to the entrance. "Come back. I just want to help."

"Yeah. By suggesting I'm overreacting. Who the hell do you think you are?" It had worked when the neighborhood bully tormented her in school. However, it took a while before she had the courage to retaliate. Then he backed down fast.

"I didn't say that. I thought you might have been near someone who had theirs open and picked up some of their stuff by mistake."

"Logical thought, but no." Now, Jack only looked hurt. An ache started at the back of her eyes. She wanted to cry, but tears didn't achieve anything.

"I happen to think you're amazing."

"So you think…oh, sorry." She wanted to vent her anger some more to stop feeling so vulnerable.

"Come, finish your coffee."

She sank onto a chair. "I don't know what I should do, Jack." She started fiddling with the spoon resting on the saucer. "No verbal threats, or attacks or anything like that. It's like some invisible stalker pops up just when I think everything's normal again." She paused and looked at him.

"The policeman asked me if I was under a lot of stress. Can you believe it?" She folded her arms and hunched her shoulders.

He reached across the booth and put his hand on hers. "I believe you. Do you think that when you had that break-in, the intruder could have put the note in your personals drawer then?"

She pulled her hand away. "I'm not a baby. Don't."

He put his hands up. "Fine."

"I'd have seen it when I packed my backpack. It must have been put there today, but how?"

"Those lockers, maybe they aren't that secure. Maybe anyone who really wants to could open one." He shrugged.

"Do you think it could have been a woman rather than a man? I should have taken the option to pay for my own locker."

"I guess it would be hard for a man to slip in unnoticed unless there was no one about."

"Jesus. You think it's a female, don't you?" She heard the opening tune of 'Nothing Compares 2 U' by Sinéad O'Connor on her cell phone and answered the call.

"Hi Steph. Where are you? I thought you were coming over," Richard said.

"Shoot. I'm sorry, I completely forgot. Something's happened. I-"

"Are you okay?"

"I found another note. This one was in my backpack at the health club." Just saying it again ramped up her anxiety.

"What? Jesus, Mary and Joseph. You're not safe."

"I'm okay. Can we talk later?" She ought to have called Richard to let him know, but she had not been thinking straight.

"Are you sure? I can jump in the car and-"

"Jack's with me. Thanks, Richard. Can I call you later?"

"I'll be waiting."

She hung up.

"My guess is that it's some male or female that likes to do this, but won't ever make contact, because that's not what they're after. They just like scaring people. It's your reaction they're after."

She shrugged. "I don't see how they could unless there's a camera in the change rooms?"

"That's not what I meant. Did you tell Jenee?"

"Maybe I should have. The cops will want to know why I didn't," she said.

Her cell phone rang. It was Bill Kennelly.

She told him what had happened.

"I'll meet you at the health club in ten minutes."

"Jack, I've got to go back to meet the cop."

"I'll walk with you."

***

Stephani told Jenee, who appeared to be more concerned about any negative publicity.

She noticed Jack looking at his watch. "Look, you don't need to stay. Thanks for your support. The police should be here soon."

"Sure you're okay?"

She nodded.

Jenee sung out a goodbye to Jack and went to chat with a muscular male working out.

She called Richard. "Hey, can I delete that conversation we had earlier?"

"Sure. What's happening?"

"I'm waiting at the health club for the cops. Could use your company."

"Be there in fifteen," he said.

That same sensation she'd had at the back of her neck started, and she glanced about. A ponytailed boxer type walked to the changing rooms while on his cell. He wasn't taking any notice of her. No one was.

Stephani was going crazy. Whoever had done this was probably long gone. She closed her eyes in an effort to relax. Her thoughts spiraled into that alien childhood again.

"The nice lady will look after you," my mommy says. "You know I have to work. We need the money."

"I don't want to stay, please. Please I'll be a good girl." My mommy has tears in her eyes just like me.

"You're my best girl."

She takes my hand again, walks me down the dirt path, and then hurries me up the front steps. I nearly fall because one step wobbles as I tread on it, but my mommy holds my hand to steady me.

"You want to knock?" My mommy says.

"I don't want to."

My mommy does it. The door opens.

"Hi." My mommy bends down to me. "Say hello."

When I don't speak, my mommy asks me again.

A fat woman smiles without showing her teeth; just sort of spreads her lips across her face but keeps them together. "How are you? Come in and let's meet this big girl of yours." She pushes on the screen door. It squeaks as it opens.

I hold my mommy's hand tighter as we go into a room with so many piles of stuff everywhere that my mommy has trouble getting around it. "Where is the nice lady, Mommy?" I say.

"Hush."

"Set yr'selves down," the fat woman says.

Some cakes are set out on a plate. The fat woman leaves us for a moment. "There's nowhere to sit," I say to my mommy.

"Hush, honey. We can sit here." She moves aside some crumpled clothes to make room for us.

I take a bite out of two of the cakes and put them back, as they are too yucky.

My mommy picks them up and finishes them off. She is always doing that, she doesn't like to see waste, she says now that we are poor we have to be careful.

The woman returns with coffee for my mommy. She and my mommy talk for a while about things. My mommy wants me to have lots of nice food to eat.

My mommy squeezes my hand. "It'll be okay."

Then my mommy gets up from the stained lounge. "Show me which room will be hers?"

The woman leads us down a short hallway and into a small bedroom. A pretty doll is sitting in the middle of the bed. I run over to it. The doll's white dress is so beautiful. I touch the soft lace.

"Take your grubby fingers off. You dirty little...."

Then the woman smiles and I see her yellowed broken teeth.

"Sorry darl'n. I know you'll be careful." She pats my head with her rough hand.

I try to smile back, but I can't because I am going to be alone here for a whole week and I'm scared.

"Bye honey," says my mommy. She starts for the front door.

"Don't leave me here," I cry. "Please, Mommy."

"This nice lady will look after you. I can't be taking you to work with me, honey. This lady will look after you, honey," my mommy says with tears in her eyes. "I promise I will come get you every Friday night, okay?"

"But I don't want to stay here. I don't want to. Don't leave me here, Mommy, please."

"You know I have to go because I have a job now, and I can't take you to work with me."

I don't know what a job is, but it has something to do with getting money. "Please Mommy. No Mommy. I'll be a good girl."

I cling to her dress and she pulls my fingers off of her. I scream and cry 'till my eyes are sore.

The fat woman goes away and leaves me in the living room. She comes and goes a few times. When I stop crying, she stops in front of me.

"Come with me." She has her hands on her hips.

"I don't want to." On her dress, she's got yellow marks under her arms.

She pulls me, and I let myself fall to the floor.

"You devil kid. I'll have to drag you."

I'm about to ask what a devil kid is but she grabs my arm. "I don't want to go," I scream.

I'm screaming so hard that I don't see that we are outside at first. Then she pushes me along a dirt track to some sort of shed.

"The chicken coop is where you'll sleep, kid."

She drags me when I dig my heels in.

She unlocks the door to the pen. "Come on, kid. I'll bet you haven't seen chickens before."

They do make a lot of noise. I nod and forgot about how sad and scared I am, and run in to touch them. They scratch and cluck, and peck in the dirt. Each time I try to touch one, it runs away. I turn to see where the fat woman is. She's closing the gate.

I run hard. "Let me out." I pull at the wire. "Let me out. Let me out."

She turns the key in the lock. "This is where you're sleeping, kid. Now don't cause any trouble, hear?"

I start to cry. Then I scream, "I hate you. You're not my mommy. I want my mommy."

"Shut up, kid. Do you hear?"

The fat woman opens the gate, and slaps me hard on the cheek. It hurts. My mommy never hits me like that. I am so surprised that I stop crying.

"That's more like it," the woman says. "You're only going to be here through the week anyways."

"Stephani Robbins?" Officer Bill Kennelly stood before her. His partner, Zamoloski joined them as she got up.

"I'm sorry?" she said. His voice broke through the visions that had flooded her mind.

"What can I do for you?" he asked.

She pulled out the note and the panties. "I found these in my backpack. I was pulling out my clothes when they slipped out. This is freaking crazy. I don't know how they got there. My bag was in a locker that I locked. No one's supposed to have a key except management."

Kennelly looked up from his notepad where he had written a few notes. "Is it your regular locker?"

"I don't have a regular locker but I did leave my shoes on the floor beside the locker," she said.

"Who's in charge here?" Zamoloski asked her.

Richard came through the entrance doors. "You okay?" he asked Stephani.

She told him everything.

"Kennelly and Zamoloski. Richard Dixon."

"Yeah, I remember from the bear incident."

"I'll get Jenee." She turned to see Jenee hurrying over.

Kennelly flipped his badge and introduced himself and his partner to the trainer.

"Can we go look at the locker that Stephani used?" Zamoloski asked.

"I need to call management before I can let you do that." Jenee placed the call.

After Jenee hung up, she said, "I got the okay, so I'll take you in after I check that there aren't any women in there. Management wants this kept low key."

"I can't promise anything, you understand," Kennelly said.

"Someone from management will be down to speak with you soon."

"Sure," Kennelly said.

Jenee went to the change rooms.

"What do you think you'll find?" Richard asked.

"Can't say 'till we take a looksee," Kennelly said.

"Are you going to take fingerprints?" Stephani asked.

"We will, but don't get your hopes up as any number of people would have used this locker," Zamoloski said.

"All clear," Jenee said.

The four of them tailed her to the female change rooms where the scent of fresh soap permeated the air.

After the locker was opened and found empty, the officer turned to Jenee, "Who would have access to every locker here?"

"Only staff."

"How many master keys?"

"Three. I have one on my key ring and the other two are in the drawer at the desk, and a full set of keys are there too in case one of the customers loses their key."

"Is the desk kept locked?" Zamoloski asked.

"I always lock it."

"Can anyone walk in and access the change rooms? What I mean is…are you on duty at the desk 24/7?" Kennelly asked.

"I'd see, 'cause no matter where I am, it's glass all 'round."

"Show me where the master keys are kept," Kennelly said

Jenee took them out of the female changing rooms to the reception desk.

She moved to the drawer, but before she could put her hand to it, Kennelly spoke. "Don't touch it."

Jenee held out the key for him. Kennelly went over and tried the drawer. "Not unlocked, huh?"

"Well, I'll be damned. I did lock it." Jenee scowled.

"Not this time," Richard said.

"It would mean my job if I didn't. I tell you I did," Jenee said.

"You think someone tampered with the lock?" Stephani asked.

"Let me handle this, Ms. Robbins." Kennelly looked up at the ceiling. "Security cameras?"

"Only in the gym and yoga rooms. The rest don't need any 'cause the one in the gym does the other areas too as it's all glass. None in the change rooms 'cause of privacy."

"I'm going to get someone over to scan the change rooms for concealed cameras. Can you let the owners know?"

"They won't like this. The club closes at 10:00 p.m. Can you come in after that?"

"We need to do this ASAP. Sorry for the disruption ma'am." The cop appeared to be considering something and gave his partner a guarded look. "Stephani Robbins, would you come around first thing in the morning and look through the mug shots? See if you can ID anyone." He closed his notebook.

She knew that look, like she was some hysterical woman who was imagining things. Her posture sank as she exhaled. She feared that scanning through the mug shots would be an exercise in futility, and that no one would take her seriously until something terrible happened.

CHAPTER 26

Stephani flicked on the lights, kicked her heels off and went into the kitchen. "I need a coffee badly."

Richard closed the front door and joined her as she pulled out a jar of olives.

Richard took the lid off. "You still hungry? I'm starving."

"I lost my appetite after I found those panties and note in my gym bag. I don't know why I'm reaching for these. Habit, I guess."

He stabbed an olive with a fork and gently pushed it between her lips. "Something stronger than coffee first."

Stephani sucked in the salty flavor. "Mmm. Like what?"

"Ouzo," he said finally.

"I'll go with that." She pulled out some shot glasses from the kitchen cupboard thinking that a drink to settle her down was just what she needed. "I've got some meatballs and pasta in the freezer. Will that do?"

"Yep. I was expecting to meet you for dinner."

"Sorry about that."

"Thanks. Initially, I was hoping this creep will move on to someone else. I know that's not a nice thing to say. But since all this has happened, I'm watching to see if anyone's following me all the time."

She pulled out the ready-to-go frozen meal and popped it into the microwave.

"It makes me angry that someone's doing this to you." He drew her closer.

"Sometimes I think that I'd want to kill this creep if I got the chance. Then…" He hugged her, then drew back and looked into her eyes. "You okay?"

She wiped her eyes as the microwave dinged. "Dinner's ready."

The phone rang.

"It could be important if someone's calling at this hour."

"Maybe the cops," she said.

Stephani picked up after the third ring, just before the answering machine started.

"Hello?" she said.

"Some bad dude's been watching you. Be careful," the male voice said.

"What?" The line was dead. She dropped the phone. The emotions she'd held in check burst forth and she sobbed on his shoulder.

"What did they say?" he said.

She sank to the sofa. "Sorry about your shirt."

"I don't care about my shirt. It's you I care about," he said. "Please, tell me who it was."

After a moment she spoke. "Some…someone who thinks…a bad dude's been watching me."

"Does he know who?"

"He didn't mention any names."

"Jesus, Mary and Joseph. How did he get your number?"

"My number's supposed to be private. I'm calling Bill Kennelly."

***

After hours of staring at mug shots, Stephani rose.

"Any luck?" Kennelly asked.

"A handful look familiar. But I'm not sure." She looked again at the ones she'd selected and shook her head.

"Thank you for taking the time to come in, Ms. Robbins."

"Who did you show the note to?"

"Jack…Jack Theed and Richard. Only Jack touched it besides me."

"We've dusted the photos for prints and found two different prints. Can you get Mr. Theed to call in as soon as possible?"

"I will. Do you have any leads?"

"Nothing firm. We're interviewing perps that like to take photos of their targets and give them gifts. They were in the mug shots, but you didn't ID any of them. They weren't even on your maybe list."

"I'll go home if there's nothing else." She usually spent her Saturday mornings catching up on laundry.

"If there is, we'll be in touch, Ms. Robbins."

She trudged out the door, dejected. She'd hoped that she'd recognize someone on those files. Then the cops could have arrested and charged the creep. As she walked to her car in the Wal-Mart parking lot, a feeling of unease had her glancing about. Someone was sitting in a white Toyota staring at her. She pulled out her cell and punched in Kennelly's number. Her heart raced.

A woman carrying some shopping bags, climbed in the passenger seat of the Toyota.

She nearly fell as she stepped in a pothole.

"Kennelly."

"I thought someone...it's nothing. Sorry to bother you," she said.

"Call me anytime."

"Thank you." She hurried to her vehicle and climbed in, still sensing that someone was watching. She slammed the door shut and in the process dropped her keys between the middle console and the driver's seat.

Scrambling for her keys, she hit the locking button accidentally and swore. When someone banged on her side window, she screamed and sat up.

"You okay, ma'am?" The male had tattoos down his arms with some showing above the collar of his T-shirt.

Stephani nodded and buzzed down her window just enough so she could hear him clearly.

"At first, I thought you were with that guy who was behind you. But when you got in your vehicle, and you locked the doors, he took off."

"You sure?"

"Yes, ma'am."

She buzzed down her window further. "Can you…describe him?"

"I can't get involved. My missus will think…I'm in enough trouble. Just wanted to see you were okay and didn't need medical attention."

"What the hell?" What made him think she needed help? Did she look sick? He must have seen her head down when she was looking for her keys. She didn't dare get out of her vehicle. "Hey, wait. Come back."

She took a photo of him with her phone as he hurried away. He may have been the stalker and just wanted to interact with her. She buzzed up the window as a scream rose in her throat, and she gritted her teeth to stop it.

Where had he gone? He'd just disappeared.

The hot, dry air sucked the breath from her lungs, Stephani turned on the air conditioning. She gulped some water from the bottle she had in her bag and called Kennelly telling him what had just happened.

"Send me the photo."

She attached the photo she'd just taken. It wasn't much of a picture with the back view of a man walking away, but it was better than nothing.

Kennelly called her. "There's little to help us ID him. You're taking his word that someone was following you."

"I got a creepy feeling when I left the local precinct. I turned around a couple of times but didn't see anyone following me."

That sounded a bit like a fantasy story, and she guessed he

wouldn't buy that. "This might help ID him. He had tattoos up his arms & chest."

"Your bystander or the perp?" Kennelly asked.

"The bystander. Well, it could be the perp."

"Come in and we'll try to recreate his face."

She should have parked closer to the local precinct, but she planned to do some shopping in Wal-Mart afterwards. Her Saturday morning shopping would have to wait. Rather than walk again, she drove and parked outside the local police station.

CHAPTER 27

The phone rang, and Stephani put down her empty glass and stumbled toward the sound.

"Hey. Do you want to catch a movie tonight?" Richard said.

She stared at the handset, and suppressed a sob that threatened to burst from her.

"Is that you, Steph?"

He sounded concerned. She took a deep breath that did nothing to clear her head, but only made it spin more. Then she slid to the floor, "I'm…can't go."

"What's wrong? Are you sick?"

The ground appeared to be rising to meet her. She pressed the palm of her hand to her forehead. "Yes, sick. Sorry."

Stephani hung up. She couldn't do the relationship thing over again and lose another partner.

***

Someone buzzed the intercom.

Stephani pushed herself into a sitting position. The living room spun, and she closed her eyes. She started to slip lower, so she crawled to the wall and leaned against it.

The sound was louder now. She still couldn't focus properly. She tried to stand, but that made the walls move, and she pressed against the one behind her, ignoring the noise. However, it kept right on going.

"Ohh," she groaned, crawled to the intercom and eased up the wall. She spoke into the microphone. "Who…is it?" The words came out more slurred than she intended.

"It's Richard. Let me in."

"Go away…please." Stephani did not want him to see her like this.

"I'm going to lean on this buzzer 'till you open the door."

"Son-of-a-biiiitch." Even the curse was slurred.

"What did you say?"

"Can't see you." Stephani rubbed her temples, and tried to stop them pounding. "Go away."

"What's wrong? I'm going to buzz every tenant if you don't let me in."

"Oh…if you mus…" The living room wasn't that far away. Surely, she could reach it. Stephani slid downwards and grabbed the empty bottle of Ouzo, then crawled towards the sofa. Her head was fuzzy again.

Stephani tried hard to remember what she was doing here. Saw the bottle in her hand and knew. She hid the bottle under the cushion as Richard entered.

"What's wrong? Are you okay?"

Tears started down her face. She hated when that occurred in front of someone, but they wouldn't stop now. She had no control.

"What's happened?" He knelt down and took her in his arms. "You're drunk. I can smell it on you. How'd you get like this?"

Stephani wished she could just vanish. Anything would have been better than to have him find her like this. "Sorry." Another sob rose from somewhere inside her.

He pulled back. "Where are your tissues?"

"Kitchen."

"I might get us some coffee going."

While he was gone, she rested her cheek on the sofa cushion and closed her eyes as the tears continued. Her head was spinning again. A reason for the state she was in was what Stephani needed, but her head was too fuzzy to concoct a lie.

He returned with a box of tissues. "Here."

He retreated to the kitchen, and then came back with two steaming mugs. "Drink this."

She sipped her coffee in silence.

He sat down at the opposite end of the sofa eyeing her. "Now you'd better tell me what this is all about. I don't think you're the type to get yourself into this state except for a good reason."

Stephani shrugged...didn't want to talk...to think, but each sip of coffee drew her back. She was that type since....

"And don't tell me you haven't been drinking. I had an alcoholic father, and I knew from the moment he entered the house if he'd been on a binge or not. I can smell it a mile off."

"Nothing really."

"I don't believe that. So what's bothering you?"

She stared at the floor, wishing it would swallow her up so she didn't have to deal with his questions nor why she was doing this.

The faucet in the kitchen dripped…dripped…dripped.

He went into the kitchen and turned it off.

"Come on. It can't be that bad, can it?" He sat closer to her this time. What's all this about?" He pulled out the bottle from under the cushion.

Her stomach churned. She bolted to the bathroom and vomited into the porcelain bowl. After rinsing her mouth with mouthwash, and splashing cold water on her face, she reemerged. "I'm sorry."

He sighed. "Stop apologizing."

She sunk onto the sofa. Fresh tears surfaced.

"You'd better tell me what's happened?"

"I can't."

He put his arm around her shoulders. "Tell me. I'm not here to judge. Let me help you."

"I'm beyond help."

He rubbed her shoulder. "We're friends, aren't we? Don't shut me out."

Richard wouldn't like her when she explained it all. Would he even want to know her afterwards? "It's about…my family."

"I won't judge."

She stared at the floor as she spoke, wishing that she could disappear. "If I'd organized to get my car serviced instead of ignoring the reminder message because I was too busy, I would still have

Allan, and Henry would be enjoying his childhood."

"What do you mean?"

Stephani told him, about her car not starting; how she'd meant to have it serviced the week before but had not gotten around to it; how she called Allan, and about how devastated and guilty she had been when told of the fatal accident involving Allan when they were on their way to pick her up from the health club. How her mother always brought the subject up and how hard it was to keep explaining it nearly every time she saw her. "It's killing me."

"It wasn't your fault. Whatever you do, don't crucify yourself. How were you to know that a single call would result in your husband's death and your son in a coma? It was an accident, an unfortunate one, and nothing or no one can change that. Did you plan it?"

"What?" The question caught her off guard.

"I said did you plan their deaths?"

"Are you mad? I loved them. They were my life." Saying the words aloud was so crushing that she found it hard to breathe.

"There's your answer."

It was better than hurting so much that she couldn't endure it. "You don't know what it's like to lose the two people that meant the world to you."

"What else?"

"I'm freaking out about that stalker. What is he going to do next? When I'm driving home, I'm thinking…has he been in my apartment again? What nasty surprises will I find when I come home? Am I safe anywhere? On top of that, Zamoloski or was it Kennelly, I don't remember, suggested that I could have hired a photographer to take those photos and that I could be planting those things. I guess that started me drinking more."

"Have you seen anyone?"

"I thought I saw someone watching me yesterday when I went for my run. Then I realized they were waiting for their dog to do...."

"Oh, dog poop. But I meant a shrink."

"I went to one in L.A. twice."

"A little therapy can't hurt. It's better than drinking yourself into oblivion."

"I'm not in a state. I can manage."

"I'm only trying to help. I see that you don't want that. Then I'll be going."

He started for the door, and then turned. "Jesus," he said softly. "What if I tuck you into bed, and you can sleep it off. And I'll see you at work tomorrow."

"I'm fine," she said.

"Didn't look like it earlier. Still...you're not so bad now."

"The cops rang. Said they might have a lead and would I be able to come in Monday morning to have a look at some mug shots."

"I'll let Ross know. Put off the meeting 'till later. Do you want me to come with you?"

"I think I can handle this."

"It doesn't look like it to me."

"Don't patronize me."

CHAPTER 28

Using a laser-capture microscope Richard dissected a cell population and placed it on a glass slide. He stared at the image on the computer-generated picture. "Huh?"

After a few moments, he pushed down his mask and whooped for joy. "I think we've got something here. You checked the growth of the sample?"

His enthusiasm was infectious. Yesterday's incident with that bystander who'd knocked on her car window pushed to the back of her mind for the moment. "Double checked it." Stephani grinned as she sat at the bench in Laboratory 1. "The contamination problem we had with the last tests has finally been eliminated."

"It's been a long time coming," Fred said as he joined them.

Melissa stopped the robot injecting the media into the test tubes, pushed down her mask and came over. "Wow. Now you'll both be rich."

"Don't start that again," Stephani said, as she rolled her eyes. "I'd have been doing this anyway. This is my life."

"Oh, come on," the brunette said. "What I wouldn't do to be in your shoes."

"Oh, sure. I'm so lucky that my husband…." Stephani stopped herself short. She was trying to move on from the loss of Allan, and Henry still in a coma after five months.

However, her problems wouldn't be buried so easily. How would

Melissa like to have a mother who loved her less than her sister? How would she like it if this mother had Alzheimer's? She turned from her co-worker and tried to focus on the desert landscape outside the window so Melissa wouldn't see how angry she was.

"Sorry, I didn't mean it like that," Melissa said.

"You're right. I'm out of line." She shouldn't bring her problems to work. It was unprofessional.

Nina opened the connecting door to Laboratory 2 and wheeled in a trolley of a dozen culture flasks that she'd retrieved from the bioreactor.

"Well, I still think we should all go out and celebrate," Melissa said.

"What is to celebrate?"

"Nina, you're behind the times. The last round of tests was a success," Melissa said.

Stephani shrugged. "The tissue growth is promising. I'm not convinced yet. I want to repeat the test a dozen times to make sure the result will be identical. You know as well as I do that if the tissue keeps growing at a rapid rate, it's of no use to us."

"That is good," Nina said, as she came over and shook Richard's hand.

Then she turned to Stephani and hugged her. "Very good," she said again.

"Thank you," Stephani said. But what happened yesterday shadowed it. The identify kit software helped recreate that bystander. Was he the one who'd been harassing her? Kennelly had entered the bystander's face on the department computers, but there had not been a match. It only meant that this guy had no prior record,

Kennelly said. She hoped that Kennelly could come up with some answers instead of more questions.

The phone rang in Richard's office. He limped over to answer it, groaning as he went.

"How's the leg?" Stephani asked.

"No good. I need a new one. I'm going to the physiotherapist this afternoon," he said just before he opened the door.

Richard returned a few minutes later and spoke to Stephani. "That was Jack Theed. He invited me to go hiking with him on Saturday."

"What about your torn thigh muscle?"

"Don't worry. There's no way I'd consider it, and I've got plans on Saturday for us."

"Oh. Now what might they be?" she said.

"I've booked Angelo's Steak and Ribs if it's okay with you."

"Great. Now my phone's ringing." She went to answer the call.

"Hi, Officer Bill Kennelly, here. We sent the photos to forensics, and I got the report back this morning with the digital footprint, the type and model of the camera."

"You can do that?"

"Yes. Just to rule you out, what make and model camera do you own?"

"So you still think that I'm doing this, for some deranged reason, to draw attention to myself," she replied, upset. She let out a sigh when the officer assured her otherwise. "I'll bring in my camera tomorrow."

CHAPTER 29

Before the heat had permeated and sapped the energy from every living thing, in the cool of the new day, the Saturday Mesa flea market bustled with people buying trinkets, handmade goods, cheap clothing, and produce. As Stephani walked with Dionne, she discreetly unbuttoned the top button on her tan three-quarter pants as she'd eaten too much breakfast. Her sister insisted on serving her the grand slam breakfast of two easy-over eggs, hash browns, toast and bacon. Iantha was always trying to fatten her up.

"Look, Auntie Steph. Aren't they pretty?" Dionne, in pink three-quarter leggings and T-shirt, pointed to rows of stacked colorful Mexican baskets.

"Let's buy the puppy first and then get something for him to sleep in later." Stephani kept walking. Iantha and Theo had wanted to come too after she told them about the latest incident. She'd be damned if she'd let some creep stop her from being normal. Although, last night she'd let her uneasiness build and she'd nearly cancelled. She fueled the anger by cussing the creep to give her courage and it had worked.

"Joe B. Dodo. I love all his songs." Dionne stared dreamily at the memorabilia of caps, pens, T-shirts, mugs, pins, glasses and other items.

Stephani had never heard of the singer. Today's children grew up too fast. She was nine-and-a-half and pop stars already mesmerized her. "Aren't we here to get you a new dog for your birthday? I agreed with your mom that we wouldn't come home with anything else."

"But I need a new T-shirt," her niece said, touching the fabric.

How her niece had sweet-talked Iantha into this, she would never know, especially with all the pets Dionne already had. "Let's keep going."

They edged through the crowd to a stall with colorful-painted wooden Hopi kachina dolls. Some wore elaborate, dyed, feather headdresses, others had masks and leather fringed clothing.

"You should get one," Dionne said.

Stephani reached for one at the back of the table, with an unusual carved mask and a colorful headdress of painted bone and leather. A white band was woven into the border of the red kilt. "Look at the detail. That must have taken hours of work." She turned to the woman operating the stall. "This one's not priced."

The Hopi Native American with hair pulled back in a ponytail frowned. "It ain't for sale."

The woman scolded a teenage version of herself as she put it under the counter.

Stephani turned to go, but the woman touched her arm with a calloused hand and then withdrew as if stung.

The Navajo's lips creased into a hesitant smile. "Please choose another. I will give you good price."

She shook her head. "That's the one I like."

"Sorry. It's for someone."

"Special medicine," her teenage daughter said.

"Go help the customers before they go away," the woman said to her daughter.

Someone called Stephani's name. She turned and waved when she saw Jack. "Hey, what are you doing here?" He was casually dressed, like her, in shorts and T-shirt.

He edged around a family and came striding towards her. "Hey. I was going to ask the same question."

"This is Dionne, my niece."

"I'm Jack. We work out at the health club together."

"Then you're not her boyfriend?"

"This one's got some great carving," the woman held up another doll.

"No thanks." Her cheeks flamed. She hated that she could blush like some teenager even now. "We're friends."

His lips turned up in an amused smile.

"She could do with one. She's lonely and-"

"Dionne, stop it," Stephani interrupted. "Out of the mouths of babes." What had made her niece say such a thing?

Someone pushed past them and Stephani waited until they were gone before she spoke. "So what are you doing here?"

"Getting a bed for my dog."

"The stand's that way." Dionne pointed in the direction they had just come from. "We're buying a puppy today."

"Thanks for the tip. Do you need help picking one?"

Dionne shook her head. "I want a Jack something."

"Just like my name. I think it's a Jack Russell. Sounds like a good choice," he said. "My spaniel is ten weeks old today. If you like, you can come around and see her one day."

"Can we, Aunt Steph?"

"Sure we can."

"See you on Tuesday night at the health club, Stephani?"

"I'll be there."

Stephani and her niece meandered past shoppers. The sound of yapping puppies grew louder as they got closer.

Her niece kneeled to gaze into a cage with four puppies: their round bodies too big for their small unsteady limbs. Some tumbled repeatedly, some ate puppy biscuits and others were curled up asleep on shredded paper. "This one, this one, Auntie Steph!" She pointed to a tan-colored puppy that was asleep in the middle of the melee of little bodies wrestling. "I love him. He's so cute."

"Are you sure?"

"See…he's awake now and wagging his tail. He likes me. I'm going to call him Milo."

They waited while the stall owner served another customer. Finally, he plodded over to them.

"I want him, please?" Dionne said.

"He's a she," the man said.

"I'll still call her Milo."

"You'll need a collar, lead, puppy vitamins, and squeaky toy. They love the toys, ya know." The man scratched his neck.

"Where do the puppies come from? Are they registered?" Stephani asked.

"Local registered breeders, ma'am. Ones I sell don't have full certification 'cause they can't be show dogs. They're pure breeds and are six weeks old. Here's the papers." He had the documents in plastic sleeves.

"We're going to need the extras as well," Stephani said.

Dionne picked up the box that held Milo while she paid and picked up the bag of goods.

As they walked past the stall selling Hopi kachina dolls, the Native American called out to Stephani. "Come, please," she waved them over.

The woman held out the doll that Stephani had admired before. "Hopi doll is powerful spirit. You need this doll to protect you." The woman touched her arm. "You are in danger. Trust no one. One that dances with the bad spirits is waiting for you."

Stephani backed into someone behind her. "Sorry," she said to the woman. Convinced that the seller was trying to make another sale, she said, "You're talking in riddles. I don't want the doll anymore." Did this woman mean the stalker? A sliver of unease pierced her thoughts.

"Please. The one that waits is cloaked and hunts in the shadows. You will not know of their black heart until it's too late. You must put it beside your bed to keep bad spirits away."

Oh, she didn't like the sound of that. She was already on edge after everything that had happened. "How do you know this?"

"This gift was passed down from my great grandmother, to my mother and now to me."

"You're just trying to scare me. Didn't you make it for a friend?"

"I can make her another. You need it now."

"My spirit guide sent me a sign. The spirit drew you to that doll. No one else picked it up today. When we touched, I felt your life force and I received a vision of a man with a black heart in the shadows just behind you. You must protect yourself."

"I…I don't know."

"You must take it."

"How much?" Stephani pulled out her purse.

The seller shook her head. "Please, it's a gift. The spirits would be angry if I take money for this doll."

Dionne took the doll that was now in a paper bag and put it beside the puppy.

"Thank you. Let's go." She took Dionne's hand.

They negotiated past people, stalls selling T-shirts, and tables of moccasins and leather goods.

"Can we get a basket?" Dionne said.

"Let's go home."

"Please."

"Okay." Now she had a creepy feeling that someone was watching her. Maybe, it was that warning from that Native American woman.

Stephani, loaded up with their purchases, struggled along while her niece carried Milo.

They had not gone far when they saw Jack again.

"Let me help you." He took one of the bags. "Isn't he cute?"

"She," Dionne said, as she stopped to admire a bead necklace.

"Isn't that sooo pretty?"

"How about I buy it for you?" Jack said.

"I can't let you do that." Stephani paid for the necklace.

"Thanks, Aunt Steph. You're the best Auntie in the world."

"No more sweet-talking, please. I'm going broke fast."

They headed back to the parking lot through the crush of people.

After they had loaded everything into the car, Jack said, "Now, you will look after her, won't you? It's important to spend time with her. She'll be lonely, otherwise."

"Dionne, where's the doll that woman gave us? I can't seem to find it," Stephani said, as she searched through the shopping bags.

"Oh. I remember now, I put it down when I was looking at the beads. Sorry."

Jack produced the paper bag from his carryall. "I saw you buy it. When you left the jewelry stall and the bag was amongst the jewelry, I was sure it was yours and took it."

"Thanks so much, Jack. See you at the health club."

"Sure thing."

***

After Stephani had left her camera with Kennelly so they could ensure that she hadn't been taking the photos herself, she drove to the hospital and went inside to see her son.

She sat at Henry's bedside. The ventilator helped him breathe, and a stomach feeder tube sustained him. "Henry, I've got a new story I'm going to read to you today. It's Winnie the Pooh. I hope you like it."

Henry didn't move except for his chest rising and falling.

She opened the book, and a nurse came in.

"Mrs. Robbins, the doctor would like to speak with you. If you could make an appointment, please. Here's the number."

"What's this about?"

"It's about your son's continuing treatment."

"I'm not allowing them to turn off his ventilator. I won't be signing any release forms."

"I'm not sure why the doctor needs to speak with you. Please don't be upset." She stroked her son's cheek. "Mommy's here, my dear. Can you hear me? I won't let them turn anything off. I love you."

CHAPTER 30

Stephani browsed the racks of dresses in the Nordstrom department store. Finally, she pulled out one dress and then another and carried them towards the change rooms.

Princie watched as she paused to collect a tag from the attendant and went in. He hoped she would re-emerge wearing one of those dresses. He stopped and pretended to admire some lingerie.

When he saw her standing in a slinky number, in front of the mirror inside the entrance to the change rooms, his breath caught. The thin material stretched across her flat stomach, hips and the soft fullness of her breasts. Even from this distance, he could see the outline of her nipples. In the few moments it took her to turn this way and that, he felt himself grow. She would be indecent in that dress and every man would want her. He hoped she wouldn't buy it.

He couldn't wait to see what she would try on next.

When she appeared, he gasped with delight at the silk number that clung to her curves without revealing too much cleavage.

A big-breasted woman glared at him. "What are you doing?"

He'd guessed she must be with security by the purposeful way she marched towards him. By now, a few women and men were staring at him. He backed into a clothing rack. Clothes swayed and some fell as he edged away.

"Are you buying those?" the security woman asked.

"We don't need your kind of filth here!" a grey-haired woman said.

Princie looked down at his hands and saw he was clutching a red lace pair of knickers. A flush of heat rushed to his face. He turned away from the accusing eyes and thrust them onto the nearest rack.

A dark-haired sales assistant rounded on him, her hands on hips. "If you aren't going to buy those…what are you doing here?"

"I wanted them for my wife but need to check her size first."

He hurried off without a backward glance, his thoughts centered on Stephani in that dress. But he had to have it. He turned and slammed into a chrome tree of belts.

The tree tittered and he grabbed for it, but missed. Belts of all styles and sizes scattered across the tiled floor. He ran headlong into a shopper and her shopping bags fell emptying their contents.

The big-breasted woman scowled. "What the hell-"

Heart hammering, he sped to the escalator, pushed past a couple, and rushed down the escalator. He pulled out his asthma atomizer to ease his wheezing. In the men's clothing section, he paused to allow his breath to return to normal. He had to find out if she'd bought that dress. He grabbed a tan jacket, and slipped it on. The sleeves covered his hands, so he rolled the fabric up. Then he tucked in the price tag. He grabbed a pair of sunglasses and put them on too. This would make him look different enough so that the sales assistant would not notice him right away. He caught the elevator to the floor above.

When the doors opened, he skirted the women's clothing department, well away from that sales assistant and the security woman, and loitered in the shoe section when he saw Stephani at the sales counter.

Another assistant was wrapping tissue paper around the dress.

When the girl at the register lifted the folded dress to slip it into a bag, he could see she'd chosen the soft flowing number. He sighed with relief.

After Stephani left, he waited ten minutes or so before he approached the counter where another assistant was rehanging the discarded clothes on a rack.

"That dress." He cleared his throat. He'd never done this before, but he had to have it. "Can I buy it?"

She smiled and calmly said, "Sure. Want to try it on, sir? But you'll have to take it to the men's department. We can't allow men in these change rooms. You understand, don't you?"

He wiped his clammy palms on his trousers. "It's for my girlfriend. Tried it on yesterday, she did."

She held it up. "You sure it was this one, sir? There's so many that are similar. Plus, the one she's tried could've been another size."

"This is the one!"

"Oh. You know there's an alteration service in the mall. Your jacket-"

"Just wrap it up... How much?" He turned up the dangling sleeves from his hands again. He hated being reminded just how insignificant he was.

"Okay, okay." She glanced at the tag, then told him the price.

It was more than he had on him in ready cash at that moment. "Just hold it for me. I need to withdraw some more money."

"We take credit cards, sir."

"I'll be back." Princie had only walked a few steps when his desire overtook his hesitation. He returned to see the dress being carried away. "I want that dress."

The dark-haired assistant glared at him. "You!"

He removed the sunglasses and pulled out his card. The disguise had not worked on this one. "I want to buy it for my girlfriend." He worried about having this transaction on record here, but the need to have that dress eclipsed this. When the sale was completed, he hurried to the escalator.

On the floor below, he discarded the jacket together with the sunglasses onto a table of shirts. Let them worry about where it should go. He'd had enough of this place. By the time he had left the store, he was shaking with nerves. He wanted to get home, feel that dress and imagine her in it.

***

Princie parked his van at the curb and went past the kids playing handball in the empty lot he used as a shortcut to his place in a small area of a crumbling building. He unlocked the front door of the disused office that he had turned into living quarters for himself, stepped inside and quickly closed it behind him. The rent was dirt-cheap, and it was rare that anyone ever rang the bell. The only ones were collection agencies chasing unpaid bills from the last tenant.

Down the dingy corridor he went, past the kitchen, a single stained basin with a faucet than never stopped dripping, a few cupboards with missing doors, a gas stove, and then into his bedroom. He sat on the sagging blanket strewn bed, and with hands that trembled with desire, he unwrapped that dress. He laid it out on the bed and began to fondle it. When he reached a crescendo of arousal, he shed his clothes, and lay beside it masturbating.

CHAPTER 31

"How's my hair look? I'm not sure if this style suits me," Stephani asked when she walked into the hotel room.

"Great," Richard said.

"Kennelly called me while I was at the hairdresser's. He told me that my camera is the same make and model as the one that took the photos."

"They can tell the make and model of the camera that took the photos? But even if you have the same camera, it still doesn't mean that you took them."

"Yup. I'm fed up with those cops accusing me of trying to get attention."

"What's that cop's number? I'll set him straight."

'I don't know if that's going to help. Let's focus on this press conference." She'd tried to explain to Ross it was too soon, as had Richard, but Ross wouldn't listen and went ahead and called it. Now they were stuck with the situation.

"Yeah, this should have been scheduled for three to four months' time. When Ross gets something into his head, you can't talk him out of it."

Stephani reached over from the lounge chair and picked up the newspaper lying on the coffee table. "Look what they're writing about you, Richard."

The press downstairs in the conference room would be waiting for their appearance. "Was this what you told them? The project has taken you two years?"

He picked up the paper. "What a load of horseshit. Any fool would know it takes much longer than that to see any research project to its conclusion, or at least near conclusion. I would never have said that. Nor this," he pointed to the next paragraph. "Can't wait to rake in the millions. I ought to sue."

He threw down the newspaper and tapped in a number on his cell phone. "Hello, Ross. Tell the organizers not to let in any reporters from that Arizona rag that printed all that rubbish about me today." He paused to listen to Ross's reply. "Yes, we're coming down in a few minutes. Everything ready?" He winked at Stephani. "Yep, she's coming too and she looks great. Yep. Not like a scientist, but a movie star." He put down the phone. "You're looking gorgeous."

Stephani slipped on her dark blue stilettos, and smoothed the teal-blue pencil skirt as she stood. "Oh, come on. Looking for brownie points, are you? Anyway, they'll just have to take me as I am."

"I'll take you, anytime."

She laughed. "Let me fix your tie." She reached up on tiptoe. "There, that's better. Has Ross said anything about our…keeping company?"

"He wouldn't dare say a word. We're worth too much money to him." He caught her hands in his, bent his head and kissed her. "Hey, good kisser," he said.

She laughed again as he held her. "I've taken a course in the art of kissing."

"And I've done a course in…the art of the bedroom tango," he threaded his fingers into her soft, thick black hair.

"And I've done a course in…oh, I can't top that one. Wait, wait…belly dancing. You know I'll have to fix my hair again now."

"You look so sexy with your hair mussed up like that. I think I might just make them wait a while." He bent his head to kiss her again when his cell phone started playing Bruce Springsteen's "Dancing in the Dark."

"What now?" Richard picked it up. "No…no. It wasn't me." He listened and his face went pale. "How could they? I can't believe it." He sank onto the ottoman beside her. "This can't be true." He rubbed his temples. "Have they…Well, tell them to get on with it. The sons-of-bitches have got to be dealt with." He slammed the phone onto the side table.

"What's happened?" Stephani asked.

"That was Ross. He said that there's another company that has announced as of today that their research has been successful, and they'll be going into testing phase at the beginning of next month."

Stephani sank down beside him, shocked. "Jesus. We'll have to fast track the trials on the mice. It's not my preferred option."

"Nor mine. Too easy to miss something and run foul of the FDA requirements," he said.

"Do they have anything stronger than soda pop in this place?"

"We've got a meeting. Let's wait until after."

"Okay, just let me splash some water on my face."

On autopilot, Stephani applied lipstick and then kissed a tissue to blot the excess while her thoughts raced on. She and the other staff would have to work weekends to get this launched ahead of time. Then she pulled out a hip flask and took one gulp and then another. The liquor slipped down so easily.

She joined Richard, and they went to the elevator together.

They stepped from the elevator into a blinding sea of flashbulbs.

"When do you expect to release the product for consumers?" a reporter asked.

"No comment."

"Is this your girlfriend?"

"Yes."

That surprised her to hear him acknowledge this.

"When's the wedding?"

"We're here to talk about our clinical trials, not personal stuff. Get out of my face. Just get that piranha away from me before I punch him," Richard said to the security guard.

"Where's the other scientist? That Stephani Robbins dame?"

"I'm Stephani Robbins." She grinned.

"You've been drinking," Richard whispered.

Stephani ignored Richard's comment. He couldn't be sure, and she wasn't telling.

"What deal did you both cut with Rigby Research on the profits from the groundbreaking formula to grow harvested breast tissue?"

"No comment."

A group of security guards kept the media at bay.

"See you all inside," Richard said.

"Oh, come on. You stand to make billions worldwide. Give us an estimate."

"No comment!" He snapped.

They were ushered through the thronging crowded foyer and into the conference room.

CHAPTER 32

Stephani walked the endless corridor of the hospital to Doctor Talia Cowan's room. Each step brought her closer to this confrontation with muscles bunched so tightly that everything ached. She'd left work early after receiving a call from Henry's doctor.

She knocked.

The door swung open. "Come in," Talia said.

"Please take a seat." The doctor went around and sat at her desk. "Have you read through our reports on Henry?"

Stephani looked at the wad of printed papers on the desk and sucked in a breath. She guessed these were a second copy in case she said that she had not received the originals. On top was a form with a pencil cross where the guardian or parent had to sign. "I'm not switching off the ventilator."

"I know how hard this is for you."

"No, you don't. He's all I have left."

"There is no brain activity. It would be a kindness. You can't want him to be a vegetable. There has not been any change to his condition since he was transferred to our facility. In fact, his condition has deteriorated."

"I've read that there are occasions where someone in a coma wakes up."

"I've known of only two patients that have woken from a coma—none with the extensive brain damage that Henry has."

214

"I'm not signing anything." She brushed away the tears as they surfaced.

"Would it ease your mind if I solicited a second opinion on his condition?"

"Nothing will. I don't want some other doctor's opinion. I'm not signing away Henry's chance of life."

"As you wish." The doctor put her pen down.

CHAPTER 33

Richard paid for the shirt and walked out of Macy's toward the stairs with his purchases. He liked to come early before the Saturday morning crowds, especially with sales in nearly every store. He saw Nina having a coffee with Vassily and went over. Nina had a few shopping bags at her feet.

"Hi. Vassily." He turned to Nina. "Giving your credit card a serious workout?"

"We got a few things at the sales."

"Join us?" Vassily moved his chair to allow Richard space.

"Sorry. I've got to get home. Mom's expecting me to take her to the hairdresser."

"How did the press conference go?" Vassily asked.

"Nina didn't tell you? It went great."

"See you on Monday, Nina and see you later, Vassily."

Richard took the elevator down to the parking lot. He selected Stephani's number in his cell and pressed dial. "Hi, Stephani."

"Hey, Richard. I'm ready."

"I've got to pick mom up from the hairdresser's and take her home. I'll be at your place in about an hour."

"I'll be waiting. I'm excited about going to my first Sun Devils game."

"I've been waiting all my life." For you…he nearly said. He'd not been this excited since he'd landed the job at Rigby.

"Huh?"

"See you soon," he said.

The parking lot was full now and he was glad he preferred to shop early. He popped the trunk, dropped in his purchases, climbed in and started the ignition.

A woman screamed. "Help. Stop, thief."

He saw the robber running away with the woman's handbag. He leapt from his Lexus and gave chase to the stairwell and opened the door when the ground trembled with a deafening explosion. He turned, ears ringing, to see flames leaping from his vehicle.

He raced towards it as screams rent the air. The heat was too intense, and he couldn't get close. Families were running in all directions. Children were crying.

His heart galloped as he stood watching. He could have been inside the Lexus. He took deep breaths to get his racing heart under control.

Drivers backed out. Cars collided.

"That's my new car," a short-man shouted. Richard guessed it was the vehicle next to his as he sank to the concrete floor.

Two security guards ran towards Richard.

The woman who had been robbed shouted to the guard. "Where were you when all this happened? My bag's been stolen."

"I'm sorry about that, ma'am. We'll check the cameras. Give me your details and I'll get back to you. Whose vehicle is that?"

"It's mine," he said.

***

He flat palmed the steering wheel. That interloper Dixon, who'd moved on his Princess, should have died in the explosion. Dixon had to die. Now he'd have to find another way to kill him.

He'd been careful to change from the woman's garb in the camera-less stairwell, go down to the lower level, let himself out and walk to his van carrying a shopping bag with the discarded disguise.

He eased from his parking space and drove away. Frustration built and built inside him as he entered the roadway in search of another young girl to kill to ease his pain.

***

Stephani's cell rang. "Hi, it's Richard." His breathing was ragged and labored.

"Richard. What's wrong? What's going on?"

"I won't be able to go to the game." He paused to catch his breath. "I just narrowly escaped being blown up by a car bomb."

"Wait. A car bomb?" She couldn't have actually heard what she thought she just heard.

"Yes, someone planted a bomb in my car. I'm lucky to be alive. If I hadn't gotten out of my car to help a woman whose bag had been stolen, I'd be dead. This happened in the shopping mall parking lot."

"Jesus. You sure you're okay?" Her heart seemed to beat out of her chest at the thought of losing him.

"Yes, thankfully."

"Do you want me to come over?" Stephani wanted to rush right over to be with him.

"A policeman is driving me home and I have to break the news to my mother. She's going to be pretty shaken up by it."

"You take care of yourself and make sure to call me if you need anything."

"I will. Thank you, Stephani."

"Richard?"

"Yes?"

She wanted to say "I love you," but hesitated. "I'm here if you need anything," she said.

"I appreciate that more than you know." He said goodbye and hung up.

She pressed her eyelids together and tried to shake the image of him being blown apart. What more could happen to her now?

CHAPTER 34

Dionne bent over the rabbit enclosure and tried to catch one. They hopped this way and that evading grasping little hands as children milled around the enclosure in the Arizona State Fairgrounds. Squeals of delight and excited young voices filled the area as they touched and patted the soft furry animals, while their parents stood waiting.

Stephani stood with the parents, thankful that Dionne had not outgrown this yet. She smiled as she readjusted her backpack. She loved spending Sundays with her niece.

She'd visit Henry later this afternoon after she dropped Dionne home. The staff had been great and let her visit Henry any time she wanted. She still hoped he'd wake from his sleep.

"They're so cute," her niece said, as she joined her.

"Would you like a juice? It's so hot in here."

Dionne nodded her head. "When are we going to see the BMX freestyle riders, Auntie Steph?"

"Do you really want to see them? I'm not sure you'll enjoy that sort of show."

"Ben's brother is one of the riders."

"Ben?"

"He's in my class."

"Get your drinks here," a man shouted.

Stephani squeezed through the milling crowd and paid for two orange juices. Her cell rang.

"Hey. Where are you?" Richard asked.

"Arizona State Fairgrounds. Doing the aunty thing. Hey, I've lost sight of Dionne. Got to go." She hung up.

"Dionne, where are you?" Stephani shouted when she lost sight of her.

Stephani stopped just short of crashing headlong into some strange man who wore a studded leather collar around his neck. She opened her mouth to apologize when she saw her niece walking to the bleachers where the BMX riders would be performing.

She caught up with her. "Dionne, don't run off like that."

***

Princie watched Stephani buy juices at one of the many food stalls at the Arizona State Fairgrounds. She looked stunning in the button-down white blouse and jeans she wore. He collided headlong into her niece as she stopped to stare at a display of soft toys. Her niece looked like she was Stephani's child, as they both had similar features: thick black hair, well-defined eyebrows with long eyelashes and oval faces with full lips and honey-colored skin. This would be a great day.

He watched Stephani turn this way and that looking for her niece.

Dionne fell and he saw her get up as he retreated quickly and disappeared into the crowd.

***

"You had me worried. I don't want to lose you here. Promise me, you won't?" she said.

"Sorry, I just wanted to get us good seats."

Stephani bought tickets, and they climbed the bleachers.

"See, there's hardly any seats left now," Dionne said.

The stunt riders appeared one by one as they were announced, and they pedaled around the circuit waving to the mostly teen crowd, which cheered so loudly that Stephani could hardly hear the announcer.

"Thanks for taking me. You're the best," Dionne said.

Stephani wrapped her arm around her niece as they settled down and waited for the show to start.

The stunt riders were spinning their bikes on one wheel. Next, they were weaving in crisscross formation.

"Look," her niece pointed excitedly.

The riders were doing flips and jumps across cars from the top of an enormous ramp.

"Ice creams, drinks," a boy carrying a tray shouted.

Stephani bought two ice creams as each rider jumped through sets of hoops.

The audience cheered as one teen flipped and twisted, landing back on his bike.

They clapped and more riders sped up the ramp and did jumps. The crowd cheered.

The show was over all too soon for Dionne.

"That was great," Dionne said.

"What do you want to do now?" Stephani asked, as they left their seats.

"Rides please," Dionne said excitedly.

"Sure."

They passed a booth selling hotdogs and drinks. Stephani stopped and bought some drinks.

"I need to go to the bathroom," Dionne said. "There's one there."

Stephani sighed and pushed the unopened drinks into her backpack. "You always wait 'till the last minute. Let's go."

Stephani rounded the corner with Dionne to discover the restrooms had lengthy lines.

When it was their turn, she said, "You go first and I'll go after you."

After Dionne came out, Stephani said, "Wait for me just outside. No, make it inside. Don't go anywhere. Okay? I don't want to lose you again."

"Okay," Dionne said.

Moments later, she stepped out of the stall but couldn't see Dionne. She'd more than likely gotten confused and was waiting outside. After she had washed her hands, she went out. Where was Dionne?

Stephani scanned the crowds for her niece. She'd have to give Dionne a good talking to about this.

Maybe, she was making her way to the rides. She hurried in that direction expecting to see her. By the time she'd reached the rides, they were more crowded than where she'd come from. Worried, she asked anyone she passed if they'd seen a black-haired, nine-and-a-half-year-old walking alone. No one had. An awful sinking feeling began in the pit of her stomach.

More frantic as moments passed, she hurried to the southeastern corner of the fairgrounds to the Floriculture building, then the McDowell pedestrian entrance and finally, the Gem and Minerals Building. Her heart pounded, her anxiety growing. Dionne wasn't there either. Calling Dionne's name, she ran towards the Southwestern Village where there were many stalls of handicrafts.

Maybe, she was still back at the restrooms and they'd somehow missed each other. She retraced her steps, but got lost and had to consult the map, found that she wasn't that far away and continued to the restrooms. More women were waiting their turn. She banged on all the stall doors. "Dionne…Dionne…Dionne? Where are you? Has anyone seen my niece? Black ponytail and her name's Dionne, and she was wearing pink shorts and T-shirt?"

People shook their heads. She stumbled out in a daze of disbelief.

"Dionne, where are you?" Tears filled her eyes, and she wiped them away as quickly as they appeared. *Don't panic, it won't help*, she told herself. Her gaze zigzagged from hot dog sellers, ice cream boys, to trinket stalls, and to passers-by laughing and talking.

Stephani returned to the restrooms again in with the hope that Dionne would be there and they'd somehow missed each other. "Has anyone seen a girl, about so high in pink shorts and T-shirt?" Faces turned toward her.

Women shook their heads and expressed their concern.

Outside again, she frantically called out her niece's name.

Where could she be? "I'm looking for my niece." She described her repeatedly to anyone who'd listen.

Then she saw a security guard. She dashed across to him. "Help me, please." She swallowed down a sob. "I've lost my niece."

Oh Jesus, she couldn't believe she was saying this.

He smiled. "Where did you see her last, ma'am?"

His calm even tone settled her for the briefest moment. "Dionne went to the restrooms with me. She came out first and was supposed to wait for me inside. But now I can't find her."

"How about I call the Lost Children's Center? Maybe she's there. You know something attracts them and they wander off and before they know it, they're lost. Can you give me a description of your daughter?"

She told him. "She's my niece, not my daughter. But I love her like my own."

He put a call through. "I'm sorry, ma'am. They don't seem to have anyone fitting your niece's description. I suggest we try retracing your steps since you saw her last."

"We were watching the BMX stunt riders. Then we were going to the rides, but on the way, we stopped to use the restrooms. But I've been there twice and no one's seen her."

"Then let's see if she's gone to the rides. Let me put a call through. They'll broadcast a bulletin."

Stephani followed him, with hope in her heart that Dionne would be there, to the rides where children screamed and laughed as rides dove and swung, twisted and turned.

He spoke to each of the amusement operators. No one had seen a lost child fitting her description.

"Please find her for me. Please." An awful feeling of dread settled in. It made her legs feel weak and her breath catch in her throat.

Then he said, "You'd better stay with me because when we locate her, she'll want to see a familiar face. In the meantime, we'll go over to the Lost Children's Center and you can fill out the forms."

In a daze, she followed the guard to the Center.

"Hi Stephani. I'm Shona. Missing niece, is it?" Shona flicked her long blonde side swept bangs from her face.

Stephani nodded. "Please, find her." A woozy feeling came on suddenly and she blacked out.

A woman was talking and shaking her. Somewhere a child cried. She opened her eyes and saw the blonde leaning over her.

"You okay, hon?" Shona said.

Stephani sat. "I won't be okay 'till Dionne's found."

"We've got a good team out there so don't you worry none. Lemme get you a strong coffee."

After the guard left, Stephani spent the next half-hour in the office listening in to all the audio traffic in case someone had sighted Dionne. Mostly, it was about misbehaving children.

After that, Stephani sat perched on a chair and the rest of the time she paced up and down the room waiting for the call that would tell her they had found Dionne. Where had her niece gone? Was someone holding…no, she couldn't think that. It was too horrifying. She should have kept a closer eye on her…and taken her into the stall.

What was she going to say to Iantha? Iantha would never forgive her.

"I'm sure she'll be located soon," Shona said.

"Can I call my sister? She should know. I've been worrying about telling her. I was hoping that when I did, I would have good news. That Dionne just wandered off to look at something and was temporarily lost." She stared at her hands, unable to meet the woman's concerned gaze. "How do I tell Iantha that her daughter's missing...that I lost her? How could I do this to my sister? I'm terrible."

The woman pulled up a chair. "I'll call her if you like. I know it must be hard."

"Hard? It's devastating. The sort of thing you read in the newspapers about someone else's child. Not my niece, not my sister's baby." Tears started down her face as she got up. "I have to go look for her."

Shona hugged her. "We have people out there looking. We'll do our best to find her for you. Best to stay put so she can see a familiar face when we find her."

"My son Henry is in a coma and Dionne's gone missing.... I'm a terrible person."

"I'm sure you're not. Let me call your sister, then I'll fix you another coffee, okay?"

Stephani didn't answer. Sobs of despair rose and rose inside her and spilled out in a flood.

When she was spent, she slumped onto the stool again and stared at the yellow walls.

Then something occurred to her. "Tell them to look in the Petting Zoo. She loves animals. Maybe she went there."

"I'll get right on it." Shona picked up the two-way and notified the team to extend their search to all the kids' animal sites.

Hope rose in her after Shona said that. Maybe, they'd discover Dionne cuddling a baby rabbit or a chicken.

Sometime later a distraught Iantha and Theo appeared.

Stephani leapt to her feet and kissed them both. "I'm so sorry. Dionne was meant to be waiting for me inside the restrooms. Then I thought she was waiting outside because I first asked her to wait outside but then I changed my mind and asked her to wait inside because.... But she wasn't there." She spread her arms, palms up. "I was only five minutes. I thought she'd be okay for five minutes. I don't know where she could have... I shouldn't have let her out of my sight. I'm so sorry."

"You should have watched her." Iantha was breathing hard and her long hair was messy and knotted.

"How could you lose a child?" Theo asked.

Stephani hung her head. "I don't know."

"You don't know. Mother of God," Theo said.

"Where's Dionne? They should have found her. She can't have gone far. She's been told not to wander off." Iantha brushed tears away as she spoke.

"What are you doing to find my daughter? Why haven't you found my baby yet?" Theo demanded.

"We've got a team out there. As soon as they locate her, we'll know. We've also notified the police," Shona said. "There's an hour left 'till closing. If we haven't found her by then, she'll soon be spotted by our search team when the Fair empties," the woman said.

"Was there anyone suspicious lurking around, Stephani?" Iantha blew her nose.

Her sister's cold had been coming on this morning so she'd stayed at home. Now, it seemed worse. It was funny how she noticed these small things now. Theo and Iantha's distress washed over her. As if she was somehow dislocated from herself.

"I don't know? It was crowded," Stephani said to Iantha. "I shouldn't have asked her to wait. I should have kept her in the stall with me. I just thought…"

"What were you thinking? What? You shouldn't have let her out of your sight."

"I'm so sorry. So sorry."

"Oh…sorry, Steph." She brushed away tears. "I know you're so careful. I can't help it."

"You have you called in the police haven't you?" Theo said to Shona.

"The alert has gone AMBER now."

Two police officers hurried in, flipped their badges and introduced themselves as Chuck Brodie and Leroy Elmer.

"Theo Sarlos, and this is my wife Iantha. It's our Dionne that's…." He appeared to be too emotional to continue.

"Missing," Iantha said, before she put her hand over her mouth, her breath coming out in gasps.

Brodie spoke, "I'm sorry, ma'am. We'll try to locate her."

"Okay. Can we get some details please?" Elmer, the Native American police officer asked.

Theo described his daughter.

Iantha pulled out her wallet and extracted a photo of Dionne. "It's one that was taken a year ago, but it might help."

"Thank you, ma'am. I'll get this circulated." Brodie, the square-shouldered one, took a photo of the photo with his cell and forwarded it.

"We are wasting time. We should be out looking for Dionne," Theo said.

"The police will look for her. We wouldn't know where to start." Stephani put her arm around her sister. At least, Iantha didn't shrug her off.

"Well, I'm going to search the Fairgrounds," Theo said.

"We have security searching the grounds for her," Shona said.

"Have you got a map of the place?"

Shona got a leaflet for him. "Here's all the public exits."

"I can't stand around doing nothing while my baby's missing. I'll go to all the exits just in case she's there waiting for Stephani or someone's...I don't know." Theo left them.

Elmer asked. "Was your daughter upset about anything?"

"No," Iantha said.

"Did anyone have an argument with Dionne? Was there something worrying her?" Brodie asked.

"Has she run away before?" Elmer asked.

"What are you implying?" Iantha asked.

"Sometimes children run away because something's worrying

them. Was something upsetting your daughter, Mrs. Sarlos?" Elmer asked.

"She didn't run away. Dionne would never do that. She is from a happy home. We love her very much," Iantha said. "How can you stand here? You should be looking for her." She wiped away her tears. "What are you doing to find my daughter? Don't tell me this stuff about her running away."

"I understand," Brodie said.

"Understand? You don't know our little girl. Where else would she go? She has a loving family." Iantha glanced at Stephani. "She has no reason to run away. We love her. She knows that."

"I'm sure you do. We must ask these questions," Elmer said.

Theo rushed in. "I can't find our baby. I've looked at all the exits. I don't know where else to look."

"We have our best men out there right now searching the entire grounds. If she's still here, then we'll find her," Brodie said.

"Also, could you compile a list of her girlfriends and their contact details, please?"

"Why?" Stephani asked.

"I'll do that when I get home." Iantha turned to Stephani. "It's okay. Let them ask. I don't care what they ask...so long as they find our baby." She started to sob quietly as she sank into a chair.

CHAPTER 35

It was six in the morning and someone was ringing the doorbell. Stephani heard her sister get up to answer it. She leapt from the bed, heart pounding. Would this be the good news they so desperately needed?

Theo had searched the grounds with Iantha and herself. By the time they had completed the circuit, everything was closing down for the night. They drove around the streets near the Fair Grounds just in case. Iantha had buzzed down her window and screamed Dionne's name as Theo drove through street after street.

Stephani had stayed with Theo and Iantha the twelve hours that Dionne had been missing. When she'd come down to check on her sister at three o'clock in the morning, she'd found Iantha asleep on the lounge with the phone clutched in her hand. She didn't wake her, but crept back upstairs and lay staring at the wall, hoping they would get a call from the police telling them they'd found Dionne.

Footsteps sounded on the tiled floor. Theo was talking to someone in the living room. As she tied her robe, she recognized the deep voice of that officer, Bill Kennelly.

Barefooted, she hurried downstairs and nodded a greeting to Kennelly. She couldn't bring herself to say good morning because it wasn't good unless he had promising news about Dionne, and the concerned look on his weather-beaten face told her he didn't.

The officer leaned forward from his spot on the sofa. "The overnight radio broadcast about your missing niece has just produced a possible lead."

Theo moved his leg from side to side in agitation. "How so?"

"Two eyewitnesses saw a man carrying a sleeping young girl to a van." He paused, then addressed Iantha. "The husband said the girl had black hair and a pony tail. The wife said it was early evening and they were in a hurry to get home from the Fair with their kids. They didn't think anything was amiss, so they didn't worry until they watched the news on TV and saw Dionne's photo. They're coming in later today for another interview just in case there's something they've forgotten to tell us."

"What did the man look like? What type of van was it? What was the license plate?" Theo asked.

"It was white. The woman didn't notice much else. I'm sorry I don't have more positive news, but I thought any news might help. That list of girlfriends and their cell numbers, addresses?" he asked Iantha, "Do you have it?"

"I'll get it for you." Iantha hurried down the hallway and disappeared into the main bedroom.

"I've come to talk to you, Stephani, to try to jog your memory some more."

"I want to do everything I can to help." She sat on the lounge chair opposite and tried to recall her last moments with Dionne. No, it couldn't be her last moments; Dionne had to be alive. Though she hadn't believed in that mystic hocus-pocus of the Hopi doll, she'd been ready to try anything, brought the doll over and placed it in Dionne's room. She hoped that the doll could protect her niece.

"Do you remember a tall man wearing a dog collar around his neck? A couple of people called last night after they saw Dionne's photo on the news. One said they saw a suspicious-looking man at the Fair hanging around a kid who was with someone who fit your description. He wore a studded leather collar. Any ideas?"

233

"Where was he seen?" Stephani said.

"Loitering near the BMX show entrance and the amusement area."

"Come to think of it…I do recall a man with some sort of a collar who bumped into me at the movies. But the Fair…there were so many people everywhere. What did he look like?"

"The only description I have is that he was Caucasian, slight build, blond hair to his collar, and around five feet eight inches to five feet ten inches tall."

"Hey, that guy crashed into Dionne when we were on our way to see the BMX freestyle riders. Oh God. Do you think…?"

"Can you come down to the station and look through some mug shots?"

"Sure. Just give me time to get dressed."

"Have breakfast. No sense in going on an empty stomach as you'll be there for hours. Also, can you bring in your camera for forensics?"

"Then you'll see that those photos of Dionne and me weren't taken with my camera."

"It's just to rule out any possibilities. You understand."

"I just want my little girl back. Please find her," Theo said.

Iantha returned with a list and handed it to Kennelly. "Please help us." She brushed away her tears.

CHAPTER 36

Stephani taped another poster of Dionne in another store window. She'd spent what was left of the Monday morning, after a fruitless search of mug shots again, at the local printer's getting fliers done with her niece's picture. She composed a short message about her being missing and the police number to call.

The café owner came out with the cello tape when she put her head in the door to ask him if he could give her some more and helped her put the posters up.

"It's terrible. I have a daughter, too. When did she go missing?"

"Yesterday afternoon." Her eyes filled with tears.

"When they find him, if the police won't give him what he deserves, let me know. I've got contacts."

Normally, she'd have been shocked that anyone could suggest such a thing but not now. "Thank you for your help, but I still have all these to put up." She motioned toward the wad of fliers she had in her bag."

She met Theo as he went into the local drugstore with some more flyers.

After the traditional greeting kiss on each cheek, Theo said. "I've put up about twenty-five so far and I've handed out some to people walking by. This has to work. It just has to. I just want her back. God, I'd do anything." Theo looked away.

The terror in Theo's eyes before he had a chance to mask it drew her fear to the surface. Her head was spinning, just the way it had when she'd found out Allan was gone.

They had to find her. Was she cold? Scared? A knot of emotion rose in her throat. "I should be doing more to find her. Just tell me what you want me to do, please?"

"I don't know myself." He glanced at his watch. "I'm meant to be at the radio station in fifteen minutes. I'd better hurry. They asked me to put out a plea to the public. I don't know how I'll go, but I have to give it a try."

"Do you want me to come?"

"Just keep doing what you're doing."

"There has to be something we've missed. Something that will tell us where she is?"

"I don't know."

Stephani could see how emotional he was though he was trying to keep it together. She watched his vehicle pull out of the parking lot and drive onto the highway, which led to everywhere and nowhere.

Her phone beeped with a message. Richard wanted to meet her. She messaged him back.

How lonely and afraid Dionne must be. She hoped that she wasn't hungry and that the person who had her…kidnapped her…. *Please, be safe Dionne, wherever you are*, she said silently.

She clenched her fists as tears surfaced; she wasn't going to give in to useless tears. She would find her niece alive, no matter what it took.

Richard pulled up in his rental car and got out. "How's it going?" he said, as he closed the door. "You look terrible. You can't go on like this."

"I'm not giving up."

"Give me a few more flyers. I'll go around Mesa and post some there."

"Thanks, but you've already helped enough, and Theo and I are grateful. Go home and have a rest."

"No way. You look exhausted, and I'm going to give you a hand, whether you like it or not. I've got a daughter as well. And I can't help thinking how would I feel if it were my Belinda," Richard said.

"Sorry. I'm out of line." She handed him a bundle of flyers. "What's happening with that investigation? Did the security camera reveal who planted the bomb on your vehicle?"

"The only person who was anywhere near my Lexus was an old woman. Seems she dropped something and leaned over to pick it up. The officer thinks that she could have planted the bomb then. But, he's also pretty sure that whoever it was, was wearing a disguise. These plastic bombs are purchased on the Internet. I'm so glad I ran after that robber, otherwise I'd be dead."

"Thank God for that. Why did they want to kill you?"

"The cops have been asking that, too. And, that's the question I've been asking myself over and over. I don't have an answer."

Richard stepped closer, hugged her and pushed her hair from her face. "Never mind about me. I'm in this with you till we find Dionne."

She clung to Richard as a well of emotion swelled in her throat threatening to suffocate her. "We've got to find her. I should have asked her to stay inside the restroom and waited for me there. I should have been more alert. I-"

"Stop it. No one could have predicted what happened. It's not your fault that Dionne is missing."

***

Stephani looked up from the microscope as Richard and Ross walked in. She'd arrived an hour ago after deciding that she couldn't go back to Iantha's and watch her sister cry. The hours she'd spent this morning at the police station staring fruitlessly at mug shots was getting to be a habit, but she'd do whatever it took to help find Dionne.

She'd gone home afterwards and had a hot shower, tried to eat something, but couldn't and decided that she might as well be at work.

"In your office, please, Stephani," Ross said.

"What's wrong?"

"Ross would like to speak with you," Richard said.

"I'm sorry to have to tell you this, but you will need to hand in your security pass. You'd better pack your things and come with me," Ross said.

She stared at Richard. "Why? I don't understand this?"

"I hate this. I tried to tell them you were under considerable stress and this was only temporary but...they wouldn't listen." Richard pointed at Ross.

She grabbed her bag and made it look like she was taking out a box of muesli bars from the desk drawer.

"What have you got there?" Ross asked.

She slammed the drawer shut. "Food. I'll leave it then."

"Just give it to me," Ross said.

"No. It's my stuff."

Ross opened the drawer, grabbed the box and pulled out a small hip flask. "So how do you explain this?" He unscrewed the lid and smelled the contents. "You know the rules. Any alcohol on the premises means instant dismissal."

"Am I fired?"

"On unscheduled leave for now," Ross said. "I'll arrange for a place in a rehab clinic for you. Then we'll see."

"What about our work? This will put us behind."

"After." Ross stormed out and went over to the elevator.

"I just needed a little help. I'm going crazy what with Dionne missing and…did you tell him? Who turned me in?"

"I don't know," Richard said.

Stephani flung open the door to Laboratory 1.

Nina slid her stool back and stood. "This is a big mistake, Richard."

"Ross wouldn't listen to me on this," Richard said.

Nina started to cry.

"See you guys later," Stephani said.

Fred looked up from his work. "I told the truth. You could have compromised the whole trial."

"What the hell are you talking about?" Stephani said.

"I told them that I saw you drinking."

"Oh thanks, Fred. Who needs enemies with friends like you?"

"It's not my fault."

Nina came over to hug her. "You have been very worried with everything that has happened." She glared at Fred. "You are not nice man."

Fred reddened and turned away.

Melissa didn't speak, but sat watching the proceedings open-mouthed.

When they were at the elevators, Richard said, "The Company hasn't officially done anything yet. It depends on whether or not you agree to the rehab. I made a deal with the Rigby Board's lawyers that you will be willing to remain at home until we can arrange rehab for you."

"Jesus. I can't believe this is happening to me."

CHAPTER 37

"Hi, Mom," Stephani said. She'd called Richard and told him that she was visiting her mother. She'd be damned if she was going to mope around at home the rest of the day, and she would have done anything to take her mind off of tomorrow.

She hoped her mom didn't notice that it was Monday, a workday, except she wasn't at work.

"Who are you?" Her mother looked up from the wicker patio chair with a blank stare. The healthy glow on her wrinkled skin belied the growing illness inside her mind.

"Stephani. It's me, Mom."

"I have a daughter Stephani."

Then her eyes brightened as if a light switched on. "Stephani! What's kept you away? You know how much I look forward to your visits."

"Sorry. I've been busy." Stephani sank into a chair opposite. She'd agreed with Iantha to keep the distressing news of Dionne's disappearance from their mother. She leaned over to kiss her cheek, but her mom pulled away as if it was a stranger trying to do that.

"Busy doing what?"

"Richard and I went to a charity ball Saturday night. The ballroom was festooned in white sheets of fabric with a black rose hanging from the ceiling. It was a great night."

"You should be looking after your son."

She steeled herself mentally. "Since the accident five months ago, Henry's been in a coma." She pushed on, not giving her mother a chance to ask further questions about him. "I'm seeing Richard now. We work together at the lab." *Well, that was until this morning,* she silently added.

Her mother asked. "What's he like?

"Oh, he's tall and good-looking. He's a professor."

"Does he earn good money? You don't want some lazyass man that makes you scrimp and save the rest of your life."

Letha was pensive. "Your father left us when you were just over two and your stepfather was always getting laid-off. Always blamed the boss for being too tough on him. We were a family, you, Iantha and I."

"I remember when you worked two jobs to put us through school."

"And that old man, what's his name..."

"Kessler."

"He was as mean as they could come. He never paid me a cent extra if I worked through lunch so I didn't have to work overtime when there was a backlog of accounts to process."

"And you packed supermarket shelves at night."

"Did I? Where were you and your sister?"

"In bed. Martha used to check on us."

"Martha?"

"Our old neighbor."

"The worst time was when your father first left us. You were so little and I had to…" Letha was choked-up with emotion. Finally, she added, "I had to leave you in that place while I tried to earn enough to keep a roof over our heads."

"What place?" Tears filled Stephani's eyes as she stared unseeing at the ornamental grasses that edged the patio. They should have been in sympathy, but instead were tears of anger, and she couldn't understand why.

"Three years was all I got with your two-timing father, and then he took off."

"What place, Mom?"

When she heard the opening notes of 'Nothing Compares 2 U,' she reached for her cell and realized it was ringing in the next room again. Then she remembered the same thing happened last time she visited her mom.

Letha frowned and stared into the distance. "I need to tell you what happened when you were little. I thought it would be okay, but that woman was a mean one. Oh, I knew that she couldn't keep house, but beggars can't be choosers. Once I came a day early to get you and you were so dirty. I don't know where that woman kept you. I never took you back there again. For a long time afterwards you used to cry. And I found out…." She appeared to lose concentration.

Stephani twirled her hair as she waited for her mom to continue, but it was as if her mother had forgotten what she wanted to say. What she had said was enough to trigger uneasiness in the recesses of her mind. There were things she couldn't remember about her childhood and she didn't know why.

Her mother stared at her. "I have two daughters, but they don't visit me. It was kind of you to come, but you must have your own family to worry about. Thank you all the same."

243

"I'm Stephani. I'm your daughter."

"You don't have to do that. You're very sweet." Letha reached out to pat her hand.

This was too much. She wanted to sob until there were no tears left. "Bye, Mom." She ran from the room and out to the parking lot.

Stephani climbed into her silver Honda. *I want my mom back*, she said to herself. Squeezed her eyes closed, and took deep breaths to calm down.

The hallucination started.

"Set yourselves down. I'll get some coffee goin'," the fat woman says.

The fat woman disappears into another room, and my mommy looks at the stains on the lounge. She tells me to sit in between them in a clean spot, and she sits on the other side of one.

"Here we are. A soda pop for the littl' un and a fresh coffee for you, Ma'am."

"What do you say?" My mommy says as I reach for the glass.

"Thank you."

A dog comes bounding in: his tail whacks the air.

She screams at the dog "Shmoo! Shmoo! Git. Git," She kicks Shmoo's back leg.

Shmoo lets out a yelp and retreats.

"Sorry 'bout him."

My mommy must be thinking it's a mistake to bring me here? Anytime soon, she will tell me to get up and we'll go home.

They talk, but I am not listening because I am trying to work out what smells so bad.

Now my mommy gets up. "Please show me her room again."

Why doesn't my mommy just say goodbye and take me with her? The smell must be going up her nose too.

The fat woman takes us down a hallway into a small bedroom. In the middle of the bed sits a pretty doll with a white frilly lacy dress, which spreads out in a circle.

"This is your daughter's room."

"She never lets me sleep in here," I say to my mommy.

"Hush," says my mommy.

"That kid has a good imagination, eh," the fat woman says and then lifts the pillow and shows my mommy my pajamas.

Why won't my mommy just say goodbye and take me home?

The three of us go back into the other room. My mommy looks sad.

"I have to be going, sweetheart."

"No, Mommy. Please don't leave me here."

"Don't make it any harder than it already is." She kisses my cheek.

"You know I'll be back on Friday night to get you, okay? Remember. First, there's Monday, then Tuesday, then Wednesday, then Thursday and then Friday. That's the day I'll be coming to take you home."

"Noooo. Don't leave me." I cry, and grab hold of my mommy's best skirt.

My mommy pulls my fingers open. "I have to go." She hurries to the front door. Opens it, and leaves.

"Mommy, Mommy, come back," I scream. Then I start to hiccup between

sobs. "I promise to be good." I told her before we came here I could stay at home alone, that I was a big girl now.

"Come on, kid. Now get back to the chicken coop."

I shake my head. "I..." another hiccup bursts out. "I want my mommy."

The woman grabs me and drags me out to the coop. She unlocks the door and pushes me in. "Listen kid, learn that tears are useless. Tears are for crybabies."

I ignore the chickens as they scratch and cluck and, peck at some seed scattered about in the dirt.

I take a couple of steps toward them and they scatter and run away. I sneeze from the dust and the feathers. I run back to the gate when the fat woman starts to retreat, but she's faster than me. She locks the gate.

"Let me out." I pull at the wire. "Let me out."

"These are your quarters, brat." She turns the key in the padlock. "Should be used to it by now."

"I want my mommy," I cry.

"Shut up. Shut up. Do you hear? Stop that goddamned noise."

Then she opens the gate and slaps me hard on the cheek. It stings. I'm so surprised that I stop crying.

"That's more like it." She starts away, and then turns back. "Another thing. If you needs to pee, then don't forget to do it in the bucket in the corner."

Stephani rubbed her eyes. Where was she? She looked up and saw she was still in the parking lot outside the nursing home. These visions had been so vivid. Were they part of her childhood, from some story she'd read somewhere, or was she going mad?

CHAPTER 38

Stephani spoke to Richard on the phone. "How are the trials progressing?"

"You were here this morning so you haven't missed much. Only that Melissa ruined the last batch. Added too much growth media to the samples. I don't know where her head is," Richard said.

"I've noticed she's been like that lately, too."

"Have the police made any progress concerning your niece?"

"Every time the phone rings, I hope."

"You're booked into the rehab clinic for Wednesday. I'll be over to pick you up and take you there about nine."

"But this isn't a good time. I want to help find Dionne."

"I want Dionne found too, but I don't think there's anything more you can do. You have to get yourself better."

The intercom buzzed. She ignored it. Whoever it was could just go away. She wasn't up to any visitors. "Jesus. Everything's a mess."

"Whatever happens, no one will think it was your fault."

"I'm worried sick. It's been twenty-four hours now."

"As you said…you told her to wait for you inside."

"Are you trying to make light of the situation?"

"Sorry. Just trying to stop you feeling like it's your entire fault."

She let his comment pass. Nothing would diminish the enormity of her mistake.

The buzzer rang again.

"Hold on, Richard, someone's at the door. It might be Iantha." She should have answered it the first time.

Stephani rested the receiver on the countertop, and hurried across to answer it. "Hello?"

"Hey. Can I come up?"

"Hey, Jack. How did you know I was home?"

"I rang Rigby, and they said you're on leave. I'm on vacation myself this week. I've just found out something that I think you'll want to know about."

"I'll let you in." Then she went back to the phone and spoke to Richard. "Jack's downstairs. I'll call you back later."

"Okay," Richard said. "But wait. I just wanted to tell you that Saturday night after the ball was really special to me."

"For me too, Richard." She smiled for the first time that day as she recalled how he took her in his arms and made love to her. They'd both been hesitant at first, but when he'd deepened their kiss, their passions erupted.

Jack opened the door.

"By the look on your face, it must be serious," she said.

Jack nodded. "I heard the news on the radio that your niece is missing. I don't know if it's anything to get your hopes up about, but I went over to the kennels where I got my puppy to get the immunization papers. I'd mislaid the ones he gave me. Thankfully, he keeps copies. The guy there, well, he and I got to talking about your missing niece and-"

"Just get to the point."

"He remembered passing a vehicle the day that Dionne disappeared. There was a young girl with black hair in the van beside this older guy. She was crying. Looked distressed, the kennel owner said. The van went down the road and turned off to a ranch, not five miles away from where he lives."

She pushed her hair back from her face. "Oh God. Do you think it could really be her?"

He shrugged.

"Have you told the police?" she asked.

"I should, but it might be nothing."

"I just want her found. So…are we going to check his story out?"

"It's late in the day and I didn't expect you to want to do this so suddenly. I don't know if it's such a good idea."

"I can't just sit here while Dionne is out there somewhere scared and all alone."

She picked up her cell and called Kennelly, but he wasn't answering so she hung up without leaving a message. "I'll call the officer while we're on the way."

"We don't have to go," Jack said.

"Then why'd you tell me in the first place? You know I'll have to go see."

"Do you want to drive or shall I?" Jack pulled out his keys from his pocket. "My van's out front."

"Let me give my sister a quick call."

"What if it turns out to be a wild goose chase? Then you've got her hopes up for nothing."

She reached for her handbag. "Let's go."

They caught the elevator down and went outside.

"I'm hoping for your sake that we locate her," Jack said, as they crossed the road and unlocked his van.

"As far as I know, this is the only lead we have. The police aren't getting anywhere and each day that she isn't found...." She took a deep breath and climbed in. "I have to keep thinking she's still okay. It's the only thing that helps." She stared unseeing at the road, not allowing herself to feel anything but hope.

He reached over and touched her hand. "If we all pull together, we might have a chance of finding her. Thirsty?"

Stephani nodded.

He pulled out two bottles of mineral water from a small water cooler from behind his seat.

"Thanks." She stared at the bottle. "This one's been opened."

"That must be the one I started to undo. I haven't drunk from it. I'll swap with you?"

"It's okay." She put hers in the bottle holder.

He entered the traffic and drove towards the Superstition Highway. "If we find anything that indicates Dionne could be there, we have to call the cops. There's no way we can handle this ourselves. Agreed?"

"Okay. How far away is this place?"

He pointed to the glove compartment. "I've got the address in there. Just open it."

She pulled out a street map, which was partly hidden by some baby wipes and a torn piece of paper. "Is this it?" She read it out.

"Yep." He glanced at her, then back at the traffic.

"It's so isolated out there."

"You're right. It might be dark by the time we get there. Just say the word and we'll turn back." He touched her hand again. "We can go there first thing tomorrow."

"I haven't had a decent night's sleep since Dionne went missing."

"Then, we keep going?" he asked.

She nodded. "She was in my care."

"You spend too much time blaming yourself." He sipped some water.

"I can't help it." Stephani was thirsty too and took a few gulps from her bottle.

They drove past vehicle sale yards, then further on, rows of boxy houses, a Wal-Mart, and side roads that shimmered into the horizon.

"We'll find Dionne…won't we? We have to find her."

Tired and drained from the circus that started the day Dionne went missing, lack of sleep, all the tears and recriminations, and guilt, Stephani leaned back. All that pent-up worry and emotion seemingly drained away. It was a strange feeling. It shouldn't be happening. They passed a school with children pouring out with their moms. "Henry was five when he was in a car accident that left him in a coma. He would have been in school, and I'd be one of those moms picking up their kid."

"Stop doing this to yourself," he said.

Somehow, she couldn't summon up any emotion. Her thoughts scuttled on, and numbness seeped through her. Maybe this was delayed shock. She tapped in Kennelly's number on her cell phone and waited for him to pick up.

Stephani blinked. "The sun's playing tricks with my eyes. I...should have...worn sun...glasses."

"Kennelly. How-"

Jack took it from her and switched it off.

"Why did...you do that? I need to...tell him where...."

"Your niece is such a nice kid. We must get her safely home," Jack said.

"Iantha...will be...so relieved." Another gulp of water slipped down her throat. Why was she talking so slowly? "I need...to...Kennelly...."

"You need rest."

Her vision blurred. When she turned to speak to Jack again, she found that she couldn't move. What was happening? The bottle slipped from her grasp, but Jack caught it before it spilled on her jeans.

While still driving, he put the open bottle between his thighs, took the lid from her fingers, and screwed it on to the bottle. "You're very clumsy today. Too much on your mind, I suppose. Or do I detect the smell of alcohol on your breath? Have you been drinking? Maybe, something stronger than water? Gin? Whisky? I'm surprised I didn't smell it on you before."

What was he talking about? She tried to speak and tell him that he was wrong. The words wouldn't form. Her mouth was frozen. What had robbed her of all will and all movement? What was making her so drowsy?

Then she heard a man speak from what seemed to be a great distance away. "Sleep then, my Princess. My one and only love."

These softly spoken words terrified her.

A darkness that she couldn't fight enveloped her.

CHAPTER 39

Richard pushed back his chair and rubbed his eyes. He'd spent hours looking at the results of the test, but it might as well have been written in a different language. He should have been pushing harder on the tests—get them finished before that thief could beat them. However, his mind was on Stephani. He loved the way he could make her smile.

He sat back in his chair, linked his hands behind his head, and stared at the ceiling.

That night they had made love had made him realize how much he wanted to keep her in his life. He'd been like a teenager, so nervous. Just like when he was eighteen and had made love to Ellen. It had been the first time for both of them. He'd not had a lover since his wife had left him. Later, Stephani had admitted to him she'd been worried too, as she had been celibate since Allan had died.

The honesty between them had brought them together with a coupling of sweetness and gentleness yet urgency that moved him more than anything that had gone before.

Suddenly, he knew he loved Stephani more than he had ever loved any woman in his life before.

Where was she? Yesterday afternoon was the last time he had spoken to her. He called Stephani's cell and home phone countless times that day and left messages, but she had not answered or called him back. He kept checking his cell just to make sure she had not left a message for him. He'd gone over their conversation repeatedly thinking that maybe he'd said something to upset her. However, he couldn't work out what. Maybe she was going crazy brooding around the apartment and had gone out for some fresh air, even though she wasn't supposed to leave without permission. Maybe she was too sick and was in bed. Maybe she'd gone looking for her niece and gotten into trouble. Oh God, he hoped not.

Richard walked in to Laboratory 1. "Stephani's not answering her cell. I've been calling her all morning. It's not like her to take off without a word."

Nina looked up from the flask of distilled water and growth media mix she'd poured into the injection robot and said in a muffled voice, "You think something's happened to her?"

Fred slipped his mask down. "She's got a sister, hasn't she? Well, call her. Maybe, she's there," Fred said. "She was supposed to call me today. I need to discuss the latest trials with her. You know I'm using her methods. You'd think she'd be checking with me all the time. She's probably at some bar drinking."

Richard rounded on Fred. "Not only have you effectively stopped Stephani from continuing her research because you told Ross about her problem, you want to make us believe that she doesn't care too. Jesus, Mary and Joseph! When will you stop your mouth going off? What has she ever done to you? Gotten your lunches that you didn't thank her for and didn't deserve."

Fred shook his head. "I don't like the way you're speaking to me. I shouldn't have to put up with that. If that's what you think, I'll hand in my notice today if you like."

"Stephani shouldn't be sitting around at home either. Her place is here with us."

"So am I still welcome, Richard?"

"Don't be a fool, Fred. Do you think we could bring some new guy up to speed without setting the project back months?" He expelled a slow breath.

By the time Richard went to his office and found her sister's number, she had called him.

"Have you heard from Stephani? I need to speak to her," Iantha said.

"You haven't seen her either?"

"Not since Monday. Is there something wrong?" Iantha asked.

"I hope not." Now he was concerned.

Iantha started to cry. "The police came over today. The man they suspect abducted Dionne," she paused to blow her nose, "is, Princie Younger. He's the half-brother to a woman who works with you. Her name's Melissa, Melissa Toomey."

"What?" he said in disbelief. "Are you sure? How did they make the connection?"

"Seems this guy's been a person of interest on a similar case a few years ago, though no charges were laid."

"Have they found the scum?"

She started crying again. "What's he done with my baby?"

He glanced at Melissa pulling out a pair of gloves from the cupboard. "You know, she's been a little jumpy lately." He'd thought she was upset about something. Now he knew what it was.

"Let me have a talk with her and see what I can find out. I'll call you back if I find out anything."

Richard approached Melissa. "Can I see you in my office?"

Nina, in the process of tipping test tubes into the biohazard trash, looked up.

"Sure, Richard." Melissa bit her lip as she walked into his office.

He closed the door after her, pushed over a chair for her, then went around the other side of the desk and sat. "I guess you must have an idea what I'm going to say."

"You tell me," she said.

"I've just had a call from Stephani's sister, Iantha. It seems your step-brother is under suspicion for the abduction of Stephani's niece, Dionne."

"I haven't seen my brother in years and don't want to see him either."

"Any idea of his whereabouts?"

"I can't help you there." She bit her lip again.

"When were you going to tell me about this? Or was I supposed to read about it in the papers?"

"I'm sorry. I just didn't know how to tell you. My mom called and told me he was under suspicion because the cops came to her place looking for him. I was hoping the cops were wrong and this would go away."

Melissa looked worried and Richard questioned if she was telling the truth. "Is there anything else you want to tell me?"

She shook her head, appearing more worried than before.

Something wasn't right, so he kept talking to try to draw her out. "You can imagine how frantic Stephani's sister Iantha must be."

She bit her lip some more and didn't meet his gaze. Definitely, she was hiding something, probably the whereabouts of her brother.

"Tell me…what's this brother of yours like?"

"He's a loner. He left us, mom and me, years ago when I was still living at home."

"If you hear from him, please let me know."

"I will."

"Do you know where Stephani is? No one's heard from her for days."

Finally, she appeared to relax a little. "Steph hasn't called me. Maybe she's looking for her niece."

"That's what I think, and that's what's concerning me. She could get herself into a dangerous situation. I'm going over to her place to see if I can find anything out." He got up. He felt for Stephani's apartment key in his pocket and was glad when his fingers closed around it. She had given it to him after she'd had that bear turn up in her bedroom.

"Good idea. I'll get back to work." Melissa retreated quickly.

***

A half hour later, Richard let himself into Stephani's apartment. The silence and stillness troubled him. He'd been hoping to find her laid-up sick with a fever, not gone. He walked into the kitchen and saw a few over ripe bananas in the fruit bowl and a plate of dried-up food in the sink. The refrigerator held a container of milk, which had expired yesterday, the usual condiments and spreads, a few vegetables and some sliced ham. He tipped out the milk.

The light was flashing on Stephani's answering machine.

He played the messages. The first was the one he'd left last night and he'd left a second this morning.

The next was shortly after from a male. "Some evil dude is watching you. Be careful."

The next was today at two-thirty. "Jack here. Do you want to meet at the health club tonight? Call me if you want to join me? I'm going anyway. Usual time."

The last time he'd spoken to Stephani was Monday afternoon when Jack had arrived. She had ended their conversation and told him she would call back but didn't. Then he played the recorded messages again; his heart pounded when he listened to the softly spoken male repeat that warning.

A walk through the rest of the apartment confirmed that no one was here. *Jesus, Mary and Joseph, where was she?* It wasn't like her to disappear. She was so methodical, so precise. He hoped that she had not gone looking for Dionne. Surely, she wouldn't do that.

Maybe, she'd been scared off because she couldn't face going into rehab and she'd gone to her sisters after he'd spoken to Iantha this morning.

He rang Iantha. "Is Stephani with you? I'm in her apartment. There's a few messages on her machine that haven't been played since yesterday afternoon."

"Nope. I haven't heard from her today. What's wrong?"

"She's due to go into rehab tomorrow morning."

"My God, is she taking drugs?"

"I thought she'd told you." Richard sighed. "I'm not the one that should be telling you. But since Stephani's not here…it's because of her drinking problem."

"I guess she didn't want to worry me."

Iantha didn't sound surprised about the drinking. Perhaps, she knew about Stephani's problem. Though, she possibly didn't know how bad it had gotten. "I've been calling her, but she's not picking up."

Iantha gasped. "Is she missing?"

"I don't know." Richard heard a muted sob down the line. "Don't cry." Then he did not know if he should tell her about the warning and upset her further. It was enough that he was alarmed himself. "I'm going to drop in to the police on my way home and let them know."

"When you know something…call," she said.

Iantha sobbed again. His stomach tightened at the sound. "I'll keep in touch," he said, but he couldn't say, 'don't worry', because now he just didn't know.

He recorded the messages to his phone, then unplugged the answering machine. He'd bring it with him to the police station as evidence.

***

After Officer Zamoloski plugged the answering machine into a power outlet under his desk, he leaned forward and hit the play button.

Richard was relieved that the messages played.

"Do you know who left that warning?" Zamoloski asked.

"I told you that I didn't," Richard said. "Stephani did tell me that someone had left a warning on the machine last week, and she'd deleted it by mistake. She did tell you about that message, but she thought without the evidence you wouldn't believe her. I don't know if it was the same person. Do you have someone that restores deleted data from these machines? It would be worth trying to restore that message to see if it's the same voice."

Zamoloski said, "We'll have to check this out."

"She was booked into a rehab clinic for tomorrow morning. I've tried calling her so many times, and she doesn't answer her cell."

"She was going voluntarily?"

"The boss told her to go."

"Then she's high-tailed it because she doesn't want to go. She'll turn up when she's ready."

"This is not like her." Richard thumped the cop's cluttered desk making the files jump. "Maybe someone took her by force."

Two officers turned towards them, and one started over.

"All okay, guys." He turned to Richard. "I understand your concerns, but we don't know that."

Richard rose from the office chair.

The phone rang and Zamoloski excused himself and answered it. "Yeah. I need you here. Dixon has just brought in Stephani Robbin's answering machine. He thinks that she's missing. Yeah. You need to listen to the message." He hung up and spoke to Dixon. "It seems that Ms. Robbins called Bill yesterday afternoon, but the call disconnected. He tried to return her call, but there was no answer. If you think of anything, anything at all, no matter how insignificant, please call. I appreciate you bringing this in."

"One other thing, I think that Jack might have been the last person Stephani spoke to. She was talking to me on the phone Monday afternoon when Jack turned up at her apartment. I don't know why he went to see her."

"Who's Jack, and what's he to her? Oh, he's the one with the prints on that note she found in her sports bag?"

"Yes."

"Even though we've called him a number of times, he hasn't been in yet to be fingerprinted so we can exclude his prints from the ones we found on the note."

"He's a sales marketing executive from a pharmaceutical supplies company that we regularly buy from. He usually calls on Stephani once a month."

***

It was late afternoon when Richard arrived at Rigby. He parked, locked the car and hurried to his office.

Fred put down the test tubes and slipped down his mask. "So, did you find her?"

Melissa closed the autoclave and straightened. "What's wrong? Is she sick?"

"Stephani's missing. There's no sign that she's been in her apartment since yesterday morning. There's a plate in her sink with dried-up food on it, and I know she's fussy about washing up."

Richard's sigh was a tense one. "Does anyone have any idea where she could be?"

"Sorry. To me, she did not say anything," Nina said.

Melissa turned back to her task.

"Melissa, you sure she didn't say something to you? Anything that might've seemed insignificant at the time, but may throw some light on where she is?"

"I told you before, she didn't." She snapped off her gloves. "I'm going to have a coffee. Are you coming, Nina?"

"I have to finish the calibrations." She looked at Richard. The query in her glance told him that she suspected something was amiss with Melissa as well.

Richard went to his office and called Jack. Just maybe, Melissa did know more about her brother than she was saying.

The call was diverted to the office. All they could tell him was that Jack was on vacation. Frustrated, he hung up and punched in Kennelly's number. "I've tried to call Jack, but he's not answering. Did you try him?"

"No luck there for us either. Do you have his home number?"

"Unfortunately, no. Can you question Melissa again? I think she may know where her brother's holed up." Richard saw Ross heading his way. He hung up.

"Just heard about Stephani. Now this may or may not have a bearing on her problem, but you have to admit it's suspicious that she's disappeared with this hanging over her head."

It was all Richard could do not to punch him. He clenched and unclenched his fists under the desk. "Get out. Get out."

263

"Now, now. No need to get hot under the collar," Ross said.

"I've given Zamoloski Stephani's machine."

"What machine?"

"Talk to him. I'm going out."

"You can't walk out on me!"

"Watch me."

He let himself out into the hallway. The anger left him suddenly like a deflated balloon as he pressed the button on the elevator.

What could he say to anyone that would help? He felt useless and helpless like when he was a boy and his father had fallen into the lake and couldn't swim. He sat in the boat screaming to his dad. "Swim, Dad, swim."

"I can't," his father had gasped before he went under.

The outboard motor carried Richard further and further away from his father. Some stranger fishing nearby had dived in and saved his father. They never went boating again.

Richard's shoulders slumped as he rode the elevator down to the ground floor. He went outside.

Through the tinted glass windows, he noticed people observing him. He didn't care. Then he found some shade under an oak tree. When he looked out from his office, which he didn't do too often, he could see the uppermost branches. He sat and squinted from the shimmering sun as he stared into the distance. The heat was making him sweat, so he loosened his tie and unbuttoned the top buttons of his shirt.

What would he do without Stephani? She had contributed so much to their project in the way of sheer commitment, brains and chutzpah. Stephani had suggested they try a new method of growing cells. She outlined the test program and to him, it had sounded stupid at the time and he'd said so, but it turned out to be their best bet.

She meant so much to him. He wanted to spend the rest of his life with her. He didn't know if he still had a job, but nothing was more important than finding Stephani.

Richard did not know how long he had sat staring into the desert, but eventually he rose and went back inside. The cool air settled on his heated skin and made him feel cold for a moment. He caught the elevator, and headed to Ross's office.

Sharon, Ross's assistant, stopped typing. "Sorry to hear about Stephani."

"Thanks. Is Ross in? I need to see him." He didn't know if she was sorry about Stephani being suspended from work or about her disappearance. Whichever it was, he wasn't going to ask.

"He's in a meeting, but give me a moment and I'll see what I can do." She buzzed her boss. "Sorry to interrupt. I know that your instructions were…but Richard would like to see you." She listened. "Yes."

She turned to Richard. "Ross won't be long, just take a seat."

He looked at the leather lounge chairs arranged decoratively in a large reception area and chose the closest one beside a potted fichus tree. Large paintings of desert scenes decorated the walls.

Had the same criminal kidnapped both Stephani and Dionne? Was it any consolation if they had? He thought not.

You only read about these things in the papers and never think that it could involve you. Jesus, it was horrifying.

Two men that he didn't know nodded a greeting to Richard as

they came out of Ross's office and went towards the elevators.

"Richard. We need to talk," Ross said, as he walked towards him. "Come in."

He stood. "I can say what I need to say here."

"Maybe, we were both a little hasty."

Richard went in and sat in a leather chesterfield armchair. Grenfeld's oak desk held a few papers, laptop, phone and, some ball tree thingy that you set off by pushing the first one and the next one hits the next one and so on.

Grenfeld sat on the other side and steepled his fingers.

Richard was about to speak when Ross held up his hand to silence him.

"The way I see it is that you believe I've been hard on Stephani. That she has been drinking due to-"

"Fuck you, Buddy." Richard stood.

"Now hear me out before you steam any more horse shit."

"You've given me no reason to stay."

Ross sighed. "You have to understand my position. I'm-"

"I don't have to understand anything." He started for the door.

"Come, sit down, please. Let's sort this out," Ross said.

"Let's do that." He sat. "You don't know her. You don't know that she's been pivotal to this whole project. Without her we wouldn't have gotten this far for at least two more years or longer."

"Those men who just left were two of my backers. I don't have the resources to raise enough cash on my own for all the projects I have underway at the moment. They're asking hard questions about all this and I'm the person who has to satisfy their answers, or they pull out."

"Just like that?"

"Yep. Just like that. So, are you with me or not? We need your commitment, notwithstanding that Stephani is missing. Do we have it?"

"As long as you leave me to concentrate on the research and allow Stephani to return after she's been in rehab. Do we have an agreement?"

"We do."

Ross stood to shake his hand, but Richard ignored it.

CHAPTER 40

He stared at himself in the rear-view mirror of the van. He looked respectable. This would do. Some females went crazy for a man like him. However, he didn't want them. What he wanted he went out and took.

Got out, and then he strolled across the concrete parking lot—past vehicles sitting in rows waiting for their owners—and into the shopping mall. He stared from store window to store window. Where did they keep such things?

Finally, he went into Dillard's and asked the girl behind the makeup counter. Young thing she was. Black bangs, thin with pert breasts. This one was too preoccupied with her multi-colored fingernails to answer right away. Finally, she directed him to a smaller shopping mall two blocks away. Looked at him with starry eyes, she did.

He wasn't going to do any of that stuff again. Anyway, she was a little older than the usual type he wanted. So was Stephani, and he still wanted her. However, she was different. She was his Princess.

Into the brightly lit store, he strolled. Two assistants were busy wasting time, as they usually do, with some bridal music playing softly in the background. White dresses lined the walls—some soft and fluffy, others all slinky, satin, lace, and sequins. The puffy inflated ones with that tulle and sparkling shiny stuff reminded him of the Christmases he didn't celebrate. He'd spent his time pressing his nose against the glass window displays wishing for this or that.

He passed by the short runway set in the middle and walked over to the rows of gowns. Before he could start looking through the rack, the store assistant was beside him. She pulled out some sleek and strapless numbers.

He said it had to be something old-fashioned. It would suit his Princess best. He snapped when she suggested that he should let his bride pick out what she wanted. He walked out. This bitch wouldn't be getting his cash. She made him feel sick to his stomach with her baggy skin: just like his mother used to.

***

Stephani blinked, disoriented. Where was she? Something was wrong.

Sunlight slid in through a shuttered window and caught the dust motes in its glow. It shone across a haphazard assortment of boxes stacked to one side of the room with an old floral sofa and an old rocking horse. Nothing looked familiar.

She tried to roll on her side, but something stopped her no matter how hard she tried, and the fog in her head made it all the harder.

What had happened? Accident? Injury? Try as she might, she couldn't work out the puzzle.

Her arms ached when she tried to move them, and her wrists were bound in-front with a zip tie. She tried to lift her head, but the movement made it feel as if there was a banging drum inside it.

Had she gotten into some S & M thing?

Her legs were tied as well. What the hell?

Then a realization filled her thoughts. Someone had brought her here against her will. Fear knotted her stomach.

Oh, God. Stephani opened her mouth to call out for help but

269

realized that whoever had brought her here might hear.

She lifted her head despite the drumming at her temples and saw each ankle chained to opposite sides of the bedpost. Anyone could do whatever they wanted to her. *Jesus.*

This was a nightmare, had to be a nightmare. However, in a dream state she was sure she wouldn't feel pain, though she did now.

Her clothes were wrinkled as if she had slept in them for a long time. The suffocating stillness washed over her.

She was alone.

This somehow scared her more. Was someone planning to starve her to death?

She twisted her wrists to try to free her hands; perspiration beaded her face. That such a task would prove such an effort made her worry about how long she had been drugged because there could be no other explanation for the way she felt.

Then she remembered being in Jack's van, and they were driving to a remote ranch to try to find Dionne. This had happened before she fell asleep.

The man who had tied her up may have captured Jack, or worse, killed him and left her here to die. An icy well of apprehension grew inside her.

She heard her ring tone on a cell phone…'Nothing Compares 2 U'. Someone was answering her cell. Was it her captor?

Then she remembered that Jack had thrown her cell out. Was Jack the one who had brought her here? Maybe, that part was a dream, too.

Footsteps echoed from somewhere below. Someone was coming.

CHAPTER 41

Stephani stiffened at the sound of a key in the lock. That sound sent nearly sent her hyperventilating. It raised terrors of dark enclosed spaces for which she had no explanation.

What was this kidnapper going to do with her? Maybe, she could do a deal with him.

Eyes closed, she concentrated on trying to keep her breathing as even as she could. Someone padded softly into the room.

This person was setting up something, maybe a table. She opened one eye and closed it quickly trying to process what she had seen as the man hurried out.

Jack…it was Jack…but it couldn't be. It had to have been the effects of the drugs that kidnapper had given her. Her brain must be muddled.

Jack returned moments later with a tray of sandwiches and a drink.

She opened her eyes and stared at Jack in total disbelief. How he could do something like this? "What's going on?"

"My Princess has woken. I've made some delicious food for my Princess."

Princess…where had she heard that…then she remembered. Jack had said that just before she blacked out in the van. Jesus, why hadn't she noticed anything odd about him before this? "If you wanted to spend time with me, we could have worked something out," she said.

"I've brought you something to eat. We can't have you getting weak," Jack said. "You'll feel better after you've eaten."

His chatting startled her. "Why have you done this, Jack?"

He didn't answer, so she plowed on, all the while her heart galloped like a frightened gazelle running from a predator. "What do you want from me? There's no need for this."

"Hold out your hands."

"Jack? What's happening here? Why have you done this? Surely we can work it out."

"Don't get any ideas. Just keep still."

She did as he asked. He cut the zip tie and secured handcuffs to her wrists.

She thought she knew Jack, had trusted him.

Stephani stared at the sandwiches realizing how hungry she was.

"Eat."

"What drugs have you laced these with?"

"I would never do that."

"Then you eat one so that I know you haven't put anything in the food." He'd drugged the water he'd given her.

He picked one up and took a bite. "Happy?"

She held up her hands. "Take these off so I can eat properly."

"Not yet."

If it tasted strange, she would spit it out. However, the first bite filled her mouth with the delicious taste of pickle and beef, and she couldn't stop eating.

"Was it you who sent those photographs and that poem?" she said between mouthfuls.

He smirked, and her throat tightened so much that she could hardly swallow. "If you let me go now, I promise I won't tell anyone. Please, Jack. Just let me go." She pushed the rest of the sandwich away.

He didn't answer.

"Come on. This is crazy. Just let me go."

He smiled. "You think me that stupid, my Princess." He ran the back of his hand down her cheek.

"Stop it." Stephani pushed his arm away.

"My Princess, my one and only love."

"Jesus, Jack. The police will put you away for this. Why'd you do it?" This wasn't the Jack that she'd come to know. Was he some sort of Jekyll and Hyde?

"This wasn't about Dionne. This was about getting me to come with you, wasn't it?"

"Eat," he snapped.

Stephani's appetite evaporated. "Why'd you bring me here?"

He didn't answer.

His silence scared her more. "Where am I?"

"Attic room in a remote location," he said.

"Just let me go and we can forget this ever happened. We can still be friends." She tried to smile.

"I won't hurt you. I will never hurt you. You are not like all the others. My Princess, my one and only love." He lifted his hand to touch her cheek but stopped when she shrank away.

Someone driving a white van took Dionne, she'd been told. Was it Jack? "What others?"

"Don't ask if you don't want to know the answer."

Jesus, had he abducted other women? He was right, she didn't want to know…couldn't handle that information. She took a shaky breath. What was he going to do with her? "Don't lock me in, please." The moment she'd uttered the words, she wished she hadn't revealed this vulnerability.

He stared at her as if he was reading her thoughts. "Why?"

"I don't like it."

"My Princess will have to wait till I can trust her completely."

Then she asked the question that she had not been brave enough to ask earlier. "Did you kidnap Dionne?"

CHAPTER 42

Richard logged out of the file he had worked on, brought up the advertisement he had run—together with a current photo of Stephani—on a missing person web site.

Missing – Stephani Robbins Height 5'8". Mid length, black hair, brown eyes. Any information received will be kept confidential. Please email.

He'd left an email address he'd created just for this.

Richard wanted to do something rather than wait for Zamoloski and his team to locate her. He might get some crackpots, the officer had said, but all Richard cared about was finding Stephani.

He picked up his cell to call Grenfeld but hung up when he saw an email in reply to his advertisement.

He opened the message.

Subject: Missing person

Hi

I'm very concerned about Stephani.

An evil dude was watching and taking photographs of Stephani when she was going for her morning jog in Iron Grove Park. I saw him following her when she was shopping last week. I am sure he's the one who abducted Stephani. He is tall, tanned with black hair. He drives a white van.

Concerned Citizen.

"Fuck. Fuck. Fuck." This couldn't be a hoax. This man knew where she went jogging. This message confirmed his worst fears. Richard reread the email, then forwarded it to Zamoloski. Meanwhile, he mulled over what his reply would be. He started to type, then stopped mid-sentence, deleted the message, then started again. He paused when he realized. This guy had been watching Stephani too, otherwise how would he have known any of this?

He slumped forward, closed his eyes and began to recite the Lord's Prayer. At the end, he pleaded with God to help find Stephani and Dionne while they were still alive.

Richard had not prayed for a long time. He'd given up going to church when he left home to board near the college where he was studying all those years ago. His father used to insist he go to God's house and he had grown to hate all that pretense. His father used to smile at the churchgoers and help the priest every Sunday, and then he'd go home, eat lunch, turn on the TV and either drink himself to oblivion in front of the set or go to the bar and down too many beers there. Some Monday mornings, he'd find his dad asleep in the car. How he'd driven home from the bar without crashing the Ford, he didn't know. He'd come inside, get cleaned up, and go to work.

It would be safer to discuss his reply to this guy's email with the officer before he sent it. He reached for his cell as he reread the message. His chest tightened in anger. That guy was a voyeur, a sick voyeur or worse. Had he abducted her and thought she was someone else? He prayed that Stephani would be found before it was too late.

***

Richard sat down beside the officer's desk. While Zamoloski eased himself into the chair on the other side, Richard glanced around the room. It held an eclectic assortment of furniture, old technology fighting with new. Uniformed and plain clothes officers colored the terrain, some in discussion, some sitting at a desk, staring at a monitor, and others with jackets discarded talking on phones. Why weren't they all out looking for Stephani?

Zamoloski broke into Richard's thoughts. "I guess you're wondering why I've asked you to come in."

Richard leaned forward. "Melissa's told you some new information concerning the whereabouts of her step-brother?"

"We are holding a suspect by the name of Princie Younger. It seems-"

"What did you say?" Richard leaned forward.

"We traced him by that email sent to you in response to your advertisement."

"He was 'the concerned citizen' who hadn't replied when asked how he came to know this information about Stephani," Richard said.

"There's been a positive ID of him outside of Stephani Robbins's apartment. But because he's a mail carrier, he has a perfect excuse to be there every day. We did a search of his premises and found a surprising collection of objects. This suspect liked to sift through trash bins and lift discarded items that interested him."

"My God, what sort of creep goes through other people's trash? He's been through Stephani's refuse? What did he take?"

"In his home, we found a hairbrush which forensics have established is hers from the strands of black hair on the brush. We got her sister to bring down one of Stephani's current hairbrushes and a few other things this morning so the lab could test it for a match. There were powder puffs, lipsticks, empty deodorant bottles, and some intimate clothing. Not all the clothing was hers. He's been at this game for some years and he has quite a collection."

"Where's this scum?"

"The suspect is being held in custody. Swears he didn't kidnap her."

"Let me see him."

"No chance."

"Please."

"I do need you to take a look at a computer-generated line-up and tell me if you recognize anyone." He logged into the program and turned the screen to face Richard.

Richard stared at the images.

After a few minutes, he paused at a face that looked vaguely like someone he'd seen recently, however he wasn't certain. "I can't recognize anyone here. I wish I could because then you could nail the guy."

Zamoloski expelled a slow breath. "Okay, we'll get together a live line-up." Zamoloski picked up his phone and asked someone to organize it. "You want some coffee. There's a machine in the staff room that makes a mean brew. We won it in a raffle. It's the best piece of equipment we have here."

"Sure." Richard rose.

"Stay put. I'll be back soon." He went to the staff room.

Zamoloski returned with two steaming cups.

He finished off his coffee while Zamoloski answered calls.

Zamoloski put down the phone and turned to Richard. "An abandoned white van that could have been the kidnap vehicle has been located. Forensics are combing the vehicle now for evidence."

"Let's hope they find something," Richard said.

The phone rang again. "Excuse me while I answer this."

Finally, the officer pushed back his chair and rose. "Okay. Can you come in tomorrow for the live line-up?"

"I'll do anything it takes to find the scum who took Stephani."

He led Richard through the clutter of office furniture, past some woman who was slumped in a chair sobbing, to some glass doors that opened into a corridor.

Uniforms were milling about. "Hey Ted," Zamoloski said to a colleague, "Let's get a meeting put together for this afternoon." He kept going without waiting for an answer.

Down the hallway, a uniform had just opened a door for a handcuffed man.

"Hey, he looks vaguely familiar." Richard stared at the slightly built man. "Is that him?"

Zamoloski said, "Hey, Mike. Get him into the interview room now."

"Sure."

Richard clenched his fists. "I knew it. Mother-fucking-scum. Where're you keeping Stephani?"

"How did I know he was going to grab her?" Princie scratched at the two days' worth of stubble on his pitted skin. "Stephani's so beautiful."

"Let's go," Mike said to the detainee, as he urged him inside.

"Come on." Zamoloski went to take Richard's elbow, but he shrugged him off.

Richard turned, ran down the hallway before the uniform could close the door. Richard grabbed Younger by the collar, wrenched him into the hall and slammed the door, temporarily locking the uniform inside.

Younger flailed uselessly.

"Where is she?" He slammed Younger into the wall and wrapped his hands around his throat.

The officer was pounding towards Richard.

Younger gasped.

"Let him go." Zamoloski grabbed his arm and brought it behind his back.

Richard eased away from Younger, who was still gasping for a breath. Richard allowed himself to be restrained. He'd have been crazy to fight a cop.

Younger pulled out his atomizer and breathed in the Ventolin.

"What the hell do you think you're doing?" Zamoloski frog-marched Richard toward the squad room where a couple of guys were talking.

He allowed himself to be led for a few moments. Then he broke free.

Zamoloski screamed for assistance.

Two uniforms standing by the entrance started running.

Richard slid into a leg-sweep, knocking Younger to the ground.

Mike flung the interview room door open.

Younger's breath came out in a rushing wheeze as Richard took the advantage, arms flying.

Younger cowered.

Zamoloski grabbed Richard by the collar, but he twisted away from his grasp.

He was about to have another go at Younger when he saw that Mike had drawn his Taser. "Raise your arms, Richard. Now."

Zamoloski got up slowly, breathing hard.

Kennelly appeared from another room a few doors down. "What's going on?"

"Get Younger outa here," Zamoloski puffed. "I'll sort this out with you later."

"Will do," Mike pulled Younger to his feet and took him to the end of the hallway and tapped in the code.

Younger and Mike disappeared into the secure holding area.

"Glad you didn't lose your head back there, Richard," Zamoloski said.

"I'm not," Richard said.

"What the fuck went down here?" Kennelly asked.

"That mother-fucking-scum has my girl. I'm not the criminal. He is." Richard nodded towards the doorway where Younger had gone.

"It's under control, guys. Thanks," Zamoloski said.

"You sure?" one of the uniforms who'd rushed to their aid asked Zamoloski.

Zamoloski said, "Yep. Appreciate this." He put a hand on Richard's shoulder. "Let's go."

The moment they were back at Zamoloski's desk, Richard shrugged him off. "I'm not going to do anything crazy."

"Damn right you're not. I should have you up for assaulting a suspect," Zamoloski said. "And this will damn sure stick. But, I sure as hell don't need any more paperwork."

Kennelly grimaced. "You're going to get hung for this if the chief finds out," he said to his partner.

"Just find Stephani and Dionne," Richard said.

"We're doing our best, but you're hampering this investigation, and I don't need to tell you that you can forget about live line-up now," Zamoloski said.

"Don't worry. I'm not going to lose any sleep over it."

"You never heard me say this, but I can understand how you feel. My brother's daughter went missing a couple of years ago, and it was all I could do to stop him shooting every guy she'd ever gone on a date with," Zamoloski said. "We found her after a few weeks with some scumbag."

Richard held up his cuffed hands. "Do I have a right to ask for these to be removed?"

"Sure. You didn't assault anyone, did you?"

"Appreciate this."

CHAPTER 43

Jack eased Stephani's breakfast onto the side table. "How's my Princess today?"

Stephani glared at him. "I am not your damned princess!"

"You are, my Princess." He said this as if it were a foregone conclusion as he centered the plate of easy-over eggs and toast on the tray and refolded the napkin.

"How can I eat with these handcuffs?"

"It will be my pleasure to feed you." He smiled.

"I'd rather starve." This was the first morning that she'd been lucid. She didn't know how long she'd been drugged. No more than a day, she guessed.

"As you wish." He picked up the tray, and started for the door.

"Please uncuff me so I can feed myself?"

His hesitation made her try again. "I promise not to try anything."

"Do you mean that you won't try to escape?"

She nodded her head.

"Then say it."

Stephani took a deep breath. "I won't try to escape. I still don't know if I should believe you that you didn't kidnap Dionne."

He laughed. "I admit it was great timing."

That didn't assuage her fears for Dionne. If he had taken her, she might have been able to make a bargain with him. "So who's got Dionne? Is the rest of my family in danger too? If you do anything to them, I'll kill you. Just leave my family alone."

When he didn't answer, she said, "And another thing…were you the one behind those phone calls?"

"What calls? Why would I bother? I have you where I want you now."

"It doesn't matter." Was it someone who was working with Jack, trying to make her more afraid?

"When we're married, will you cook for me?" he asked.

"Married? You're joking?" He looked serious, and she could see he wasn't. "Is that why those wedding dresses are on the back of the door?"

He stared at her as if she were naked. What perverted things did he want her to do? "Oh sure, I'll cook. Then let me eat now. Do you want a bride that's sick and starving?"

He picked up the knife and fork and cut the toast and eggs. "Open wide."

She'd choke before she'd let him feed her.

"Open your mouth!" He screamed.

Startled, Stephani jerked backwards.

"How long have I been here?" she asked between mouthfuls.

He didn't answer.

"I haven't washed in days. My hair's dirty. I need a shower." It worried her that he might want to be there when she washed, but she had to convince him to let her out of this room.

He grimaced. "I'll think about it."

***

A while later, he came back. Stefani couldn't be sure whether one or two hours had gone by.

In his hands, he held a chain and padlock. "I can't take a chance that you'll escape."

"I told you I wouldn't."

"Keep still so I can blindfold you."

"Please don't cover my eyes." She cringed at the thought of being led somewhere in darkness. 'The dark scares me', she nearly said but didn't. She always slept with the bedside light on.

As he drew closer with the blindfold, she swung at his head with her cuffed hands.

Jack groaned as his head snapped backwards from her blow.

Damn, she should have hit him harder and knocked him out.

He glared at her. "My Princess doesn't know how to behave. I will have to teach her."

One blow sent her backwards against the mattress, and the next one felt like her cheek was exploding.

"My Princess will keep still while I blindfold her."

The intense pain and his raised fist forced her to back down from her fight.

He wrenched the cloth over her eyes.

Stephani gasped. "I can't breathe. I can't..." The blindfold made her feel like she was locked up in some dark hole.

The pain of a slap on her already swollen cheek brought her back suddenly.

"Pretending to faint won't get my sympathy, my Princess."

Jack must have freed her legs because they were now dangling over the edge of the bed.

Disoriented and claustrophobic, she stumbled as Jack pulled her along. "Where are we going?"

"Bathroom, unless you want to go to my bedroom?" He paused.

"Bathroom."

"You're shaking, my Princess. You can't be cold. I've turned off the air conditioning."

The dark terrified her. However, she'd never admit this to him, for he would certainly use this to his advantage.

"A few steps...careful. Take it slowly. I don't want you falling, my Princess."

A door creaked open and a musty odor assaulted her senses.

"We're here." He took off her blindfold.

She breathed and blinked to adjust her eyes to the sunlight flooding in through a small cracked window in the bathroom.

"It's not the Hilton but adequate for your needs." He undid one cuff. "So you can get your clothes off."

He secured the chain to the pipes under the green hand basin while she took in the original fifties sparse décor of the bathroom. A clean white towel hung over the bath and a chrome and shag-pile stool was beside it.

"I can't get my clothes off while I'm still connected to that chain," she said.

"Just ease them far enough so they won't get wet. If you think I'd be stupid enough to remove the cuffs, then you're wrong."

"Shampoo?"

He opened the mottled mirrored cupboard above the basin. Bottles of deodorant, shampoo, conditioner and face cream stood like soldiers in a row. "It's all here."

They were all unopened bottles. My God, how long had he been planning this? He was staring at her. She glanced behind the door, relieved when she saw a key in the lock. "I need some privacy?"

"Why? You've been married and had a child." He lifted her chin with the tip of his finger. "Nice body under those clothes."

Stephani swallowed. "How would you know?"

"I saw you walking around your bedroom. You know you should close your blinds."

Holy hell, he'd been watching her. She tried to remember if she'd walked about naked in the bedroom and guessed that she probably had. "I'm not getting undressed while you're here."

"I'll let you off this time, but when we're married.... I'll be vacuuming and dusting your room while you wash." He slammed the door as he left.

Stephani sank onto the ledge at the back of the green bath badly shaken. Then she remembered about the door and went over—chain dragging nosily on the old tiles—and locked it. She carried the stool over to the window and climbed up so she could reach the latch. Her heart hammered for fear that he would burst in and catch her. She undid the catch, tried to slide the window up and saw that the frame was nailed down.

She pressed her face against the pane. A few trees, cactus, and an old barn were all she could see.

That warning the Native American woman had given her entered her thoughts. *You are in danger. One that dances with the bad spirits is waiting for you. This one that waits, is cloaked and hunts in the shadows. You will not know of their black heart until it is too late.*

She wished she had questioned that woman more. Maybe then, she wouldn't have been in this predicament.

CHAPTER 44

Stephani finished off the cereal he'd left on a small table beside her bed and drank the lukewarm coffee. He must have snuck in while she was asleep early this morning. And he was always cleaning. The attic was spotless now. It had been dusty when she'd arrived.

Those wedding dresses were still hanging on the back of the door. One looked smaller than the other. What did he have planned? Tears welled up and she blinked them away.

Feeling sorry for herself wouldn't help at all. She put her hand to her sore and swollen cheek and gritted her teeth to stop from crying out. She'd forgotten how hard he'd hit her.

Her sister was probably worrying about her as well as Dionne. How long had she been here? Who would tell her mom that she was missing? Better not to distress her. She hoped Iantha didn't say anything. She hoped Henry was safe from this monster, Jack.

Jack didn't to chain her leg irons to the bed after her morning trip to the bathroom. Had he forgotten or was there another reason. Was it a test to see if she'd try to escape and he'd set a trap for her? She hobbled slowly over to the shuttered window and tried to move the dusty slats so she could see out. However, the window was boarded up and through the wide gaps searing sunlight slanted in. She blinked to adjust her eyes and stared out.

Car tracks led to an old barn and its doors were wide open. Had he gone out?

She stood listening just in case he was still home. The sounds of mocking birds twittering, and the rustle of leaves in the breeze was all she heard.

Stephani shuffled to the door. She called out. "Is anyone there? Is anyone out there? Please help me."

She was met with silence.

***

Princie, who had been cleared of any wrongdoing as far as Stephani was concerned, was glad to have a seat to himself on the bus. He sat looking through the window at the passing parade of people, cars, dogs and children as the bus continued toward Mesa.

At the next stop an old guy that smelled as if he'd never washed in his life, took the spare seat next to him. Princie was relieved that his stop was next and he could stop covering his nose to stop the odor.

A couple of hours after Dixon's attack, the cops had let him go and told him that he wasn't to leave town. He was lucky.

His cell rang just after he got off.

"Is that Princie Younger?"

"Speaking."

"This is Brad Jenesie."

"Hi, Mr. Jenesie." This wasn't his immediate boss; it was the head of the department. What did he want with him?

"The police called yesterday to inform us that you were a person of interest in the abduction of a young girl, and I gave them your home address. I'm going to have put you on extended leave without pay pending our investigation."

"But...but. I need that job."

"You must understand that we cannot employ anyone with an unsavory background. You'll get any outstanding pay deposited in your bank account at the end of the month. Good day, Mr. Young."

He was about to speak when he realized that Jenesie had ended the conversation. He knew that once they delved into what he'd been doing, his employment would be terminated. Even the unions couldn't help him with this.

Man, what was he going to do? He had very little in savings and rent to pay each month. It wasn't fair. He'd have one of those frozen meals in his freezer and start looking on the Internet for another job.

He called his sister. "Hi, Melissa. Can we meet someplace?"

"I told you before. Don't call me. I don't want anything to do with you. Don't come to my place. Stephani's missing and the cops have been hanging around my place. I don't know where you live and don't want to know."

"I lost my job and I don't know how long before I find something else. If you could help me with the rent-"

"I'm not giving you any more money. No money. Do you hear me? I don't know what sort of stuff you're involved in and don't want to know. As far as I'm concerned, you're a lowlife. Never call me again."

Stephani was a sexy dame with those long legs and lovely buns, he especially liked her buns, but she was a trouble magnet. Look where his good deeds had gotten him. He wasn't going to bother with looking out for her any longer.

He walked down the alleyway towards his rental in the neglected multi-story office building. He opened the front door and dropped his keys and cell phone on the side table. He needed a stiff drink after what he'd been through today and went toward the cupboard. He heard a noise behind him and turned.

That bad dude he'd seen watching Stephani was standing before him.

"Younger, isn't it? Dump of a place." He kicked aside one of the refuse bags.

Princie tensed, nervous that this guy had sought him out. "You got no right to come in here."

"You invited me in. We're going to have a few drinks to celebrate." The bad dude pulled out a bottle of wine and two glasses from a cooler bag on the floor.

"How'd that get in here?" He pulled out his asthma spray and sucked in its healing mist.

"I came over earlier but you weren't home so I let myself in."

"The door was locked…how'd you know that I'd come home today?"

"Your face is on the front page of all the newspapers. Seems the police have been questioning you in connection with the abduction of that young girl and Stephani. I knew they'd release you sooner or later, and I got lucky. I've got a proposal for you. First proposal…we join forces. You find the girls, and we can both watch them and compare notes."

"Get your ass outa here. What I do, I do alone." He had a gun stashed in the drawer under the sink if he needed it.

"You know you ought to clean this place up." He brushed the

haphazard pile of newspapers and clippings from the Formica table.

"Why'd you do that?"

"We're going to celebrate, and I need to pour out the wine." He set the glasses on the table and filled them. "This one's for you."

"Say, what's your name?"

"Jack." He pushed the glass toward Princie. "Second proposal…I have a job for you. You can earn more money than you ever dreamed of."

"What sort of job?" Now he was interested.

"Let's have a drink and discuss it." Jack pulled out an aluminum chair, sat at the table and took a gulp. "Drink up."

Princie had been about to say, 'it's your fault that I lost my job', but kept silent and joined him. Any hesitation that the wine could be tainted or drugged dissipated when he saw Jack drink. He picked up the glass and tasted. "Not bad."

"I only buy the best for my employees. I've got a client who needs a courier. He wants you to deliver parcels to various places. Since you've been a mail carrier, I thought it was right for you."

Princie drank some more. "Why you helping me?"

"I like your style. You and I are the same sort of guys."

"Say…what's in the parcel?"

"Don't ask questions. You get paid a grand on delivery. With four deliveries and sometimes five a week, that's four grand at least. Are you in?"

He nodded. This was sounding better and better. It was his lucky day after all.

Jack refilled Princie's empty glass.

Princie downed that one too and attempted to rise from his seat, but his legs gave way and he tumbled to the floor. "What's going on?"

"You think I could stand by knowing that you'd been watching my Princess. Even went through her refuse and picked up some of her personal stuff. You're nothing but sewerage."

"Stephani? You've…drugged me." The words came out slurred. "How…"

"You're going to die unless you get help. Too bad you can't call anyone." Jack picked up Princie's cell from the side table, threw it down and crushed it under his heel. "Got any more phones?"

Princie stared at him. He wasn't going to tell him where it was. He tried as hard as he could to move and succeeded in moving only his finger.

"Stay there. No need to get up." He laughed. "I know you can't anyway." Jack disappeared down the hallway.

Princie struggled repeatedly to no avail. Whatever Jack had put in his drink had paralyzed him.

Jack returned with an old sixties phone, cord hanging from it. "Found it. See, that wasn't too hard."

"How…" His jaw was refusing to work. He couldn't even swallow.

"I coated the inside of the glass with a fast-acting poison. If no one finds you soon, you'll drown in your own spit and, or stop breathing first. I've got to get back to my Princess." He picked up Princie's keys and stared at the gas burner on the bench top. "Don't want you getting cold. Let's fix that now." He lit the burner and hauled a bag of refuse over. You should have tidied up this place. But, it doesn't matter now." He undid the bag and tipped the contents over the burner and down the sides of the cupboard. Jack added a few newspapers on top of the smoldering mess. At first, the food fizzled and spat until some paper bags and newspapers ignited.

"Don't…leave…me…" Princie could hardly get the words out.

Smoke poured from the burning refuse.

He heard Jack let himself out and lock the front door.

Princie looked at the crushed cell and the old phone on the floor. If only he could plug the phone back in. He tried to shout, but the sound came out in a whimper and drool ran down his cheek. This wasn't his lucky day.

It was his last day. He wasn't ready to die.

***

A car door slammed, making her jump. *Oh God, he was back*. Stephani had been drifting off to sleep.

The heavy tread of Jack coming up the stairs set her nerves on edge. She prayed that he wouldn't harm her as the door opened.

He turned on the lamp, and came over to her, his fingertips tracing the curve of her thigh through the blanket. It took all her willpower to keep her breathing even and not shrink away.

After a few moments, she could hear him rustling nearby. She opened her eyes the tiniest bit and saw him sorting through the basket he had provided for her dirty laundry. Jack pulled out her underwear, rubbed it against his groin, and groaned. He was getting off on this.

As suddenly as he entered, he retreated, but not without pausing at the door to say, "Sleep then, my Princess, for soon we will be wed. My sweet Princess will be mine forever." Then he was gone.

CHAPTER 45

Richard leaned back in his desk chair and stared at the glass wall separating him from Laboratory 1. The excitement he should have been feeling, now that final trials were underway with the first successful samples they had produced, was absent.

Stephani should have been part of this. However, those officers were no closer to finding her or Dionne.

He couldn't stop thinking about Stephani. Was she okay? Was she being kept locked up in a cage: cold and hungry? Dear Lord, was she still alive? She had to be. However, each day she was missing made him sink deeper into despair. The police had not been able to make Princie reveal her whereabouts. And since he ruined his chance of identifying him in a line-up by attacking him, Princie had been let go. Maybe, the man was telling the truth. There had to be someone who had seen something.

He picked up the phone and dialed Jack's business cell phone again. He'd left messages so many times that he'd lost count. Jack was probably the last person to have spoken to Stephani. There could have been something she said to Jack, something that didn't seem important at the time, which could help.

"West Labs Equipment, good morning."

"Hello. I'd like to speak to Jack Theed."

"I'm sorry, sir," the female receptionist said. "He's on a month's vacation. Would you like to leave a message for him?"

"No. I need his home number. I need to contact him urgently.

I've left a dozen messages for him already."

"I can't give out any personal details of our employees."

"It's urgent. I've been trying to reach him on his cell phone, but he's not answering. He was the last person to speak with my girl, Stephani. She's missing. Please help me." He had not called her his girl to anyone before, and he now knew he wanted her to be much more than that if he got the chance.

"I'm sure she'll turn up soon enough if she wants to, sir."

Richard could imagine the junior filing her nails while she talked. "Don't you listen to the news? Stephani's been kidnapped." He thumped the table in frustration and temper.

"Oh, that girl. That Stephani. Oh, it must be terrible for you."

"It's…. Just help me please."

"Please don't tell anyone where you got the number, or I'll be out of a job…his details are on the screen now." After she gave him the number, she said, "Tell you what, I used to think he was a stud. Kinda acts like it too. Someone told me that he's a bit of a loner. Probably just shy underneath." She sighed.

"Thanks for your help. I'm sorry-"

"Shucks, it ain't nothing. If I can do anything more, just give me a call. Oh, here's a bit of gossip. Not that I go in for that sort of thing. Anyways, he bought acreage out near Camp Verdi. Could be there right now. His mom died two weeks ago. Sad really. Probably wanted to get away for a while."

So Jack's mom had died. Poor guy must have been still grieving. However, a feeling of unease gathered in his chest. "Do you have a phone number or address?"

"Naw. It's only that I overhead the boss giving the bank a reference."

"Thank you," Richard said.

"Anytime. You sound nice. By the way, the name's Gabby."

He hung up. Richard called the number the receptionist gave him. The phone rang, then switched to a recorded message. Frustrated, he left a short message and hung up. A moment later he tapped in Kennelly's number.

"Good morning. Kennelly speaking."

"Hi, I got Jack's personal cell number and another bit of information that might be worth investigating. Jack's recently purchased acreage out near Camp Verdi." He gave the officer the number.

"Do you have an address?"

"The receptionist didn't know it. She only overheard her boss speaking with the bank manager about approving a mortgage."

"I see. Thanks for this. Keep in touch."

"I just want Stephani found ASAP."

CHAPTER 46

Stephani scratched the wall behind the iron headboard so she could keep count of the days, and it was going on three days since he'd kidnapped her...assuming her calculations were accurate. Days that she'd been cut off from the rest of the world and didn't know what was happening with Henry. Had Dionne been found? She was crazy with worry.

Every night, she was sure, Jack drugged her evening drink because each morning she woke feeling as if she'd fallen into a black hole and couldn't even remember falling asleep, even though she'd tried hard to stay awake. Last night, she'd poured out the mug full of coffee onto the mattress. Her leg chain was just long enough for her to go to the window, but not as far as the door. She'd searched under the bed, the mattress and under the faded floral sofa and even lifted the cushions for something she could use as a weapon and found nothing.

When the barrel turned in the lock, hurriedly, she perched on the edge of the bed.

"Is it time for lunch?"

"How are you, my Princess?" Jack stood at the foot of the bed.

"Oh fine, considering I'm chained up. Held against my will."

"I've been thinking…"

That didn't sound good. Her heart upped its beat as the silence lengthened.

"About the cooking. See my mother…I hated her cooking."

Jesus, and she was thinking from the way he looked at her that he wanted to do perverted things to her. Stephani stared at the faded sofa…anything not to have to look at him. "Maybe, she was trying her best, and there was no pleasing you." The words were out before she could stop them.

"Shut your mouth. I didn't ask for your opinion. I don't like greasy food. Mother always cooked the pasta first. The pasta was cold when she served it, and she never skimmed any of the fat off the beef sauce." He stood still and then screamed at the wall. "Mother, I told you not to call me that. You filthy stinking bitch…bitch…bitch." Then he raised his fist. "No more Pud, hear?"

Holy shit. He was crazy. "I'll make it just how you like. I should meet your mother since we'll be man and wife soon. When can I meet her?" Maybe this woman could talk some sense into him, or help her escape.

"She's dead."

"I'm sorry."

"I'm ecstatic."

"You don't care?"

He shrugged. "Why should I?"

She tensed. "You helped her along, didn't you?"

He didn't answer her question, but instead asked, "Will my Princess cook for me when we get married?"

He'd killed his mother as if it meant nothing. How long before he would do the same to her. "What did she do to you?"

"None of your god-damn business. Hear?" He jumped to his feet.

"Don't you question me about her, ever!" He stomped out, slamming the door after him.

A dog barked somewhere. It had to be Jack's spaniel, Rocky. She couldn't understand how Jack could have been so kind to his dog and do what he did to his mother.

Henry needed her, she had to be brave, but she didn't feel that way now.

The door flew open. Jack, hands clenched at his sides, shouted. "Don't ever speak to me like that again. Hear!"

Stephani flinched.

"Now, my Princess cook for me?" he smiled as if he'd been planning this event for some time and finally it was happening.

"Do I have a choice?" Stephani wanted to scream...I am not a princess...you murderer, kidnapper. However, she wanted to live. Why the fuck did he obsess over cooking?

"I've bought a cut of prime roast beef, some pumpkin and potatoes. I'll take my Princess to the kitchen."

He pulled out a blindfold.

"No. I don't want to fall or break a leg."

He was thoughtful for a moment. "Then you won't be able to escape, will you?" He finished tying the cloth over her eyes.

Stephani tensed. "I'm not going down those stairs if I can't see."

"I don't recall asking. I'll undo one of your leg irons."

He was touching her legs. "Get away from me." Both hands swinging as one, she felled him and tore away the blindfold. She swung again, but he rolled away, just out of reach.

It was time she took a stand. "I told you, I'm not putting up with that," she said.

He lunged knocking her to the floor and punched her swollen cheek. Pain exploded there.

He grabbed her arm and wrenched her up. "Don't try it again, or you'll really be sorry. Keep still unless you want more of the same."

As he forced the blindfold over her eyes again, a scream swelled in the back of her throat. "Get it off. Get it off."

When she tried to tear the fabric away, he caught one of her still handcuffed hands and wrenched her toward him.

"You're hurting me. Let me go." She tried to twist away.

"Then do as I say." He unlocked the leg irons and skimmed his fingertips up her inner thighs. She jumped backwards to escape his touch and nearly fell.

"I was only undoing them." He cuffed her wrist to his and led her out of the room.

She stumbled. *Don't think about the dark*, she told herself. However, it didn't help; she stumbled again and cried out.

"What's wrong?"

"I can't see."

"That's too bad." He jerked her downwards.

"Hold on," she said, after going down about seven steps.

"I have to catch my breath," she lied. She'd secretly begun a regime of exercising when she was sure he wasn't in the house.

The smell of old wood and unused rooms, mingled with the

whisper of a breeze that floated up the staircase.

Stephani stumbled again on the sixteenth step down, which creaked badly.

He grabbed her elbow.

She wrenched herself free and tore off the blindfold as she tripped on the last tread. She took note of a hallway that appeared to be in the center of the house with a number of closed doors on either side.

"My Princess is strong-willed. But I will crush this spirit from her."

No, you won't, she thought. He had the blindfold back on before she could take in anything else.

"Can't trust you until after we're married, my Princess."

"I can't believe someone would marry us."

"I have it all arranged."

The way he spoke left her with no doubt that he would be the master and she the slave…if he let her live.

When they finally stopped moving, he removed the blindfold.

Gleaming pots and pans hung in neat rows on the wall nearest the stove. In the center of the light-filled kitchen stood an island-bench, and all the windows had security mesh. He'd thought of everything.

He bent down to pat Rocky who was asleep on a dog bed by the back door.

Again, she couldn't reconcile that he could be so kind to a puppy. "I don't cook so much anymore, not since…"

"Since you've become single again." He pulled out a cut of beef from the refrigerator.

Rocky opened his eyes and wagged his tail. He trotted over to her. "He likes me." She bent down and stroked his head.

"Now you'll have to wash your hands. By the way, don't bother to try and escape. All exits are locked…the vegetables are in the pantry. Try the door on the left." He unlocked his handcuff and locked it to a chain attached to the draw handle on the island bench. "Don't worry the chain is long enough for you to reach anything you need."

So why did he bother to cover her eyes on the way down? She walked into the pantry, which was big enough to hold provisions for a large family, but it was half-empty. Tins of spaghetti sauce, peaches, pears and various condiments were lined up like soldiers.

He opened the refrigerator. "Cook enough for four," he said, as he pulled out some potatoes, pumpkin and broccoli.

"Are you expecting visitors?"

"Don't question me."

She opened a few drawers, most of which were empty. "I need a knife to cut the pumpkin and potatoes."

"I've removed all the dangerous equipment. Here's a potato peeler. Any slicing or cutting will be done by me."

She washed her hands and set about preparing the meal. When she was throwing the peelings into the waste bin, she saw a discarded paper clip, and concealed it in her jeans pocket. She wanted to take the potato peeler too, but knew he would check.

After the meal was cooking in the oven, to her surprise, he sat her down at the table with a bottle of red wine, and two glasses.

Stephani stared at the full glass in front of her. Jesus, she had to try to be civil to him. "Trying to get me drunk, or is it drugged?"

"We are going to enjoy a good wine like a proper courting couple." He smirked. "If you'd rather skip the pleasantries, we could-"

"I think we should wait until we're married." Rather than lifting the glass and betraying her shaking hand, she pretended to study the goblet.

"As you wish, my Princess. Our mating will be sweeter for the waiting. There will be a small surprise for you on the wedding night. It will just add to the enjoyment."

Apprehensive at the thought of Jack using some deviant sex toy on her, she said, "You talk in riddles. Why not tell me now?"

"A surprise is just that. Raise your glass and let us toast to it."

"Just tell me." She turned the glass with her fingers and stared at the way the light made the red translucent. *Think of something pleasant to say to him*, she told herself.

"I will not be persuaded to reveal it. Our wedding night will be magnificent. It will make you feel a virgin all over again. Don't blush on my account. I know you've had three lovers in your bed, and you have borne a child."

Alarmed, she asked, "How do you know that?" He was wrong about the number of lovers, as she'd had four, the first one in her sophomore year. It was a relief that he didn't know. She took the smallest sip of wine to avoid him telling her to do so. She kept the liquid on her tongue for as long as she could. Nope. It didn't taste strange but then, some drugs had no taste.

The wine slopped in the glass and she caught him eyeing her shaking hands.

"I have forgiven you for them. You didn't need either of those men. And your family, they were millstones around your neck."

"My family was my life." Stephani slammed down her glass making the stem snap from the goblet.

"My lovemaking will make you forget all that went before...You've broken it." He reached for the stem.

She didn't like the sound of that...perverted men with their perverted fantasies. "I could never forget my family."

"That life ended when your husband died on that road. That man wasn't right for you." His lips turned up into a sly cold smile. "Nor that child you gave birth to, lying in a coma."

"I love Henry. Don't you do anything to him."

He smiled. "He's as good as dead anyway."

"Don't say that. How dare you say that! Don't you lay a finger on him. Promise me that you won't touch Henry."

"If you behave, then you've nothing to worry about." Deceit was in his smile. "Give me the glass." He disposed of it in the waste bin, returned to the table and poured her another glass of wine.

"I only met you when I started at the Scottsdale branch of Rigby...You know about the accident, yet I didn't tell...oh, I did, in the van on the way to this...this..." *Nightmare*. It took all her willpower to stop herself throwing the wine in his face.

"I know everything I need to know about you already. How your mother was left practically destitute, had to take menial jobs to support first you and later your sister. She didn't choose husbands well."

Stephani was so tense, she wanted to twist her hair around her finger, which she had not done since she was a child.

"You were transferred to Scottsdale because of a fire at the branch in L.A. and that Asian guy who worked in the lab here at Rigby accidentally electrocuted himself. You had no lab in L.A. and Rigby was short one person and you had little choice but to come to Scottsdale."

"You know how Lee Chew died?" Did he orchestrate this man's death?

"Your sister lives near you and your mother is in a home for the old and forgetful. Your father lives in San Francisco with a new wife. Your stepfather roams without settling. But that bit of information you told me."

"How did you find all this out...you know where my father, my real father lives?"

"Stop twisting your hair! He wasn't too hard to find, my Princess."

"You have no right to pry into my private life." For as many years as she could remember, she'd speculated if he were still alive and why he'd disappeared from their lives.

"Where's my father?"

"This I will tell you after the wedding. I know all your secrets. You were a working girl, pleasuring men."

"You said I had three lovers." Her cheeks flamed at her guilty secret exposed. Moreover, she'd thought no one would ever find out. Paying clients weren't lovers.

"Paid sex isn't lovemaking. Don't bother to lie to me. You worked at the Diamond Escort Agency in L.A."

"I…I've never heard of that agency."

"You escorted bankers, corporate clients, and even Japanese high flyers. Whore."

"I was laid off from my part-time job at the local café and I still had a year to go to complete my degree. I was an escort for only a year. Why am I telling you this? What I did was my business." She'd hated that sordid job. "My God, how did you find out? Did you hire a private eye?"

"Not telling."

Not even Allan knew. "You're the person who's been making those calls."

"Who's been calling you?"

"Why the hell are you pretending it wasn't you?"

"My princess is confused."

"Don't tell me what I am." Was or wasn't he the one making those calls?

"Enough of this. No more children for you! They'll make you old, and my princess must be young and fresh."

"What do you mean?"

His lips turned up at the corners in a threatening smile.

CHAPTER 47

After shuffling to the window and watching Jack drive away in a blue van, Stephani wondered what had happened to the white van in which he'd brought her here.

Stephani tried to pick the lock to the leg-irons with the paperclip she'd found in the garbage bin. After a while, she gave up. Then she started on the door and was relieved when the barrel clicked. Her hands were shaking when she opened it.

Finally, this was her chance to escape. She'd go directly to the hospital to ensure that Henry was safe from this monster. Her heart was leaping in her chest with apprehension.

She started down the stairs, but the leg-irons prevented her from taking a proper step and she stumbled, twisting her foot. She grabbed hold of the handrail as pain flared in her right ankle.

She hobbled downwards trying to ignore the throbbing in her ankle. When she finally reached the bottom, she stopped to listen for any sound that would indicate Jack was back. He could have driven up the road and come back to check on her.

"Help." A muffled child's voice.

She gasped when she realized. "Dionne? Dionne, is that you?"

A sob drifted up from somewhere.

She sank to the floor, relieved that Dionne was still alive. "Oh, God no! He's got you, too."

She couldn't leave her niece behind. "Hell, what am I going to do now?" she said aloud, as if the telling would offer her a solution. "Where are you?"

"Don't know. Help me."

Stephani rose and shuffled as fast as she could towards the back of the house. Closed doors confronted her. "Dionne, where are you?"

She opened the first bedroom door carefully in case it was booby trapped. A white throw draped the bed and an easy chair sat in the corner. Dionne wasn't here. The next door wouldn't budge and she couldn't pick the lock. "Are you in here?"

"Help me." Dionne's voice was coming from the other direction.

She moved on to another room, which had a black throw on the bed. A pair of shiny black shoes stood beside a dark suit hanging on the robe door-handle.

The sound of a vehicle outside stilled her. "Dionne. He's back. I'll try again tomorrow. I promise, honey."

Her niece sobbed.

"Oh, Dionne, don't cry. I'll get you tomorrow." She hated herself for having to say that. The slide of a van door outside made her gasp in fright. If he caught her here, would he take it out on her or her niece? *Please, not her niece.* She would beg him to hurt her, not her niece.

She crawled up the stairs as fast as she could. When an external door opened somewhere downstairs, she tried to rush the last few steps at the top, and fell; first two steps, and then a third. Her ankle throbbed.

Stephani tried to stand.

"How'd you get out?" Jack loped up, and wrenched her to her feet.

"My ankle hurts."

"Do I look like I care? How'd you get out?" He pressed a penknife at her throat. "Want to see if you bleed?"

"Don't."

"My Princess had no right to leave her room. I was out planning our wedding, and you were going to run out on me."

Something in his look warned her to be extra careful. "I'm sick of being cooped up."

He gripped her jaw with his strong hands. "Look at me! Now tell me again."

Her hands shook. "I...."

"So you wanted to find Dionne."

"My niece?"

"Don't bother trying to pretend that you don't know she's here. Why didn't you escape when you had the chance? You think I'm stupid. Just remember this. If you leave, Dionne's death will be your fault." He closed the penknife.

Stephani straightened but kept her right foot slightly off the ground so it didn't hurt so much. "I don't believe you, Jack. Show her to me."

"Just shut up. Shut up and get to your room." He pushed her up the few steps to the landing.

"It hurts. Please, stop." She wished she'd kept her mouth shut. This morning she'd come to a decision to stop being a wimp. *Come on, she told herself, be strong 'cause Dionne is depending on you as is Henry.*

"Stop. I hear whining, whining, whining. Mother! Don't you whine! Don't you call me Pud. Hear!"

He raised his hand to slap her and she shrunk back.

"Jack, it's me, Stephani." That seemed to bring him back from wherever he'd gone.

He rubbed his temples. "That filthy whore never stopped whining. If I could kill her again, I would."

The menacing edge to his voice terrified her. It was all she could do not to cower. She had to be strong to survive.

He half pushed and half dragged her back to her room. Shoved her in and locked the door between them. "Will you take me to see Dionne?"

"Just stop whining, hear?"

A few minutes later, Jack returned. He had the blindfold in his hands. "Get up."

"My ankle's sore. Can you wrap a bandage around it?"

"Turn around."

"It's too tight, Jack." She wanted to pull the blindfold from her eyes. A scream of panic swelled inside her, and she gritted her teeth to stop it surfacing.

"Then you'd better get used to it."

"Where are you taking me?"

He didn't answer.

She jerked backwards when she felt his hands at her ankles

undoing the leg irons.

"Hold still." Jack wrapped something around her ankle, possibly a supportive dressing, because it wasn't so painful when she had her full weight on that leg. Then he dragged her from the room and into the hallway.

"Stairs," he said.

At each downward step, pain shot up her leg.

At the bottom, he took her along the hallway and stopped to open a door. "Stairs," he said again.

This time he gripped her shoulders from behind and propelled her downwards. She reached out to find the railing for stability and descended.

The odor of clay soil and dust assaulted her as he opened another door.

Her stomach tightened at Dionne's muted whimper. "Take this off. I can't…" She tried to pull off her blindfold.

He whacked the side of her head. She screamed as she fell.

"Get up, whore!"

Her head throbbed.

"Didn't you hear? I said get up. My Princess will be respectful. Hear! Did you hear me?" He hauled her up.

"You're hurting me," she said.

The creak of a door opening had her trying to guess which direction he was taking her now. She'd thought they were in a cellar, but there was no way to tell as she had lost her bearings.

"Careful, the steps are uneven," he said.

She submitted to his manhandling; she would do whatever it took to see her niece.

Four steps later, he stopped and unlocked a door that creaked when he opened it. He pushed her inside.

"Aunt Steph?" Dionne whispered.

Jack removed the blindfold. Stephani stood in a lamp lit windowless space. Tears welled in her eyes, as the shock of a bedraggled and grimy child tethered to a large wooden pole assaulted her senses.

"Dionne." The cry came from somewhere deep inside her.

She stumbled toward her niece.

"Hold it right there." Jack grabbed her arm. "No, you don't. I could make a nice pattern on her face and she won't be so pretty anymore. You know, she reminds me of you when you were young."

"You lay one finger on her, and I'll come after you, I swear it, Jack." *What was he talking about...knowing what she looked like when she was younger?* She dismissed the thought as the ravings of a lunatic.

Dionne got up from the dirt floor. "Auntie Steph, please, please, help me," her niece cried. "I don't like it here."

Stephani's heart contracted. "Why don't you let her go? You only took her as a way to get to me. Now that you have me, surely you can let her go."

"If you want to see her pretty face again, then you'd better do exactly as I say."

"Son-of-a-bitch," she spat at him. "She's only a child."

315

His knife was at her throat again. "My Princess, will do as she is told." The pressure of the blade directed her backwards toward the doorway.

Her niece ran toward her, but fell to the dirt floor when the chain snapped her back. "Please, don't leave me. I don't like it here. Please...Auntie Steph." Dionne screamed. "Please."

"I'm sorry. I'm so sorry, Dionne. I'll be back soon." My God, how she hated Jack for doing this. She would get even no matter what it took.

"Empty promises. You don't know what I'm going to do with you or her." He laughed and pushed Stephani through the door, and kicked it shut behind him. "I think we'll have a double wedding," he said. "It'll be so much fun for the three of us."

Her niece's soft voice pleaded. "Auntie Steph, please...don't leave me. It's dark in here. Please...don't leave me. Please...please...please."

Stephani pulled free.

Jack lunged and pressed the knife at her neck. It stung as he cut her. It mattered so little...her niece was more important. "Dionne, I'm so sorry, honey."

She wrenched the door open.

Dionne screamed.

Before Stephani could step into the room, he pushed her aside, locked the door and pocketed the key.

She brushed away her tears. "Please, don't leave her here. Jack, you can't leave her like this. You can't do that. No one will marry you to a nine-year-old."

"It's all taken care of. Let's get you back to your room, my Princess."

She started her ascent, limping as she went. "Leave her out of it, or I won't marry you."

"My Princess will do as I say."

He'd forgotten to blindfold her. "I won't marry you if you hurt Dionne. You marry me and only me." She didn't care what happened to herself if Dionne was safe. "Just let her go. You have me. I'll do anything if you let her go."

"After all the lengths I've gone to, you demand, you shout. You could be dead now but I saved you for our wedding. Remember this. You are mine—all mine. You are my Princess."

"What lengths? I don't believe you," she said, as he opened the next door to another room and a staircase.

"That fire in Los Angeles. The timing was perfect. You didn't have a laboratory anymore, no staff in L.A. Then that guy accidentally electrocutes himself. Perfect again."

"My God." She turned to face him. "Innocent people died in that fire. Lee accidentally electrocuted himself in the shower." The hallway seemed larger than she remembered from this morning. "Didn't you hear what I said? Innocent people died. Died."

"So what."

"How can you say…?" Stephani found it too horrifying to admit to herself what she knew must be true.

A momentary smirk crossed his face. If she'd had not been studying him, she'd have missed it. She was sure he was pleased with himself.

"That fire was your doing?"

"It was a great success."

Was it possible that he'd misinterpreted her question? However, she had to know. "And Lee's death?"

He nodded.

She put her chained hands to her face. "You're making this up just to…to…," She'd almost said…scare me.

"Do you really want me to tell you how I did it?"

Her worst fears became a reality. He was one of those serial killers that they wrote about in the newspapers. She was too stunned to speak.

"Did you stop to think how well things fell into place for you after you became single again?" he said.

"You used Dionne as bait."

"You're bleeding. Let me tend to the wound."

"You cut me. What did you expect?" He went to touch her neck, but she jerked away as his fingers brushed her wound.

"I'll put a Band-Aid on it," he said.

Jack licked his bloodied fingertips.

Disgusted at his hunger for blood, a gob of bile rose in her throat.

"Blindfold first before we go back to your room."

Somehow, she had to save Dionne. Iantha would never forgive her if she didn't, and she wouldn't forgive herself. However, she had no idea how she would execute this, but she had to find a way for them to escape.

CHAPTER 48

Kennelly drove the off-road vehicle along the interstate highway towards Camp Verde. Zamoloski was in the passenger seat beside him.

The landscape was mostly populated with Teddybear Cholla, which found purchase on some of the rocky outcrops, and more grew on the flats where the earth looked like it had never felt the touch of rain.

"The turn off is coming up just about…now," Kennelly said.

After a while, the cacti grew sparser, and long grasses covered the ground at this higher elevation.

Kennelly glanced at the cloudless sky, which was such an intense aquamarine that it seemed unreal. He loved the desert.

The vehicle left the smooth tarred surface and started along a dirt road. A column of dust rose in their wake.

Kennelly stopped at a ranch gate.

"I'll get that." Zamoloski eased himself out to open it and closed the gate after Kennelly drove through.

"It's hot as hell out," he said, as he climbed into the cabin.

They bumped along for another twenty minutes before seeing a cluster of police and SWAT vehicles.

"Looks like they've been here a while," Kennelly said.

"Let's go see," Zamoloski said.

They joined the huddle of dark clothed men and women.

"Seems that the rancher on the next property noticed some Caucasian, who moved in about six months ago, coming and going a hell of a lot. The rancher saw the man carry a young kid towards the house. The kid was screaming. He thought it was a girl, but wasn't certain 'cause it was nearly dark. Never saw the kid before and never saw them again. When the guys asked what he was doing on the property, he said, he was walking his dog. He never saw anyone else with the Caucasian and when he read in the newspaper about the girl going missing and all, he decided to call us. Two of our team scouted the area. Didn't see a soul. The ranch seems deserted."

After an exchange of information, the team clambered into their vehicles. The first of the police vehicles drove down the track, which meandered past some sage and creosote bushes until it came to the house. The others followed a distance behind.

They changed from their shirts into their bulletproof vests, and slipped their shirts back on.

"Let's go," Kennelly said.

They climbed in, and Kennelly tailed the last vehicle down to the old ranch house. Cars and off road vehicles had stopped here and there in an untidy jumble.

By the time Kennelly had parked, two guys, wearing full body armor and guns drawn, were ready to approach the porch. Six SWAT team members were in position behind their vehicles, guns aimed at the door and the windows. Five other team members, ducked behind bushes as they zigzagged to the back of the house.

"I want all team members in position now," Randall, the chief of operations said.

Zamoloski and Kennelly listened to the exchange on the two-way.

They waited behind their vehicle.

"Don't be a smart ass. Don't get your ass shot off either. On my command," the chief said. He paused. "Go."

The two guys who'd been waiting to storm the ranch house, ran up the steps and banged on the front door. "Police. Open up."

After waiting for a moment, one of the team members tried the handle. However, it didn't budge. He banged hard against the wood again, and then listened.

The chief shouted over the loudspeaker. "Open up. Police."

No answer.

No one moved.

The chief shouted his message again and waited. The silence, except for the odd birdcall, charged the dry air with tension.

Finally, he spoke into the two-way, "Shoot out the lock and force the door. Watch out for booby traps."

Two team members shot out the lock and shouldered the door, but it didn't move.

"Smash the windows," the chief said.

The guys clambered in one after the other.

A few minutes later a small explosion had Randall shouting. "Fall back. Fall back. It's a 10:80. Calling the bomb squad."

Moments later, one of the team members who had gone through the smashed window emerged from the front door carrying his partner. He stumbled down the steps.

Smoke poured out through the broken windows.

"Get an ambulance," the guy shouted.

Two of the team ran across to the officer and gave assistance.

"Harris, advise 10:70 and 10:52. Fire brigade and an ambulance on the double," the chief shouted. Kennelly and Zamoloski crept closer to the house. "If it was my kid in there, I'd have to get her out now," Zamoloski said.

Kennelly nodded, but kept his gaze on the open doorway for any movement.

"I've gotta save her," Zamoloski said.

Kennelly turned to his partner and saw that he'd gotten as far as the front porch.

The chief's voice came through the two-way. "You follow orders. Do not enter. Is that clear! Do not enter."

"Don't," Kennelly screamed. He had a bad feeling about this. He took off after his partner as he disappeared inside. Kennelly wasn't going to let him go in without covering his back.

Kennelly couldn't see. The smoke was so thick. He coughed and felt his way along the hall and found himself in a kitchen with chipped vinyl tiles and a couple of blue painted cupboards. The smoke wasn't as bad at the back of the house. He took a breath and went back to the hall.

He could just make out a door. When he tried it, it wouldn't budge. Kennelly coughed as plumes of pungent smoke filled his lungs. He took out his mini LED light to see if he could spot his partner. "Hey, Zam? Where are you?"

He couldn't hear anything but the crackling of burning wood.

What was behind the door? His conscience wouldn't leave him

alone. It might be a victim and he had to save them if he could. He took a step back, coughed, shouldered it and nearly dived down the stairs when the door splinted and fell. When he reached the bottom, he shone his LED light around. Stained concrete walls, dirt floor and piles of discarded furniture. The smell was like something was rotting…and…it couldn't be, he thought in disbelief. A child was tethered to the wall. He couldn't tell whether it was a girl or boy as it was dressed in rags. Its hair was matted. It pressed itself further against the wall and turned from him.

Kennelly crept closer, shone the beam around some more, and saw a cage beside the child. Inside was a bunch of rags and a blanket on the floor. He coughed again.

He had to save the child. He crossed the room. "Hi, kid."

The child shrank back even further and whimpered.

"I'm Officer Kennelly, and I'm here to take you back to your mom and dad. Just let me get you free."

The child turned slowly. Its face was grimy, and the black hair matted and dirty. The child was shaking. "I want my mommy."

The cry was uttered softly.

That's when he knew it was a girl. "What's your name?"

The child didn't answer.

"Now, don't be scared, I'm going to shoot the lock so I can get you free. Okay?"

She nodded.

He took aim and squeezed the trigger. It took two bullets to break and a bit of tugging to free it completely.

"Don't worry. You'll be soon with your mom and dad."

"Sky, it's Sky." She trembled again.

"Anyone else in here?"

"Onnie was kept in that cage."

The name sounded like Dionne. Kennelly hurried over and opened the door just in case the rumpled blanket concealed another child. He edged aside the blanket with his toe. "No one here now."

"Where is she now?"

The child shook her head and started to cry.

"Let's go, Sky." His stomach knotted. He hoped Dionne was still alive. The child was crying in his arms. He kicked the door out of the way and carried her up the basement stairs as he heard another small explosion.

The heat hit him as he reached the top. *Holy mother of God*, he thought. The walls were on fire. It stole his breath and he fell to the floor with the child.

He forced himself to crawl along the hall. His back felt like it was on fire too. It was hurting, but he huddled the child to himself and kept going.

It seemed like an eternity, but someone was dragging him out into the fresh air and Linda from the swat team was cradling the child. A paramedic hurried to the child.

Someone pushed an oxygen mask to his face, but he pushed it away and coughed. "Where's Zam?"

Randall shook his head. "Sorry."

Kennelly hauled himself up.

"You can't go in there. That's an order!"

"Try and stop me." Kennelly ran coughing to his vehicle, popped the trunk and grabbed an old blanket.

He saw a hose nearby and turned it on, drenching himself and the blanket.

Two officers ran towards him.

Kennelly raced up the steps of the house before anyone could stop him. He burst inside. A figure was lying in the hall. He lurched towards it and threw the blanket over the figure. Then he fell, gasping for a breath. The air was better near the ground. Slowly, he dragged his partner toward the entrance before passing out.

***

When Kennelly came to, he was lying on a stretcher. Sky was being consoled by the policewoman as she was led to an ambulance.

The second policewoman walked over to Kennelly. "My name's Marilla. From the photo we've got, it's not the girl you're looking for?"

"Her name's Sky. I'll never get over seeing that poor child," Kennelly said. "Did she say anything?"

"Not a word." Marilla said.

Randall joined them.

"How's Zam?" Kennelly asked.

"Ambulance just took him to the hospital. Superficial burns. He's lucky," Randall said. "And you're lucky that your vest saved your back," Randall said before he was called away.

"It's still sore."

"If you weren't wearing that vest…and your hair will grow back," Marilla said.

"What?" He touched his head and could only feel clumps here and there. "What the hell happened to the rest of my hair?"

"Lucky you were nosing the floor when a flash flame came through, I think that's what they call it…that singed your hair but your scalp's okay. Didn't figure you'd miss it as your hairline was a little far back anyways."

"Cut that out," Kennelly said.

"Just wanted to lighten up a bit," Marilla said.

"Poor kid's been locked up in that hell hole, my partner's gone to hospital and you think about joking." He didn't like Marilla at the best of times. Her timing was off, as was her attitude to the crew. "Did any guys find anyone else in there?"

She shook her head. "We'll have to leave it to the forensic guys to sift through the rubble."

"Poor kid. These monsters should be locked up for good."

CHAPTER 49

"Love your new hairdo. Sexy." Zamoloski's bandages covered his arms from elbow to wrist.

"Lay off. I had to shave off what was left. My wife thinks it gives me a whole new look. Like she's got a new man. Makes it more interesting in the bedroom and I'm not complaining." Kennelly had raised his voice to drown out the frequent dispatches that burst into the cabin. "How come you're back at work so soon? You were supposed to have the rest of the week off."

"Overnight in a hospital bed with nurses fussing was enough. The thought of a day at home with the wife doing the same... I can't even fart without her taking my temperature. How much more can a man take?" He glanced at his bandaged arms. "I'm lucky it wasn't my hands. The burns aren't that bad. A nurse will be coming every morning to dress them." He turned off Main Street, Mesa onto a side street.

"Don't fart in the cabin. I don't have any gas masks with me."

Zamoloski gave him the "not amused" look.

"At least the kid you rescued noticed the type of vehicle her captor drove when he grabbed her." Zamoloski turned off the engine.

"Yeah. Only thousands of white vans. That really narrows it down. A license plate would've been great." Kennelly sighed.

"It's damned frustrating with the lack of leads on Dionne Sarlos and the Robbins woman missing nearly four days. We've been asked to work the weekend."

"Fucken hell. All our new chief wants is more kudos so he can climb the ladder," Zamoloski said. "My wife won't be happy, but I feel for those folks. Missing kid and that Robbins dame."

"He's only been on the job a month."

"That's long enough for me to know."

"I don't know if we can pin our hopes on Theed? Let's see if we can jog his memory about that empty block behind his mother's old place in LA?"

"It's a long shot."

"Those two cadavers that were found in L.A. haven't talked to the forensic guys yet," Kennelly said.

"Some job. It's bad enough when we find a stiff. I can't stand the thought of having to sift through the remains, that putrid smell is overpowering." Zamoloski opened the driver door of the Ford and swung his bulk out.

"These cadavers are years old. No smell left." Kennelly clambered out of the unmarked police car, and joined his colleague. "I remember when you were still green and the first time you attended a 10-54d and puked all over the captain's shoes. It was the talk of the precinct for weeks."

"But hey, that cadaver was really ripe."

"It used to be a living person. Think of those poor kids lying in some unmarked grave until that construction company…. Anyhow, let's hope he's around."

"No response from Theed to the numerous messages I left. Maybe his answering machine crapped out. Who knows?"

Together they went up the path to a neglected clapboard house.

Zamoloski went first, up the two steps to the porch because the spikes of a mature prickly pear cactus would not allow two people to pass by it side-by-side. It appeared to reach out as a warning to any visitor.

When he tried the doorbell, he found it did not work. He banged on the front door and listened. All he heard was the occasional car driving by on the dry dusty road, and then his partner going back down the wooden steps.

"Going for a quick look-see." Kennelly's footsteps crunched on the dry grass as he went round the back.

Zamoloski tried the door and found it locked. He peered through the porch window where the curtains didn't meet in the middle. A floral lounge, a sagging easy chair and a coffee table were the only things he could see.

Kennelly returned about ten minutes later pulling cobwebs from his shoulders. "No sign of anyone back there. The place is locked-up tight. Looked through the kitchen window. No dishes in the sink. Nothing on the counter. Not even a bowl of sugar. Maybe Theed's gone on a holiday, now that his mother's passed away."

"Could be."

The neighbor across the road shuffled out, letting her screen door slam and stared at them. She sat down in a rocking chair on the porch. Kennelly shielded his eyes from the glare of the afternoon sun so he could get a better look at her, and crossed over with his partner in step beside him. He stood at the bottom of the three steps that led to a small wooden porch, flipped his badge, then returned it to his top pocket. "Good morning, ma'am. Mind if I ask you a few questions about your neighbor?"

"Guessed it. Cops. So why'd you come sniffing around here?" She started to rock backwards and forwards. Her crochet shawl slipped sideways. She pulled it back over her thin legs.

"Aren't you hot?"

"Come to think of it, yeah amight."

She made no move to uncover her legs.

"Do you know where Jack Theed is?"

"Nope. But, eez not bin here for days now that his mother's dead. Lazy old bitch she was. That cowboy was always bringing the shopping home and doing the laundry. I think eez got another house somewhere."

"Did you know her well?"

"Kept to herself. Used to holler at that boy of hers."

"What were the fights about?"

"Search me. I don't meddle in other people's affairs."

"So you never heard what they argued about?" Zamoloski said.

"That cowboy was always yelling at her about how dirty she was, and she was yelling at him about how ungrateful he was. Calling him strange names but I didn't really hear."

"What sort of names?" Kennelly asked.

"Hearing's not so good. But, she was a goddamned mean one. He used to storm out of there slamming doors and would roar up the street in a temper."

"Did they have any visitors?" Kennelly asked.

She laughed. "No one in their right mind would go near that

place. She never cleaned and he was always doing the jobs, but he wasn't allowed to touch her stuff. I heard them arguing one day 'cause he had moved her stuff to clean the floor. Never saw no gal there neither. Don't like that cowboy. He's a bad un if you ask me. Just like his mother."

Kennelly asked. "How long have they lived here?"

"'Bout a year and a half."

"If you think of anything else, here's my card. Just give me a call," Zamoloski said.

"Thanks for your help." Kennelly nodded to his partner and closed his notepad.

They returned to their vehicle.

Zamoloski opened the door and then reached inside for the mike. He was about to speak into it to request a search warrant when a blue van pulled up behind them.

A muscular man with a prominent jaw climbed out. "What do you want?"

"Are you, Jack Theed?" Kennelly showed his badge.

"What's this about?" Theed eyed them suspiciously.

There was something about Theed that didn't seem quite right, but Kennelly couldn't work out why he had this feeling. "Officer Bill Kennelly, and this is my partner, Zamoloski. We've been trying to call you for days."

"Now that you've seen me, you can go."

Defensive and cagy! What was he hiding? "We'd like to interview you about the old place your mother owned in LA," Kennelly said.

"She sold it to move here. Look, I haven't been there since she bought this place and I moved her out."

A puppy started to bark inside the cabin.

"Can we come inside to continue our discussion?" Kennelly asked.

"Anything you want to ask, ask me right here."

Zamoloski sighed. "Have you got something to hide in there?"

"Oh hell." Theed reached into his van and picked up a spaniel puppy. "Rocky's getting worried." He turned to the officers. "Fine." He climbed the front steps as he cradled the puppy in his arms and then unlocked the door.

The predominant odor in the house was one of disinfectant. The bare floorboards held an eclectic assembly of furniture casually arranged in the living room.

Zamoloski stopped to stare at a showcase full of snow globes. "You got kids?"

"Hey, no way any kids would get their hands on these. They're valuable. Most of my globes and figurals are eighteenth century rare collectors' pieces. The flitter in this globe is meerschaum filled with water."

"I guess people collect all sorts of stuff."

"Your mother sure kept this place neat," Zamoloski said.

"I was devoted to her. Rocky needs some water." He took the spaniel into a back room.

Either the old woman across the road lied or Theed lied, which made Kennelly wary. He stared at the old-fashioned bow-fronted china cabinet. His grandmother used to have one just like it. It came with her all the way from England.

When he returned, Zamoloski said, "Mind if we take a seat?"

"No," Theed said.

"The reason we're here, as we said, is about the empty block behind your mother's old place in LA." Zamoloski lowered himself into the easy chair. "What can you tell us about it?"

"Not a thing. Ask some of the other old neighbors."

"I believe they've been interviewed. Did you ever see anyone regularly hanging round that empty block?" Kennelly continued to stand.

"Fuck. I don't have a memory that good."

Kennelly noted how suddenly his anger surfaced. "We know it's been a while, but we would appreciate if you could recall any small detail."

"Kids used to play games on that block. I did as a kid myself. It's been empty, always." Theed shrugged. "Cops find something there?"

"What makes you think that?"

"Why else would you be here?"

"We are not at liberty to discuss that. Did you see anyone suspicious hanging around there?" Zamoloski asked again.

"Hell, no. If I had, it would've been long forgotten. I haven't lived there for years now." Theed stood. "Look, I'm busy, so if there's nothing else…"

"Did you notice anything unusual on that block?"

"Like what?"

Zamoloski shrugged. "Did you spend much time on the block when you were older?"

"Played ball. That's about it."

"Any strangers stand out in your memory?"

"It's been too long ago."

"How come you were living with your mother?"

"I didn't for a long time, but she was sick and I wanted to look after her."

"It's amazing what forensics can do now. With just a drop of dried blood or a hair shaft, they do a DNA profile."

"The cops found a body?"

"I didn't say that," Kennelly said. "Where were you based eight years ago?"

"Let me think. That would have to be San Francisco."

"Were you with the same company then?"

"I was with East Coast Medical Supplies then."

"Sales as well?"

He nodded.

"Would you have a schedule of calls you made then?"

"I threw all that stuff away when I left the company. Why?"

"The police are checking every neighbor who had lived there. Can we have the company contact details?"

He recited the company phone number while Kennelly wrote it

down.

"We'll be going then. Thank you for your cooperation." Zamoloski rose. "I guess it was nice to be able to go on vacation. Where did you go?"

"Huh. Oh, just visited friends at Hoover Dam. And we went across to Las Vegas for two days."

"Win anything?"

"No. I was lucky to come out square." He went past the coffee table to the front door. "Like I said, got lots to do." He opened the door.

Kennelly said, "Mind if we call on you again if something comes up?"

"No."

"I believe you've purchased a ranch house out near Camp Verdi. Can I get the address?" Zamoloski asked.

A fleeting look of alarm crossed Jack's face. His composure in place again, he said, "Still in the process. I don't have the address on me. How about I get it to you later?"

Kennelly followed Zamoloski to the porch. "Guess you must be worried about Stephani," Kennelly said.

"What do you mean? What's happened to her?"

"She's been missing since Monday afternoon, as far as we can establish."

"I didn't know."

"We're currently following up some leads." Theed didn't look too concerned that Stephani was still missing, thought Kennelly. Jack had looked more concerned that his partner had asked for his new address.

"Maybe, she's on vacation."

"She hasn't answered her calls since Monday morning," Zamoloski said.

"Let me know if you locate her."

"Sure," Kennelly said. "Except you never answer the phone."

"My friends live so far from civilization that I couldn't get reception on my cell."

"I left a number of messages on your company cell before you went away requesting you to come in to be fingerprinted so we could eliminate your prints from the ones found on the note Stephani found in her sports bag. You didn't answer that cell either."

"I was busy."

"Will you come in tomorrow to be fingerprinted?"

"I guess I can."

After they left the porch, they heard the front door slam.

"Don't like him," Zamoloski said, as he opened the door of the Ford. "I don't know why, but I don't like him. It's a gut feeling."

"He didn't ask any questions about Stephani," Kennelly said.

"The place smells of disinfectant. Like he's trying to erase any trace of his mother."

CHAPTER 50

Stephani awoke to find Jack standing over her like an apparition caught in the early morning autumn sun.

He was holding that wedding dress.

How long had he been there? "What do you want?" She tried to sound gruff, but her thick sleepy voice let her down and sounded croaky instead.

How did she not notice he was crazy until he'd kidnapped her?

"Today we will be married, my Princess. Then my Princess will be all mine."

He had that strange look in his eyes again.

"This is sudden. I remember you said soon."

"I don't want to wait."

"This is short notice. I've got to get my hair done. You'll have to book me into a beauty parlor."

"You are beautiful as you are, my Princess. I've purchased everything you need…makeup and hair styling products."

"This marriage can't be legal. Who'd agree to come out here and marry us?" She just wanted to keep him talking. Maybe he would reveal something she could exploit. "What you are you wearing?"

"Did you not hear me, my Princess?"

"You're getting a celebrant."

"Don't play with me."

"How many days have I been here? I'm guessing it's Friday today. Means I've been here four."

"You will cook for me always." He continued speaking about cooking as if he had not heard her question.

He had a fixation with food. "Jesus, Jack. How long?"

"I don't like greasy food. Mother always cooked the spaghetti before the ground beef and she never scooped out the fat. Mother would have sullied my Princess the way she sullied everything she touched."

"You murdered her."

"Mother didn't treat me nice."

"That doesn't justify killing someone." Talking about this as if it were an everyday thing was appalling. "What did she do to you?"

"Don't you ever ask me that!" He wiped his face with his hands. "When we're married, we'll go on vacations together...somewhere secluded. I don't want to share you with anyone."

That sounded like he didn't intend to include Dionne. "Let Dionne go. Just drop her off at the local police station."

"Don't tell me what you want. Why don't you ask me what I want? You should be asking me what I want! No one asks me what I want! Why doesn't anyone ask me what I want! My mother never asked me what I wanted. You ask me what I want. You hear?"

Just breathe, she told herself. Somehow she had to get through this. "Can I go to the bathroom? I want to look my best for our wedding."

He went over to the door and hung the dress on the back of it. "How do I know that you won't try to get away?"

"I'll need to wash, put on some makeup and do my hair and loads of other things. I'll be too busy to try and escape." Stephani would never desert Dionne. She reached out and touched his hand. "I can't wait until I can call you, husband." The words were acid on her tongue.

"You'll have to earn my trust. Kiss me." He leaned towards her.

"What?"

"Kiss me. My Princess said she cares for me."

She propped herself up on her elbows. "I haven't cleaned my teeth. They're furry from sleep. Anyway, we should wait until we're married."

He flung off the sheet covering her. Twisted up around her thighs, her nightdress revealed more than it covered.

Her heart thudded in fear as he stared hungrily at her. He wanted more than straight sex. She was frightened of the "*more*" as she imagined her spent body lying in some shallow grave.

"I'll be back soon to take you to the bathroom. Get yourself ready." He turned and walked out, slamming the door behind him.

CHAPTER 51

Richard rang the doorbell at Iantha's home.

He didn't know what he hoped to achieve by coming here, but at least he was doing something. This inaction was driving him crazy.

"Come in." Theo, face unshaven, stood by the door—his brow furrowed from worry.

Iantha hurried into the living room. "Any news? Please tell us there's been a development. Something? Anything?"

Richard stood awkwardly. He wished he had not been so needy for company and for someone who knew Stephani well. "I don't have any. I just wanted to go over Stephani's movements before she was kidnapped."

"I was hoping…maybe someone had come forward about Dionne? Please take a seat," Iantha said, indicating the leather lounge.

"Sorry. Maybe I should leave."

Iantha shook her head. "Stay. Please…I haven't been able to sleep. I keep thinking that my baby-"

"Hush," Theo hugged her for a moment. "You see it's been terrible. You think you should have done more to find her. Why me? Why my daughter? Is she okay? Is she cold and hungry? How could anyone possibly want to hurt her?"

"And the hope, the hope that she's found alive and okay. But each day, that hope gets less. Then I think that maybe the person who took her hasn't hurt her but…that if he's taken…" Iantha let out a sob. "Taken her life…that it's been quick and painless. It feels like my heart's been torn from my chest. It hurts so much." As fast as Iantha wiped her eyes, more tears came. "Then I feel guilty that I'm not worrying more about Stephani. Hoping…that both of them are still alive."

Theo said, "Sometimes, I get so angry that I just want to tear those kidnappers apart. If only I could get my hands on them."

Iantha said, "He's worrying about someone he loves, too. You think he doesn't know how it feels. Look at him; wearing yesterday's clothes, yesterday's shave. Does he look like someone who isn't hurting, Theo?"

"Please forgive me, Richard," Theo said.

"There is nothing to forgive. You are suffering, and I've come at the wrong time." It was hard enough for these people trying to deal with the disappearance of their daughter. "I had no right to show up on your doorstep." Richard started for the door.

"Please join us. We're about to have some coffee and cookies," Theo said.

"Please," Iantha said.

"Thank you." Richard sat on the lounge while Iantha disappeared into the kitchen.

"She's hardly slept since it happened," Theo said. "Blames herself she should have gone to the Fair with Stephani. She was supposed to go, but she had a cold."

"It's not her fault that this happened," Richard said.

"It's not Stephani's fault either. It doesn't make it any easier. I keep hoping the police find her soon. Hope is not the right word, because it means that I think she is still alive…and I don't know what some monster's done to her."

Theo paused to take a shaky breath. "When the police raided that farmhouse, we hoped they would find Dionne. But it was some other girl."

"I read in the papers that the poor kid was in a terrible state," Richard said.

Theo glanced toward the kitchen and whispered, "Don't tell Iantha this, but just between you and me...I've got a gun now. I didn't go to the gun shop with that thought. I...well...just thought I'd look at them and...before I knew it, I'd bought one. I've never wanted to kill anyone in my life before." He drew in a slow breath as if it were painful for him to admit this.

"We can't get on with our lives until we know what's happened to our girl. I've been to work half a day since.... I can't stop thinking...what's happened to our Dionne...and what's happened to Stephani. I feel like my head is going to explode with worry."

"We both love Stephani and to have her missing is killing me," Richard said.

Iantha came in carrying a tray with cups of coffee and a plate of cookies.

"Thank you," Richard said, as she handed him a cup.

The dog woofed once at the back door.

She put down the tray on the coffee table. "I'd better let Milo in. She's been sad and sits by Dionne's bed all day if I let her. She hasn't been eating much since..."

"You haven't either, Iantha. You're losing weight." Theo stirred a heaping teaspoonful of sugar into the steaming liquid.

"I'll eat when I'm ready," she said and left.

A moment later, Iantha was back with the dog one step behind, and she slumped into an easy chair.

Milo raced over to Richard and started to lick his hand.

"She's cute. When did you get her?"

"Do you remember, Iantha? Was it at a dog breeder's somewhere?" Theo took a gulp of coffee.

Iantha shook her head. "Stephani and Dionne bought her at the market. That's where they bumped into...now what's that man's name? He and Steph go to the same health club."

"Jack? He was the one at the market, wasn't he, darling?" Theo asked.

"He was buying something for his dog. He'd bought the puppy at a breeder's out past... I don't remember exactly where," Iantha said. "Dionne would remember, but...."

Richard sipped his coffee. "Can you try?" He didn't know why, but he suddenly knew that it might mean something.

She put down her cup with a thud nearly spilling the contents, and leaned forward. "Do you think it might be important?"

"It's just an odd feeling I have."

"Do you know the man?" Theo asked.

"He's a sales representative who calls at Rigby regularly. I have a feeling that Jack might know something that might help us. I know he has another property somewhere near Camp Verdi, and I believe the police are contacting the owners of about forty properties that have sold in the past three months in that surrounding area to see if they can locate him. I managed to get his cell number but it's done me no good as he never answers."

Iantha's tears surfaced again. "Let me check Dionne's room. Jack gave her a business card from the breeder." She hurried out.

"We live in this aching despair. When we hear something that might lead to finding our baby or Stephani...I start to hope again. But I'm telling myself that I shouldn't get my hopes up too much because ...." Theo said.

"Me too."

Richard finished his drink.

The beagle ran over to Theo and curled up at his feet. He patted it absent-mindedly.

"I go in to work, but can't focus on the research we're doing. Once, it was just about all I thought about. And now I just sit and think about Stephani all the time."

Iantha hurried in with a business card in her hand. "I've found it, Richard. I hope this guy might know something."

"Please call him now." She went over and picked up the phone.

***

"What are we standing around for?" Richard said to Kennelly, who was sitting at his cluttered desk.

"Just lemme get my partner." Kennelly dialed Zamoloski's cell phone. "Forget your lunch and get your ass down to the parking lot. We got an address for that dog breeder."

"Huh," Zamoloski said. "How'd you-"

Richard was tapping his foot impatiently. "Oh, for God's sake. I'm dealing with the Keystone Cops."

"Just watch your mouth…"

"What the hell are-"

"Not you…I'm talking to Dixon. Never mind. Just hurry up. I'll be waiting in the parking lot," Kennelly said, as he grabbed the keys from his desk.

"I'm coming with you," Richard said, keeping pace with him to the back door.

"No, you're not. You stay put." Kennelly pushed the door open and went outside.

Richard started to sweat as the heat of the day battered him. "I'll follow you if you don't let me come with you."

Two uniforms strolled past as Kennelly said in a low voice, "I can't stop you. I never said that."

CHAPTER 52

Jack had left her in a downstairs bedroom to prepare for the wedding. The room was furnished with a double bed, a wardrobe with a few items of clothing that were her size, and a dresser. He'd appeared agitated since yesterday, but she didn't know why.

Stephani tried to pick the lock on the interconnected door, but it wouldn't budge. She despaired that she was taking too long, and that he'd return soon. However, she ignored the voice in her head and kept poking it with the paperclip she'd found.

When the tumblers turned, Stephani hooked the train of the wedding dress onto her little finger and pushed the large paper clip she had just used for the task into the hem of her dress.

The adjoining bedroom had a large queen bed, two bedside tables with colonial lamps and a full-length mirror. She caught her image and realized just how much weight she'd lost. The spaghetti straps couldn't hide her bony shoulders.

The room was immaculate, as were the few she had seen. She hobbled to the polyester-curtained window, as it wasn't boarded up with planks of wood like the one she'd just come from. She tried the window and found it nailed down. Through the glass, she saw a large old barn and his van parked beside it. When she saw him come out of the barn, she let the curtain go and let out a frustrated sigh. She tried the closet, opening first one door and then another to see if it held a weapon.

His clothes all hung in neat rows and were color co-coordinated: shirts, ties, trousers, jackets. The next door opened to reveal a descending row of drawers.

The first drawer held an assortment of socks, but no gun or the knives he'd removed from the kitchen. She slid open the next and found hair clips, slides and hair-ribbons. They were female items unlike the previous one. The third held what looked like old school report cards and the like. A quick sift through the contents yielded some photos of…. She stepped back, shocked and shaken.

Allan and Henry? Where did he get these photos of her family? And, there was one of her when she was…fifteen or sixteen.

This strange collage drew her. There were identical photos of the ones in the picnic basket and more of herself with Dionne. As she picked up another, a half-covered photo captured her puzzled gaze.

The child in the picture was about two or three. Dionne? She reached for it. The girl was naked except for underpants, barefooted and standing near a chicken coop.

Jesus…where did he get these? Who was this child? Her hand shook and she dropped the photo. Stephani slid to the floor as her thoughts spiraled into a frightening vision, that this time was more real than ever before.

My feet are bare and I am in my underpants and T-shirt. "Don't touch me. Or I'll tell my mommy." I scream and clutch my bear tighter.

He tears it from me.

"That's mine. Give it back." I say as I twist strands of my dirty hair that the fat woman washes it only when my mommy is coming.

"Let me near you. Let's see what little girls are made of." He laughs. His shirt is so tight across his belly that his buttons look like they might pop right off and his shorts are tight on legs 'cause they are too fat.

"I'm going to tell my mommy." I edge backwards and some chicken poo

squishes between my toes.

"No, you won't. Your mom won't believe you."

"She will to believe me."

He steps closer. "She'll think you're making it up and you'll get into trouble for telling lies. Are you hungry?"

"Yes." My stomach makes a little noise. I had a piece of bread and some water when I woke up. It's getting dark now. I want to cry 'cause I don't like him...he's mean to me...but I hold it in.

His lips break into a twisted smile. "Don't you want to be friends with me? Come on." He holds out an apple.

It is a shiny red one. My stomach reminds me how hungry I am. I reach for it. As I do this, he starts to pull at my panties. "Noooo." I back away, and try to hitch them up. "I don't want you to..." I hiccup and wipe away a tear. "...to do that. My mommy said it isn't nice for boys to do that." Further and further, I back away 'till I am in the corner. The cobwebs tickle my legs, but I don't care, I just want to get away from him.

"Come on. My mother lets men look at me, but I don't like that. I won't hurt you like the men hurt me. Promise."

"Give me back my teddy...please." I whimper. It is darker here; a chicken is sitting on her eggs. She makes a squawking noise because I nearly step on her.

"You're a cry baby." He comes closer. I am so scared that I wet my pants.

"Just stop it, cry baby. It never does me any-" Then I see why he's stopped talking. His fat mother is standing in the doorway with her hands on her hips. A chicken escapes past her.

"Leave the kid alone. Do you hear? If I catch you pulling at her pants again, I'll whip your hide."

He turns to face her. "I was trying to be friends."

"Keep your grubby hands to yourself. Get inside. Dinner's ready."

"Then you should keep those terrible men away from-"

She kicks him and he stumbles as he backs away. She saved me. She is nice, after all. "Can I come in for some dinner too?"

"Don't get any ideas, kid. I'll bring yours out."

Her dress is all wrinkled and stained down the front, like she's been eating or drinking something messy.

"Please."

"Listen, kid, I said I'd bring it out. You ain't setting foot in the house. Hear?"

"I want my mommy now."

"Shut up, you stupid kid. Your mom will be picking you up on the weekend. Just stop your sniveling!"

"Please, I want my mommy now," I cry.

"Pud. Lock her up 'till she stops that noise."

"But you said I can't touch her."

"Just shut your mouth and do it."

He takes my hand and starts back to the chicken coop.

"Let me go." I jerk my hand free and start to run.

She grabs me. I scream.

"You stupid bitch. Think Hertha can't catch you. Huh? You need to be taught a lesson. Doesn't she, Pud?"

The stinky woman pulls me up and then starts to drag me.

"Don't do it, Mother."

"You want it to be you instead?"

"Just don't."

She punches him hard and he falls clutching his stomach.

"I don't want to go." I kick her.

She hits me, and I scream again.

She drags me to the chicken coop. Hens squawk and scatter.

In the darkest corner is a little room with a door that is always locked. Hertha opens the door and pushes me in.

She slams it shut and locks it. "See how you like it in there for a while?" Then she laughs. "You're no trouble now. I'll be sure to tell your mom that."

"Please let me out. I'll be good. Please don't leave me here. I don't like it here."

The woman starts to laugh. She makes a hee-hawing sound through her missing teeth.

"I want my mommy. I want my mommy. I want my mommy…please…it's dark in here."

Familiar footsteps propelled Stephani back to the present.

She pushed the photos down the front of her dress.

One small cupboard that she had not opened beckoned. Logic told her to retreat before he caught her, but she had to see inside as it might contain a weapon. However, she found it locked. She crept back to the first bedroom, that he'd taken her to this morning so she could finish doing her makeup and sat on the chair in front of the old colonial dressing table with her heart pounding.

"Are you ready?" Jack asked through the door.

Oh God. She had not relocked the connecting door. Had she closed the closet?

She sat restlessly waiting for him to burst in.

"It's unlucky for the groom to see his bride in her wedding dress. So you'll have to wait until the ceremony."

"I don't suppose you'll want your lunch then?"

"Just slide it in." Stephani breathed again.

"Not 'till I have some photos of you in that dress."

"After the ceremony you can-"

The key turned in the lock.

He smiled as he came in carrying an assortment of lenses, a tripod and a camera.

Her stomach tightened. How was she going to live through this nightmare? Somehow, she had to, for Dionne's sake.

He set up the equipment.

"Turn to the left a little," he said.

Stephani did as he asked, while he took yet another photo of her wearing that wedding dress.

"My Princess is beautiful." He clicked. "My Princess is just as pretty as a picture. Turn your head to the left. Lift your chin. That's it."

"Now take the strap off your shoulder."

"Why?"

"Just do it. That's better," He clicked. "Now take the other off and pull down your top a little."

"I don't want to. Anyway, I don't have big breasts."

"Do it. A little more, so I can see almost half of your breasts but not the nipples. More. That's perfect, my Princess."

As soon as he had taken the shot, she hitched up her straps feeling like a whore even though he had not touched her.

"Pull the train over this way."

She lifted it, pushed, and pulled as he instructed.

"The chains are showing."

"It would be much better if I could take them off."

"What do you think I am? Stupid? After we get married…maybe." He set up the tripod for another shot and came to stand beside her. "Look into my eyes as if you love me."

That would never happen.

He'd set the camera on automatic, and he pulled her into his arms as it clicked. "Now smile and pretend you love me, my Princess."

"And again," he said.

She did as he asked for Dionne's sake.

"Now kiss me."

Repulsed, she kept her lips closed as he pressed his mouth against them.

"Kiss me again as if you're hungry for me."

"Put your arms around me." All the while, the camera was going off.

"Not like a rag doll," he said. "Hold me. Okay. That's better."

"You've got photos of Henry and Allan. Where did you get them?"

He pushed her away as his cheeks flamed. "You've gone through my things. My private possessions."

"They were there in the dresser. I thought you meant for me to see them," she lied as her heart pounded. She had to know. "Where did you get them?"

"You dare to question me? You whore who slept with other men. Had another man's child. I was willing to overlook that. Because of your beauty, because of your honey skin and-" He touched her hair. "Your soft, lovely hair." He grabbed a handful and yanked. "Should I accept soiled goods I asked myself? She's not a virgin."

His laughter was an empty sound without joy. What had she started?

"But I have loved her for so long, I tell myself. Therefore, only I have the right to my Princess. I will make her pure and she will be mine forever."

When she looked away, he asked, "Didn't you hear me?"

"I need to rest up for the ceremony."

"Shortly after the wedding you will be going to a private hospital in Mexico."

"Why?" Was this somehow connected to how he was going to make her pure? She shuddered.

"Surely you can guess."

"Face lift?"

"And no more children. And…."

"What else?"

He shook his head.

"Tell me what else. Jesus, it's my life we're talking about here." Her palms were sweaty now.

"You will be made a virgin again."

"Is that what you call making me pure?" Stephani folded her arms. "You can't make me sign the consent form."

"I can…but then we don't need a consent form for where you're going."

"I'm not having any operations."

"Oh, you will when the time comes. You'll be willing do this for me and more. I took those photos to remind myself of that man who soiled you, that child who would have taken you from me. I helped you free yourself of them. Forget them. They were unworthy of you, my Princess."

"What? You can't mean what I think you mean." A low, hollow, mournful sound came from deep in her throat. "Did you do something to Allan's car? Is that why Henry is in a coma?"

"I have saved my Princess and my Princess should thank me. No questions. Shut up now, or your niece-"

"Don't you touch her! Don't you ever touch her!"

The urge to kill him coursed through her veins. "You robbed me of my family, and you tell me I should thank you!" In a blind rage, she launched herself at him, screaming, punching him anywhere and everywhere.

He thrust her away as if she was nothing more than a rag doll. She fell backwards, tangled in the dress and chains.

"Don't you ever lay a finger on me if you want to live!" He wrenched her dress up.

Stephani tried to shove his arms away as he yanked her legs apart as far as the chains would allow. "Get off me."

Jack ripped her panties away. "I think now is a good time for me to consummate our impending marriage."

He started to undo his belt.

"Do this now, and I'll never willingly go to your bed."

He put his elbow on her throat and pressed.

Stephani struggled, unable to breath and tried to push his arm away.

"Lie still."

She gasped in a breath as he eased up on her throat.

He unzipped himself. "My Princess will do as I say. You are lucky that I love you."

"Do this, and I'll never love you."

"What did you say?" He raised his hand to hit her.

"Never. Do you hear? I would rather die than love a man who's raped me."

Then he lifted himself a little and stared into her eye; his nostrils flared.

What had she said? Was he contemplating killing her? What would happen to Dionne?

"I have waited too long for this. It will be all the sweeter when I take you, my Princess." He eased back and half rose.

Stephani pulled down her dress to cover her nakedness.

"What's this?" He grabbed the photos of Allan and Henry that must have slipped out of the dress. "You stole them!"

Stephani reached for them. "They're my family."

Jack's blow set her cheek on fire.

"Stole!" He screwed up the photos and threw them across the room. "They were nothing, nothing. Do you hear?"

Breathing hard, Stephani's fury gathered inside her. "My family meant the world to me and you…killed Allan and as good as killed Henry." She was trembling all over with anger.

Jack seized the camera and thrust it into its case with more force than necessary.

"We'll have a meal after the wedding. I'm off to get the preacher." He took the equipment and left, turning the key in the lock after him.

Shattered, she drew up her knees and rocked backwards and forwards. A little while later, she heard the jangle of keys and the door slamming.

She rose from the floor, hobbled to the window, and saw a blue van disappearing down the dirt road.

Now that she knew who had robbed her of her family, her guilt that she'd carried all these months, fell away. Given the chance, she would kill him without hesitation. A life for a life. No mercy would she show him.

Again she stared at the picture of the little girl…the little girl that she once was. She knew now what her mother had tried to tell her. This monster and his hideous mother had looked after her, if that's what it could be called, when she was a child. She must have blocked it from her mind and couldn't recall any moments of her early years, except for those terrifying visions.

How long had he stalked her? He must have imagined he had a connection with her…feelings for her. How could anyone be that way? It was too horrific. She closed her eyes and again told herself to breathe.

Stephani didn't know how long she'd stood motionless, but she knew it had been too long. She was missing the best chance she had.

They would both be dead if she didn't act. She gathered the photos up and pushed them into her bra. Then she pulled out the paper clip from the hem of her dress and tried to pick the lock.

When the tumblers finally fell into place, she paused to check that he had really gone.

The house was silent.

"Dionne, where are you?" She stumbled from the bedroom.

Then she heard a sound and stood ready to retreat. The tapping noise sounded again and she realized it was a bird hopping on the roof outside.

Smells of baking pumpkin, potatoes and turkey wafted through the air, making her stomach rumble, reminding her she had not eaten breakfast and it was well past lunch.

She hobbled out of from the bedroom that had been her dressing room, towards the first doorway she could see and then tried it.

Locked. "Dionne?" First one way and then another she went. Nothing felt right. Which route had he taken when he'd led her to Dionne? All the while, the chains clanged in time with her motion. She closed her eyes and tried to imagine which way she had taken when she had looked for her niece the other day.

At least, she knew where the kitchen was with the smells of roasting meat and vegetables. She opened and closed a few drawers until she found some scissors, as there were no knives here. After she cut the train from the wedding dress and tore the bottom off the skirt, she looked around for keys...any keys that would unlock the leg irons. She opened cupboards, and more drawers, tipped out utensils and more. It was no use.

Stephani shuffled as fast as she could back the way she'd come, hoping that Dionne wasn't too hard to find.

One door after another yielded nothing other than a few pieces of furniture.

"Dionne. Where are you?" All she could hear was the sound of her own laborious breathing.

Her hands were trembling when she tried the last door. It opened onto a stairwell leading down into darkness. She searched for a light switch and then flicked it on. "Dionne. Are you down here?"

She stumbled downwards. The stairwell opened into a large cluttered room with a corridor off to one side leading into darkness. She recalled that earthy odor when he led her to her niece, which must have been two days ago. However, she wasn't sure of the time as it was getting harder to keep track. An old rug lay crumpled next to a post in the middle of the room. It did look like the place he'd taken her to see her niece. "Dionne,"

After looking around, Stephani hurried back up. She'd been certain that she'd been led down some stairs when taken to see her niece.

Had he moved Dionne to the barn or an outhouse?

When Stephani tried the back door, she was surprised that Jack had not locked it. He must be getting careless. Squinting against the harshness of the sunlight, she hobbled across the dry brittle grass. She tried to ignore the way the grass pricked at her feet as she made her way to the barn.

The padlock was hanging unlocked on the barn door. What was going on? Jack was usually meticulous. Had something or someone unsettled him? The thought worried her further, but she had to find Dionne.

Inside, an old pickup stood beside a dusty tractor, and an antique motorbike with a missing back wheel, was propped up on bricks and a few two by four planks of wood. Light filtered in here and there through the gaps in the old wooden planks.

A muffled noise stilled her.

Where?

There it was again. Then she started towards it...stopped and listened again. It had sounded like it was coming from the upstairs hayloft but now she wasn't sure.

Then she heard it again and knew that she was going in the wrong direction.

"Who's there?" After a moment, her eyes adjusted to the small amount of light and she saw another door at the far end of the barn. She banged on the door. "Dionne?"

"Help me," Dionne said.

"Hold on. Just let me get this door unlocked." She felt the

sidewall for a light switch and knocked down some tools hanging on the wall in the process.

She tried using the paper clip but that only bent the clip. She jammed a screwdriver into the lock and hammered until she was panting. Then she tried the handle and was surprised when the door opened. Jack had not locked this door either.

Her niece's grubby bedraggled appearance, tethered to a post in the middle of the dirt room, squeezed at her heart. "Oh, my God," she whispered. It was all she could do to hold back the tears. "Oh, Dionne."

It was too shocking to think about what he might have done to her niece. *Jack will pay for this*, she resolved.

"Auntie Steph. Please," Dionne sobbed.

"Oh, Dionne. Let's get you out of here," she said, as she hugged her and brushed away the matted hair from her face. "It's okay now."

Her niece started to cry. "I'm scared, Auntie Steph. I don't like him. He's nasty."

"It's okay now. Let's get you free. Then we'll get you cleaned up and-"

"He wanted to give me a bath…but I didn't let…didn't want a bath with him…and then he…he…and then he tried to undress…he left me here. And he came in sometimes and just stared at me." Dionne cried a little, then continued. "Said I would enjoy it. Don't know what…. He said after some wedding, I would have to do…something."

"Hush." She rocked her for a few moments and then tried to pull away from her niece.

"Don't go away. Please, don't leave me. I'm scared."

"There's no chance of that. I just want to find something to get you free. I'll be back soon."

"No. Don't leave me."

"Hush. I need to get you free. Okay?"

She went out, took the axe hanging on the wall, grabbed a brick and hurried back to Dionne.

"I'm going to cut the chains on my legs first and then the one securing you to the post."

At the first swung the axe bouncing off. The second broke the brick.

Stephani pushed the bike from the wood supports and dragged a plank of wood back to Dionne.

Finally, with all her weight behind her next swing, she had managed to make a start. After a couple more swings, she was free. Then she started on freeing Dionne.

When the chain broke, she said, "We have to hurry. It's taken so long that I'm afraid he'll be back soon."

"I'm scared," Dionne said.

"I won't let him have you. He'll have to kill me first."

CHAPTER 53

Zamoloski, Kennelly and Richard stood on an old timber veranda.

"So, do you have his address?" Richard asked the spaniel breeder over the chorus of barking dogs. The house was a low structure in a mix of styles of Mexican and plain old country farmhouse. If it had seen a lick of paint once, then it wasn't evident.

The breeder stared into the valley for a while. A fly buzzed lazily at his face, and he took a swipe at it. "Don't rightly know if I ought to give it to you. See, stuff like that is confidential like."

Zamoloski spoke. "This is a police matter. You wouldn't want to obstruct the course of justice, would you?"

The breeder shrugged. "S'pose when you put it that way. Lemme go into the office."

When the breeder swung open the screen door, they followed. It didn't take Richard a second to work out that Zamoloski and Kennelly didn't trust the guy and thought the breeder might disappear if they didn't watch him, so he moved almost in unison with the two cops.

The breeder noticed them behind him as he slipped off his boots to reveal socks with worn out heels. "Git. You all can wait out there."

"Now you listen up good," Kennelly said. "Theed just might be able to help us in our investigations, so we aren't letting you out of our sight until we have his details."

"Then you all better take off your boots. I don't like dirt on my floors."

The trio followed him along a hallway. Two spaniels ran to greet their owner.

Richard speculated how long the carpet had been threadbare and if the breeder noticed its condition or the smell of dog that emanated from it. He was the last to enter a room that was set up as an office. It seemed to be from a different era...no fax...no computer and the only modern piece of equipment was the phone on a beat-up desk that was loaded with invoices, folders and other debris.

"Jesus, how can you find anything in that mess? And you made us take our shoes off," Zamoloski said, wrinkling up his nose.

"Look, I didn't invite you in."

"Just give us the details, and we'll be on our way," Kennelly said.

"Can I help?" Richard asked.

"I know exactly where everything is." He opened a folder and started leafing through it. "Here it is. Can't give you this but you can copy down the address."

Zamoloski pulled out his notebook. "Now don't go calling him up to tell him we're going to pay him a visit."

"Now why would I do a thing like that? What's he supposed to have done?"

"He may be able to help us with our investigations. Just don't call him or we just might have to check your breeder's license," Zamoloski said.

"What is this about?"

"We're not at liberty to say," Kennelly said.

CHAPTER 54

Stephani pushed open the door to the barn and hurried back to the old pickup.

"Jump in, Dionne." She helped her niece up and hurried round to scramble into the driver's seat. When she saw the keys were dangling from the ignition, hope ballooned in her chest.

She tried to turn the key, but it was stuck. Maybe the lock had seized up. Her fingers hurt, but she kept trying the key and moving the steering wheel, which also wouldn't budge.

"He's going to catch us." Dionne started to cry.

"Hush. Everything's going to be fine." She remembered how her first car used to lock up and that doing this helped. Stephani kept worrying the steering wheel this way and that until finally it turned and so did the key.

The pickup finally started.

She tramped on the accelerator and stopped short at the barn entrance. A blue van obstructed their path. She was about to ram the van when Jack jumped from the vehicle and took aim.

She reversed back into the barn and swung the wheel toward a sidewall.

"Don't try it," Jack shouted. "I'll shoot Dionne."

Stephani braked and gripped the steering wheel.

Jack stepped closer. "Get out or I'll shoot."

"Get on the floor, Dionne." She stepped the gas pedal.

As she closed on the side wall, a bullet pierced the side window, stung her cheek and showered her with glass.

She jammed on the brake. Dionne screamed.

Stephani turned off the engine. "I'm sorry, Dionne," she cried.

"Get out and stop that sniveling." Jack stood at the barn door aiming his weapon at her.

"Don't let him touch me, please," Dionne said.

"Run to the back of the pickup," she whispered, swung open the door and slid down, almost falling as she did so.

Dionne jumped out and ran.

"Not so fast. You stay where you are, Dionne," Jack said.

"Auntie Steph."

"Do as he tells you."

"Sensible advice. Now let's get back to the house. I've got the preacher inside waiting for us."

Stephani walked to the front of the pickup and Dionne followed.

"Come here where I can see you," Jack said.

She slowed her pace so that Dionne was slightly ahead of her and he was a step behind.

Stephani spun round and used the momentum to stab toward his eyes with pickup keys.

He grabbed her wrist and aimed the gun at her niece. "Don't, or I shoot Dionne. Give me the keys."

"Just let her go. Please."

"I should make you pay for this. But, it's our wedding day, my Princess. The keys." He held out his hand.

She stabbed his open palm with the pointy end of the keys.

"Fuck you." He grabbed her arm and she kneed him in the groin.

He cried out as they both hit the dirt with her on top.

Stephani tried to roll off. Jack rolled with her and struck the side of her face with the gun. She cried out in pain.

He half rose. "My Princess is making me angry."

Dionne took off to the barn entrance.

"Stop," he shouted to Dionne.

Dionne kept going.

"Don't." Stephani jumped up.

He fired. The bullet punched the dirt at Dionne's heels.

Dionne screamed and crumpled to the ground.

Stephani grabbed a broken brick and swung at his gun hand. He dropped the weapon.

Jack lunged for it at the same time she did and they both fell with Jack half on top of her.

She clawed his face, his eyes.

"Whore." He shoved her aside as he scrambled for the weapon.

She jabbed the base of his throat and pressed her fingers to the small triangle there. He made a choking sound as he wrenched her hands away.

He rolled, and she went with him struggling all the while.

Stephani saw the gun and seized it. Jack lunged at her trying to knock the weapon away.

Stephani felt for the trigger.

As Jack tore it from her grip, the gun discharged.

Her niece screamed again.

He punched Stephani and went to rise as she rolled into a tight ball in case he was going to kick her again. But, he appeared to be looking at Dionne crying.

He went to take a step, she shot out her leg and tripped him. As he fell, she ripped the weapon from him.

"You son-of-a-bitch." Stephani fired.

Jack stared at her as if he couldn't comprehend what had just happened.

Stephani dropped the gun and ran to Dionne's side.

Jack's fingers closed around the weapon. He rose slowly and smiled. "I will take Dionne for my wife. Sleep then my Princess. You were…so beautiful."

Stephani saw him look down at the growing bloom of red at his mid-section. The gun fell from his grasp and he put his hands on his wound to try to stem the flow.

"What have you done?" His face paled as if he was in pain. "How could you? I loved you from all those years ago when my mother looked after you."

Red blood, now turning black, pumped even faster from the wound. "We could have…" Jack started to crumple. His gaze held hers for what seemed like the longest time before he fell.

"My Princess, my one and only love." He attempted to rise, then gave up the struggle. A spreading pool of black colored the dirt around him.

"It hurts. Make it stop," Dionne said.

Her niece went limp in Stephani's arms.

"Dionne, Dionne. Wake up," Stephani screamed.

CHAPTER 55

"Looks deserted," Zamoloski said to his partner as he gazed at the ranch house from their vantage point behind a clump of mesquite. "Don't move from the vehicle, Dixon."

Richard could see that a blue van stood in front of a barn and a Hyundai next to it.

"But-"

"I'll handcuff you to the door if I have to. We've called for backup. When they arrive, someone will take you back to Scottsdale."

Richard buzzed down the window and the searing heat flooded in. The silence was deafening.

"You can't just sit here. She could be in a bad way. You have to find her," Richard said.

"We wait for backup," Zamoloski said.

"Just get her out."

"Listen and listen good. We follow procedure, and that procedure is to wait for back up."

"You sons-of-bitches. You'd let Stephani and Dionne die before you'd disobey orders."

"Hold it right there. You don't bad mouth me or my partner and get away with that. I am cautioning you."

"Jesus. What will it take?"

Zamoloski glanced at his partner.

"Okay, let's go." Kennelly drove down the track to the homestead, turned off the engine and let the vehicle coast to a stop near the house.

Zamoloski closed the vehicle door softly, unclipped his gun, and slid it out of the holster in almost one movement.

Kennelly joined his partner, and tripped on the unevenly laid rock path that led to the house.

"You take the front and I'll go around the back," Zamoloski said.

Richard was itching to join them. He saw that Zamoloski had disappeared around the side of the ranch house. Kennelly climbed the front porch and knocked on the screen door.

The officer knocked again. "Police. Open up."

When no one answered, he tried the door. "You wait back there. Understand?"

"Sure," Richard sung out.

Kennelly came out a few minutes later with a short football-shaped grey-haired man.

Richard stepped from the vehicle and hurried across.

The older guy's gaze darted this way and that. Dressed in jeans and plaid short-sleeved shirt, he had flushed cheeks, and he smelled of whisky. "Git your hands off of me. I'm Chumlee Crow, renowned celebrant. I were asked to peeform a weddin' here. I ain't done nothin' wrong."

"Where's Jack Theed? Have you seen Stephani? Or Dionne?" Richard asked.

Zamoloski appeared from around the back.

"Who are you?" Crow pushed his hair from his forehead.

"I'm asking the questions," Kennelly said. "Richard, you were told to stay put."

Richard shrugged.

"Is there anyone else in the house?" Kennelly asked.

Richard noticed that the Crow's hand shook. This guy was just like his father, a heavy drinker.

"Ah, wouldn't know," Crow said.

A gunshot from the barn rang out. Seconds later, a child screamed.

Then another shot pierced the stillness.

"Stay put, Dixon and you, Crow." Zamoloski drew his weapon. "I'll go first."

Richard could see that Kennelly with his arm bandaged wasn't up to this.

Zamoloski started away.

"I'll watch your back," Kennelly said to Zamoloski. Then he said, "Get your ass back to the vehicle and stay put until I say different. Is that clear, Crow, Dixon?"

Crow nodded and slipped into the police vehicle while Richard stood beside it. He didn't want to be sitting helpless in the cabin if Stephani was fighting for her life.

Zamoloski crept to the barn and past the blue van, with Kennelly tailing him.

Richard watched the officer open the barn door wider.

"Police. Hands up." Zamoloski flattened himself against the wall and edged in with his gun cocked.

"We're in here. Call an ambulance. Dionne's been shot."

Zamoloski disappeared into the semi darkness.

When Richard heard this, he broke into a run.

"Hey. Get back to the vehicle," Kennelly shouted and slipped inside.

"Don't get any crazy ideas. I don't want a dead hero on my hands," Kennelly said.

Richard leaned in and as his eyesight adjusted, he saw a pick-up and a woman cradling a child on the dirt floor in a far corner with Zamoloski bent over them.

A man lay face down nearby.

"Stephani."

"Hold it," Kennelly said. "This is a crime scene. I am cautioning you to wait outside or you'll be charged with tampering."

Kennelly was calling for an ambulance on his mobile as Richard raced inside.

Stephani was pressing a cloth to Dionne's thigh. "I'm trying to stop the blood."

Richard hurried over to Stephani. "You're bleeding. Are you hurt?"

"I'm okay, but I don't know about Dionne."

Her niece began to whimper.

"You okay?" Stephani asked her niece.

"It hurts so much."

"Anyone else here?" Zamoloski asked.

"Where's the medics? Dionne needs help," Stephani said.

"Sorry, ma'am. My partner's called them. Be here ASAP."

"Is that Theed over there? Who shot him?" Zamoloski asked.

"He shot Dionne. We struggled…and the gun went off."

"Self-defense," Zamoloski said. "We'll need a full statement from you."

"I don't want Dionne moved," Stephani said.

Richard knelt down. "Did he hurt you? Your cheek's bloody and swollen."

"He fired at the pickup." She touched her cheek. "I think he grazed my skin."

Kennelly joined them.

Dionne clung to Stephani. "It hurts."

"Just hold on a bit longer. Your mom and dad are going to be so happy to see you. Everything's going to be okay."

Kennelly came out of a room at the back of the barn and looked at Zamoloski. "You should go look in there after we sort this."

Police, vehicles parking and doors slamming permeated the barn.

CHAPTER 56

Iantha, Theo, Stephani and Richard hurried into the hospital room where Dionne was asleep with an I.V. in her arm.

"What did he do to our baby?" Theo asked the doctor.

"Is our baby going to be okay?" Iantha asked, wiping away tears.

"I've removed the bullet. She's one lucky girl. A fraction over and her femoral artery would have been severed. She should be coming around soon, and I'm sure she'll be happy to see both of you."

"Dionne!" Iantha whispered when her daughter's eyes fluttered open.

"Mommy, Mommy!"

Iantha kissed her forehead and started to cry.

"Are you okay?" Iantha asked.

Dionne nodded and clung to her mother.

Theo squatted down to his daughter. Tears wet his face. "How are you, Pumpkin?"

"Daddy, I missed you so much," Dionne said.

"Oh Jesus, I missed you too."

"You've brought her back to me. How can I thank you, Steph?" Iantha said.

"I'm sorry, Iantha. It was my fault that he took her in the first place."

"No one blames you. We're just so happy to have Dionne back," Theo said, as held his daughter's hand.

Richard squeezed Stephani's and stared into her eyes.

A hard lump of emotion formed in the back of her throat. "How's Henry?"

"The same," Iantha said.

"I was hoping that he'd show some sign of improvement."

"There's nothing anyone can do. Sorry," her sister said.

"I guess. It doesn't make it any easier. Jack knew where my real dad lives. I'm going to see him when I get the chance."

"Not your dad too, Iantha?" Theo asked.

"No. He divorced mom before mom married my dad."

Richard wrapped his arms around her. She blotted her eyes. "I was so scared for Dionne, and I'd never have forgiven myself if something bad had happened."

"Thank God, you're safe. I nearly went crazy with worry." He pulled her to him and kissed her.

***

Richard had just driven Stephani home from the hospital. "I asked Iantha and Theo over because I have something to tell all of you."

Richard stared at her in query but didn't say anything.

The intercom buzzer went, and she let her sister and Theo in.

"Thanks for coming over," she said to both of them.

"Dionne should be clear to come home in the morning. I want to know what the cops who interviewed you in the hospital said. What's their take on this Princie guy and Jack Theed?" Iantha asked.

"I planned to tell you anyway. Please get comfortable first before I start," Stephani said.

"Let me make us some coffee." Her sister went to the kitchen, started the coffee machine and returned.

"Princie's remains were found in a recent office block fire. They suspect that Jack Theed set the fire. A homeless guy saw a man that fitted Jack's description enter the derelict office block where Princie lived about a half hour before the fire was started. Apparently, Princie left me those warning messages. He wasn't all bad. Though, it seems that he was stalking me and other women too."

"Forensics studied the security camera footage and they are sure Jack set that bomb off in your car, Richard."

"Nearly God-damned killed me too," Richard said. "I did get a call from Kennelly and I'm going to see him later."

"I guess Jack didn't want any competition for my attention."

"I told the cops that he as good as admitted to killing Lee Chew."

Richard's face drained of color. "Electrocuted Lee? Are you sure?"

"Yes. And I knew I had to do whatever it took to keep Dionne safe and get her out of there."

"What did that scum do to you?"

"I'm okay. He just knocked me around a little."

"My God. I thought I'd never say this…but I'm glad that scum is dead," Iantha said.

Never again would she need to feel responsible for Allan's death. Henry was another matter; she still couldn't bring herself to let the hospital disconnect him from the machines keeping him alive. "I seem to remember that she treated him badly when he was a child. His mother baby-sat me in appalling conditions when my first dad left and mom had to work to keep some money coming in. I kept having these visions about a child kept in a chicken coop. I know now that child was me."

Her sister gasped. "Oh, Steph, how terrible for you."

"In addition, he also set fire to the lab in L.A."

Richard put his hands to his head. "Jesus, Mary and Joseph."

"He's a serial killer. You did the world a favor, Stephani," Theo said. "Who was sending you those things…poem, rose and photos? Jack or Princie?"

"Jack did. The cops think that he's been abducting young girls for a long time. They've searched the house where he kept me and Dionne and the house his mother owned. Searched his computers and found some of the houses he's rented. Kennelly said that it may be months before they find where all of the girls were kept. It's beyond belief."

Iantha went to the kitchen. Set up the coffees on a tray and placed them on the coffee table.

They sipped their drinks in silence.

Stephani put down her nearly empty cup. "There's something else. I have a confession to make."

"What do you mean?" Theo took a sip of his coffee.

"There's more to this…horror? Whatever it is, I don't know what that monster might have done to Dionne if it hadn't been for you."

Richard sat looking at her. "You'd better tell us."

"It's not about Dionne or me being kidnapped." She sat in the easy chair and looked at the tiled floor.

"Jack had been stalking me for years. It still shocks me to know this even though he's dead. He found out something about me that I'd kept secret."

"What do you mean?" her sister asked.

"I'm ashamed to tell you." She took another slow breath to give her courage. However, it didn't seem to help. "I worked as an escort when I was in my last year at Berkley. I was desperate for the money. I needed to pay the fees and I'd lost my part-time job in the café. My cards were maxed out."

Iantha gasped. "Steph…you mean…like when a guy needs a date for a special event?"

"You were an escort?" Richard said. "Please tell me that's not what I think it is."

She couldn't meet her sister's gaze. "For the last year of college I was a paid…escort…for…well…."

"Steph. You were an…an escort?" her sister said in a voice that told Stephani how shocked her sister was. "You could have asked me for a loan."

"You weren't exactly flush at the time yourself if you remember," Stephani said.

"You're right. Sorry," her sister said.

Richard gripped the arm of the chair.

"We've got the picture," Theo said.

The look on Richard's face made her wince. He was disgusted. However, he'd never had to decide to miss breakfast so there would be enough money for dinner.

"Comes easy, does it?" Richard said.

His words made her want to disappear.

"Don't speak to my sister like that."

"Thanks, Iantha." She turned to Richard. "What do you know? You've never had to scrimp to put yourself through college."

"Actually, from what Stephani's said, she had no choice. I know how hard it can be to scrape up enough bills for the fees," Theo said. "My parents were dirt poor."

Stephani looked at Theo in surprise.

"Oh hell, Steph. I don't know what I'd be like in that sort of situation." She went over and wrapped her arms around Stephani.

Richard sat in brooding silence.

"I'm sorry, Richard. You probably don't want anything to do with me now." She pushed her sister away, ran down to the bedroom and threw herself on the bed.

A little while later, Richard walked in. She couldn't look at him.

He sat in the chair beside her. "I'm sorry. It was a shock to learn…"

She didn't speak, but buried her head into the pillow again.

"I guess what I'm trying to say is, that you did what you had to do."

"I've spent too much of my life blaming myself for all the things that have gone wrong, all the things that I should have done differently." She sat up. "Now that I know I wasn't to blame for Allan's death and Henry being in a coma, I can let go of that guilt trip."

He reached for her hand. "Can we start over?"

She didn't put her hand in his. "What are you saying?"

"That I'd like to give us a second chance."

"What about me being an escort? How can you overlook that? Do you remember that hooker when we walked back to the car after the movies and what you said? I was cringing inside at the time…thinking that if I told you this, you wouldn't want to know me."

He winced. "I said get off the streets and find a decent job. I guess I wasn't looking too deeply at the girl's circumstances."

"I resolved to tell you, Theo and Iantha, no matter what. Honesty is something I value. So I wasn't valuing myself very much by keeping it back." Many times she'd planned to tell Allan but had backed out. When she'd finally decided, it had been too late.

"You were very brave."

"The way I see it, I didn't have a choice."

"My reaction earlier makes me feel like a real jerk." He shrugged. "I can't imagine what it must have been like to see your dream evaporate if you didn't have enough money. My family has always had plenty of that."

"I've just spent the last fifteen minutes on the phone with Ross.

He's been worried about you, too. Ross said that he wants you back at work on Monday. I've explained that you'll need time to get yourself together before you return. The rehab is still on hold, and you can go there when and if you need to. He's on his way over now."

"Now?"

"Yep."

"He was ready to have me locked up in rehab before, Jack..."

"Let's finish this project together. You can work for whomever you like afterwards. I'm sure plenty of companies will be falling over themselves to get you on board. After this we'll have more than enough money to start up a research company together."

"What are you saying?"

"I'm furious about what Ross did to you, but a contract is a contract, and I'm bound by that. But I'll do my best to see that he pays dearly for putting you through the mill."

"Really?" He would do that for her.

"Yes. Now about that second chance? Can we give it a go?" He gazed into her eyes.

She had to be sure. "Can you accept me knowing that I've been an escort, and that I have a drinking problem?"

"That's a big yes. The past six months, you've been through more than most people would in a lifetime." He drew her into his arms and kissed her.

THE END

Thank you for reading my story.

I hope you enjoyed this story. If you did, please support a writer and leave a review on Amazon, Createspace, Goodreads or Booklikes. Reviews help potential readers decide if they should invest their time in a new author.

I listen to my readers and if you find something that you enjoyed or that I can improve on, please let me know via email. Many thanks.

You may be interested in reading my first thriller

The Deadly Caress: www.getBook.at/B00I0DI0MY

If you'd like to be notified when my next book comes out or you want to contact me –leave me a message on my Author Central Page on Amazon
http://www.amazon.com/-/e/B00I68JS3S

or my website http://onstefan.weebly.com/ . I love to connect with my readers.

LINKS:

AMAZON AUTHOR CENTRAL: http://www.amazon.com/-/e/B00I68JS3S

GOODREADS:https://www.goodreads.com/book/show/sleep-then-my-princess

PINTEREST: https://www.pinterest.com/olgaolha/sleep-then-my-princess/

TWITTER: https://twitter.com/olgaolha

WEB SITE: http://onstefan.weebly.com/

BLOG: http://onstefan.blogspot.com.au/

My next thriller will be out late 2016.